LONDON CALLING

EDWARD
BLOOR

ALFRED A. KNOPF   New York

Published in the United States by Alfred A. Knopf, an imprint of Random
House Children's Books, a division of Random House, Inc., New York.

KNOPF, BORZOI BOOKS, and the colophon are registered trademarks
of Random House, Inc.

www.randomhouse.com/teens

Educators and librarians, for a variety of teaching tools, visit us at
www.randomhouse.com/teachers

Library of Congress Cataloging-in-Publication Data
Bloor, Edward.
London calling / Edward Bloor. — 1st ed.
p. cm.
SUMMARY: Seventh-grader Martin Conway believes that his life is monotonous
and dull until the night the antique radio he uses as a night-light transports
him to the bombing of London in 1940.
ISBN-13: 978-0-375-83635-0 (trade) — ISBN-13: 978-0-375-93635-7 (lib. bdg.)
ISBN-10: 0-375-83635-7 (trade) — ISBN-10: 0-375-93635-1 (lib. bdg.)
[1. Time travel—Fiction.   2. London (England)—History—Bombardment,
1940–1941—Fiction.   3. Catholics—Fiction.   4.Schools—Fiction.
5. World War, 1939–1945—Great Britain—Fiction.]   I. Title.
PZ7.B6236Lo 2006
[Fic]—dc22 2005033330

Printed in the United States of America

September 2006

10 9 8 7 6 5 4 3 2 1

First Edition

For Spencer

We'll meet again,
Don't know where,
Don't know when,
But I know we'll meet again
Some sunny day.

PROLOGUE

John Martin Conway
United States Embassy
Grosvenor Square, London
January 2, 2019

Each life, in human history, begins when a person starts to walk down a path. At first it is the path that our parents tell us to walk down. Then we come to certain crossroads where we have two choices—remain on the one path or step off onto another. Sometimes our paths cross the paths of others at crucial points. This is where things can get uncontrollable, weird, unexplainable.

There is a lot more you could say about life, but that's basically it.

History *repeats itself* only in that, from afar, we all seem to lead exactly the same life. We are all born; we all spend time here on earth; we all die. But up close, we have each walked down our own separate paths. We have stood at our own lonely crossroads. We have touched the lives of others at crucial points, for better or for worse. In the end, each of us has lived a unique life story, astounding and complicated, a story that could never be repeated.

I am thinking about life and history today because of a pair of coincidences. Consider:

I am looking through a window at a statue of President Franklin D. Roosevelt. Sixteen and a half years ago, as a seventh-grade student at All Souls Preparatory, I was doing exactly the same thing.

I was just handed a note. The same thing happened at All Souls, and the note concerns the same person. Here is what it says:

> To all Embassy staff: I regret to inform you that Henry "Hank" Lowery IV, great-grandson of General Henry M. "Hollerin' Hank" Lowery, died in an automobile accident yesterday in Bethel, New Jersey, when his car crashed through the railing of the Millstone River Bridge. Information on the funeral arrangements will follow.

Now, depending on what you knew about Henry "Hank" Lowery IV, you could conclude that
—it was a tragic accident;
—it was his latest, and last, drunk driving incident;
—it was a suicide;
—it was all of the above.

I guess it doesn't really matter. It happened, and I just heard about it, and now I am looking through the window with a flood of memories coursing though me as strong and as clear as the waters of the Millstone River.

I have a story to tell about that time. It begins with Hank Lowery. Then it moves off onto another path, a path that only I have walked down. I have told this story only one other time, to one other person. That's because no one else would have believed it, not all of it. It is a unique story, astounding and complicated, and I am ready to tell it again.

ALL SOULS PREPARATORY SCHOOL

Established January 1, 1888

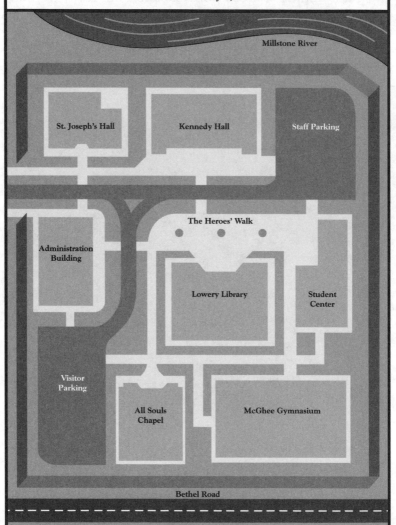

Millstone River

St. Joseph's Hall

Kennedy Hall

Staff Parking

The Heroes' Walk

Administration
Building

Lowery Library

Student
Center

Visitor
Parking

All Souls
Chapel

McGhee Gymnasium

Bethel Road

THE HEROES' WALK

Looking back now, I can see that I spent my seventh-grade year in a state of depression, imprisoned behind the red-brick, black-iron walls of All Souls Preparatory. All Souls is a private, mostly Catholic school in Bethel, New Jersey, about twenty miles east of Princeton.

Back when I was a student, All Souls had two prominent statues on the campus. Franklin D. Roosevelt stood outside the Student Center, which was a little strange since the real President Roosevelt couldn't stand. Yet there he was, with one hand on a cane and the other hand raised in a friendly wave. John F. Kennedy, the first Catholic president, stood outside Kennedy Hall. He was pointing energetically into the air, as if he were speaking.

On the last day of school that year, I was sitting in class in Kennedy Hall and looking through the window at FDR. Across the road, the Lowery Library was nearing the end of a major renovation. As part of this, Father Thomas, the headmaster of the school, had decreed that the statues of

Presidents Roosevelt and Kennedy were to be moved to join a new statue of General Henry M. "Hollerin' Hank" Lowery in an impressive new entranceway to the library. The entrance would consist of the three statues, a brass informational plaque about each one, and a slab with the words THE HEROES' WALK carved into it.

That was why Father Leonard, my history teacher, was spending one last class period droning on about World War II and the heroic efforts of General Henry M. Lowery to alert America to the dangers of Adolf Hitler and Nazism. Father Leonard was the twin brother of the headmaster, Father Thomas. They had both attended All Souls Preparatory some thirty years before; now the paths of their lives had circled around and brought them both back to their beloved alma mater.

I hated All Souls Preparatory.

I hated the uniforms; I hated the snobbery; I hated the tradition. I was an outcast there, and I associated only with other outcasts. One of them, sitting immediately to my left, had just raised his hand.

Father Leonard pointed to him warily and said, "Mr. Chander, I trust this comment is pertinent."

"Oh yes, Father. It is most pertinent."

"Fine. Then you may proceed."

"I read that General Lowery was not really opposed to the Nazis. In fact, he thought the Nazis would win the war easily, and he advised President Roosevelt to make a deal with Hitler as soon as he could."

Father Leonard looked pained. "I don't think those are facts, Pinak. But if you would care to do some independent study in that area, I will give you extra credit for your research."

"I don't need any more credit, Father. I already have an average far above one hundred. I just wanted to perhaps start a discussion."

"No. We need not discuss rumors and half-truths and falsehoods. The historical record is perfectly clear about what the General wrote and said at the time."

Pinak gave up. "Yes, Father."

Father Leonard always looked uncomfortable when talking about the late General Lowery. Fathers Leonard and Thomas both believed, faithfully, in the legend of Lowery as a fierce Hitler-hater and Nazi-fighter. In return for that faith, the Lowery family had established a million-dollar trust fund for All Souls Preparatory. All Souls had been General Lowery's prep school, back when it was all boys and they all lived there. Then it was his son's and his grandson's prep school, and now it was his great-grandson's prep school. That great-grandson, Henry M. Lowery IV, was seated in front of me and to the left. Hank Lowery was what is known there as a "legacy."

I, on the other hand, was what is known there as a "scholarship." Worse than that, I was an "*employee* scholarship*." My mother worked as Father Thomas's secretary, and, thanks to that, I was allowed to attend the school tuition-free. My mother had worked the same deal for my sister Margaret, who had excelled at All Souls and then gone on to Princeton, where she earned a degree in history. My future prospects, however, were not so bright. Unlike Pinak, who was an academic star, I barely scraped by with C's.

7

The only other kid I really associated with was Manetti. I knew him from sixth grade back at Garden State Middle School. He was an employee scholarship, too. His father was in charge of buildings and construction at All Souls, which meant that Manetti actually had it worse than me. At least my parent was hidden away in an office. His was very visible—always walking around on campus in an orange hard hat, or driving around noisily in one of his company trucks. I was watching one of those Manetti Construction trucks unload equipment when the girl in front of me turned and handed me a note.

There was no name on the note, so I set it on the corner of my desk, temporarily ignoring it until I heard a sharp, throat-clearing noise. I glanced up and saw the red, erupted face of Hank Lowery IV. He pointed a stubby finger at the note. I obediently picked it up, opened it, and read this printed message:

You're dead.

I looked back at Lowery, puzzled. He clenched his jaw and then shook his large head from left to right. He pointed first to the note and then to Pinak. When I finally understood his message, I passed the note over. As Pinak opened the note and read those two words, his dark Indian complexion turned pale with fear.

Shortly after that exchange, Father Leonard's lifeless lecture, and the school day, and the school year, all came to an end with the ringing of the bell.

As we did every day, Pinak, Manetti, and I walked

together to the Administration Building. Manetti and I had to wait for our employee parents to finish work; Pinak simply had nothing better to do. He asked his mother to pick him up later so that he could hang out with us. On that day, he probably regretted that arrangement.

Even before we got out of the classroom, some kid muttered to Pinak, "Lowery's gonna kick your ass outside."

When we got downstairs, Pinak hesitated in the doorway of the building, but a quick look left and right revealed that Lowery was nowhere in sight.

Manetti told us, "He ain't here. The rugby team's meeting in the gym about summer workouts. Lowery and his boys'll be over there."

Pinak then led us on a brisk walk across the road toward the Administration Building. Manetti, with his usual tact, started in on him. "I thought for a minute that a girl was sending Pinak a note. Then I thought, Wait a minute. We don't have any blind girls in our class."

Pinak snarled, "Shut up, Manetti."

"I figured the girl must have been sending *me* a note, but it got detoured."

"The note was not from a girl!"

"Ha-ha. I know. It was from Lowery. Don't worry about him, Pinak. He's a big nothing."

"Oh? He's nothing? So why do I never see you standing up to him?"

"I'll stand up to him anytime. Just me and him. But it's never just him, is it? That Lowery's nothing when he's by himself."

The three of us pushed open the heavy wooden doors

of the Administration Building. We stood facing the two huge paintings on the back wall of the lobby. One was *Washington Crossing the Delaware,* and the other was some even bigger thing by the same artist, with pioneers marching across it.

Pinak turned to me, anguished. "Martin, tell me what I can do."

Manetti answered, "Pray."

"That is not funny."

Manetti clapped him on the shoulder. "Hey, you're not gonna see Lowery for three months. What do you care?"

"I care about seeing him today."

"Then why did you say that thing about his great-grandfather? That was stupid."

"That was the truth. What's wrong with that? Is nobody allowed to state the truth about the great General Lowery?"

Father Thomas entered behind us, nearly hitting Pinak in the back with the door. He waited as the three of us shuffled out of his way. Then he suggested, "Why don't you boys move down by the Rembrandts? That way you won't keep getting hit by the door."

Pinak answered for us. "Yes, Father."

Father Thomas continued into his office. As the door opened, I caught a brief glimpse of my mother seated at her desk, staring miserably at a stack of blue files. She didn't look up.

Pinak, Manetti, and I moved farther down the hallway toward the boys' restroom. We settled into an area with plastic chairs known as "the Rembrandts" because it was dominated by two huge framed paintings by Rembrandt.

(The hallway to the girls' restroom had two huge framed paintings by van Gogh.)

Pinak looked directly into my eyes. "Seriously, Martin. Tell me what I can do."

I answered honestly. "I think praying might be the way to go. We could stop into the Chapel for a while and, you know, pray. I still pray for things."

Pinak looked appalled. "Really? And do you ever get these things?"

"No."

"Then why do you waste your time?"

"I don't know. That's what Catholics do, right? When all else fails, they pray."

"And you wait for some magic abracadabra thing to happen?"

"Yeah. I guess."

Pinak looked up at one of the Rembrandts. It was a very scary painting showing a boy on a woodpile. A crazy old man was trying to cut his throat open with a long knife. Pinak shuddered and looked away. "All right. Forget it. Let's get out of here. It's the last day of school; maybe my mother has come early."

We exited the building and turned right. The construction work on the Heroes' Walk had stopped for the day, so Manetti stepped over the yellow strand of "Caution" tape to check it out. I followed him, but Pinak stayed in the roadway. Three large marble pedestals, still in their wooden shipping frames, had been placed there in a straight row. I reached out a hand to feel the cold, smooth stone. Then

Manetti did the same, commenting, "My dad says they import this stuff from Italy. It's way expensive."

"You two should not be in there," Pinak complained.

Manetti pried back part of a wooden frame. "We're not bothering nothing."

I sensed some commotion, so I turned and looked toward the Student Center. Four boys in yellow-and-black rugby shirts were walking rapidly toward us. Hank Lowery was in the lead. I mumbled, "Pinak. Watch out."

Pinak's jaw dropped in horror. He started backing toward the roadway. "Do . . . do I have time to run?"

Lowery and his gang, perhaps sensing Pinak's plan, beat him to it. Two of them sprinted around us and cut him off. Pinak stepped over the "Caution" tape and stood right next to me.

Lowery started shouting at him from ten yards away, his hands clenched menacingly at his sides. "You're gonna apologize to me for that remark, A-rab."

Pinak's voice quavered. "I spoke the truth. That is all. But if I offended you, I apologize."

Lowery's boys now had the three of us encircled, like a wolf pack. Lowery jabbed a finger into Pinak's chest, causing him to exhale a burst of frightened air. "You need to show some respect, A-rab, or I'll kick your Muslim ass right here."

Pinak answered with as much dignity as he could. "I have told you. I am not Arab; I am Indian. And I am not Muslim; I am Hindu. These are lies that *you* continue to tell about *me*."

Lowery pretended to throw a punch at Pinak's face, causing him to flinch spastically; causing Lowery's boys to laugh out loud. I had finally had enough. I said, "Why don't you go to your rugby meeting? Leave us alone."

Lowery looked at his boys again. Then he stepped toward me until he was within hitting distance. I felt my throat go dry and my face and hand muscles start to quiver. Lowery cocked his head in mock disbelief. "What did you say to me?" He glanced toward the Administration Building. "You think 'cause your mommy's in there, you can talk to me like that?" He turned to the boy next to him and shook his head back and forth, sadly.

Suddenly, before I could react, his right hand shot forward and his open palm struck my face with a resounding slap.

The noise was so loud that it echoed off the marble. I staggered back a step. I doubled over and pressed my hands against my ears, feeling the blood rushing through my head; hearing a horrible ringing.

I looked up at the faces encircling me. Lowery's boys were laughing, but nervously, like they had seen enough and wanted to get out of there.

Then, out of the corner of my eye, I saw Manetti. He picked up a jagged block of concrete about two feet long and six inches thick. He heaved it with all his might at the back of Lowery's head.

It missed its target, glancing off Lowery's shoulder blade before crashing into one of the pedestals, chipping off a large wedge-shaped chunk of white marble.

Lowery reached back dramatically, like he'd been shot. Then he dropped to one knee, screaming and crying in pain. His boys exchanged a quick glance and took off running as fast as they could toward the gym. The rest of us remained in our positions for another half minute until Father Leonard walked out of Kennedy Hall. I listened through the ringing in my ears as he got on a walkie-talkie and told his brother, "You had better come out to the Heroes' Walk right away."

Ten minutes later, after examinations by my mother and Father Leonard determined that no one had been seriously injured, the four of us were lined up in front of Father Thomas in his office. He pointed to Lowery first. "All right, Hank. Tell me what happened."

Lowery stretched his shoulders. Then he thought for a moment and answered. "We were all on our way to the rugby meeting."

"Who is 'we'?"

"Me. Uh, Ben Livingstone, Joey Mayer, and Tim Connelly."

Father Thomas pointed to my mother. "Add those names to the list. I want statements from all of them. Written statements. Continue."

"Okay. So he"—Lowery suddenly pointed at me—"starts making fun of our shirts to his buddies. He starts calling them gay."

My face must have expressed astonishment, because he felt compelled to add, "Oh yeah. He was. He was saying, like, 'They're way gay-looking.' Those were his exact words. So then, yeah, I got up in his face about it. I was mad. I'm proud to wear the All Souls uniform, you know? I'm not gonna let him make fun of it." He pointed at Manetti.

"Then this kid, this psycho kid, hits me from behind with a big piece of concrete. He tried to kill me!"

Pinak could remain silent no longer. "Father Thomas, that is a pack of lies. Nothing in it is true."

"What? Are you saying he didn't throw the concrete and hit me?"

"No one said your shirt looked gay! No one said anything to you at all. You attacked us."

Father Thomas raised his hand to stop them both. "All right. That's enough. It's immaterial how this fight started. What matters is the result. You boys damaged that marble pedestal. That is a serious and . . . indefensible act of vandalism. Vandalism! At All Souls! The Heroes' Walk belongs to everyone at this school. It is a place that we can all treasure and take pride in. This is unacceptable. Totally unacceptable."

Father Thomas pointed out his window to the row of pedestals. "Your behavior today jeopardizes the construction schedule. That means that it jeopardizes the dedication of the Heroes' Walk on New Year's Day." He pointed at Manetti. "Mr. Manetti, how would your father feel about that?"

Manetti bowed his head. "Not good, Father."

"Mr. Lowery, how would your father feel about that?"

"Not good, Father."

Father Thomas threw up his hands in exasperation. "That was Carrara marble, boys! Do any of you know what that means?"

Pinak halfheartedly raised one hand, but Father Thomas ignored him. "It is the finest marble in the world, imported from Italy. It is the same marble that Michelangelo used to sculpt his statue of David, and his Pietà." He looked at my mother, and then back at us. "Do you have any idea how hard it will be to repair it? And to get the construction back on schedule?" He paused to compose himself. Then he turned back to my mother. "I'll need to get some figures on repairing that pedestal. I'll meet with these students again, and their parents, after we have determined the exact cost of repairs. Sometime before the start of next term." He pointed toward the door. "Now go. All of you."

My mother had to work late, presumably getting estimates for Carrara marble. She made me sit across from her and write out my statement about the incident on a sheet of All Souls stationery. When I was finished, she looked it over quickly. If she was surprised at all by what she read, it did not show on her face. She just sealed the statement in an All Souls envelope, addressed it to Father Thomas, and placed it in a blue file.

We finally left the campus at about seven p.m. The ride home was, predictably, worse than usual. Instead of just hearing about how I had to apply myself harder to measure up to my sister, and my grandfather, and President John F. Kennedy, I had to hear about how I had nearly destroyed All Souls Prep School, and my family's reputation, and my own future.

I wasn't really listening. All I could think about was that slap in the face. What should I have done about it? Should I have hit him back? Yes, I should have hit him back, or at least tried. So why didn't I?

When Mom finally stopped ranting, I answered her briefly. "First of all, it wasn't me. It was Manetti who threw the concrete. Second of all, he chipped off a little piece of a corner. So what?"

"So what? You heard Father Thomas. That was Carrara marble."

"I'm sorry. It wasn't a piece of a corner, it was a piece of supermarble. So what? So superglue it back on. Nobody will ever know."

"Martin, you *will* take this seriously. This is your life. How you will live in the future depends on . . ."

And blah, blah, blah. I had heard this too many times before. How I will live in the future depends on how I live now, in the present. She says that over and over, but she doesn't really mean it. Mom doesn't live in the present at all. She lives in the past and in the future, but not in the present. She hates the present. The present is all bad for her; it is a punishment time that she has to endure. She lives in the glorious past of her father and mother, and in the glorious future of her daughter and son. Well, forget about that. There's no glorious future for me, not the way she has it planned. I told her, for the thousandth time, "I don't want to go back to All Souls Prep. I want to go to Garden State Middle School."

Our house was hidden from the street by a row of skinny bushes and leafy trees. In the fall and winter, however, it became clearly visible, and clearly an eyesore. After we pulled in to the driveway, Mom turned off the ignition and yanked out the key. "Fortunately for you, you don't have to go back to All Souls on Monday, but I do. I have to go back there

17

every day, to work to ensure that you have a future. You will, though, be going back there in September."

"No, I won't."

"Yes, you will."

"No, I won't."

We left it at that, like we always do. We walked through the front door of the faded green Cape Cod house. Mom headed into the kitchen. I veered off and went straight downstairs to the basement, to my bedroom.

Cape Cod houses come to a point on the second floor. That means the upstairs bedrooms have ceilings that slope to the sides. Once you grow to a certain height, you can start to bump your head on the ceiling in your own bedroom. My sister Margaret reached that height at age ten, but she never bumped her head. When I reached that height, though, I immediately started bumping mine. I demanded to move down to the basement.

Our basement had a finished bedroom to the right side of the stairs and a computer room to the left. The rest of the space was unfinished; we used it for laundry and storage. The bedroom in the basement had been built originally for my uncle Bob, which was something we rarely talked about. Its second tenant was my father, which was something that we *never* talked about. I became the basement's third dweller.

Mom and Margaret helped me move down my furniture, which consisted of a double bed, a dresser, and a nightstand. Mom allowed me to decorate the room any way I wanted, which meant that its four green walls remained completely bare. As the room only had two narrow windows near the ceiling, level with the ground outside, and as I was afraid of the dark, I kept my father's little TV down there to use as a night-light.

Just across the way, in the computer room, the walls were fully decorated with photographs of family members. By that I mean members of my mother's family, the famous Mehans. My father's family, the not-famous Conways, were represented only by a crowd photo from my parents' wedding day. Most prominent on those walls were the black-and-white glossies of my grandfather, Martin Mehan, for whom I am named. He was shown posing in a group with President Franklin D. Roosevelt; posing alone with United States Ambassador to London Joseph P. Kennedy; and posing alone with General Henry M. "Hollerin' Hank" Lowery.

When Margaret came downstairs to get me for dinner that evening, I told her that I was not coming up because I wasn't feeling well. I must have dozed off shortly after that, because the ringing of the telephone startled me. I rolled over toward the nightstand, checked the name on the caller ID, and picked it up. I answered, as cheerily as I could, "Hi, Nana. It's Martin."

"Martin! Hello! It's London calling!"

"Yes, Nana. How are you?"

"That's what the overseas operator always used to say. Every night. When your grandfather would call from England."

"Yes, Nana. I know."

"London calling."

"Right."

"Did that little boy ever find you?"

"What, Nana? What little boy?"

"A boy was looking for you. At least, I think he was looking for you."

"I . . . I'm afraid I don't know who you're talking about. Do you mean a boy in Brookline?"

"Tell me something, Martin: Do you like to listen to the radio?"

"Uh, sure. I guess."

"I love to go to sleep with the radio on. I always have. I had a dream about a radio, a beautiful old radio that your grandfather put in the attic years ago. I asked Elizabeth to bring it down for me, and now I have it right here. It's a Philco 20 Deluxe radio. Would you like to listen to it?"

"Yeah, I guess."

I suddenly heard a click on the line, followed by Mom's voice. "Martin? Are you on the phone?"

"He's on talking with me, Mary!"

"Oh, hello, Mother. I didn't know it was you. How are you feeling today?"

I interrupted. "I guess I'll get off now."

Mom assured me, "You don't have to, Martin."

"No. That's okay. I'll talk to you later, Nana."

"Goodbye, Martin!"

I clicked off and replaced the phone in its stand. When I looked up, I found myself staring straight into the mirror on the dresser. What I saw made me sick at heart. If you looked at just the right angle, at just the right spot, the red imprint of Hank Lowery's hand was still faintly visible on my white skin. I sat there staring at that imprint until it was too dark to see it anymore.

20

NINE FIRST FRIDAYS

Certain days from the past come back to me perfectly clear, like a strong radio signal. Other days, even weeks, are a complete blur. I remember that I spent most of the next month in the basement. I slept a lot. I did some instant messaging. (I had a very short buddy list; only Pinak and Manetti were on it.) I also pretended to read the books of the All Souls Prep summer reading list. But mostly I did absolutely nothing. My days were empty and pointless. I took to napping twice a day—midmorning and midafternoon—and going to bed as soon as it got dark. During the day, I moved through the summer heat like a sleepwalker.

While lying in the basement, I sometimes had dreams that were actually set in the basement. I call these "real-place dreams." Real-place dreams are the scariest kind because you have no way of knowing if you're dreaming or not. Some of my grandmother's phone calls that summer seemed like real-place dreams. She got into the habit of calling me late at night. Sometimes her words made sense; sometimes I couldn't figure them out at all. On Friday,

July 5, she called me very early in the morning. I groped for the phone on the nightstand, not sure if I was really answering it or if I was dreaming about answering it. I heard the question "Martin, did you make your nine First Fridays?"

"Nana? Is that you?"

"This is very important, dear. Did you go to mass and communion on the first Friday of each month for nine consecutive months?"

"Yes, ma'am. Mom had me do that in first grade. Then she had me do it again in second."

"Are you sure?"

"I'm sure."

"At St. Aidan's Church? In Brookline?"

"No, Nana. Down here. At Resurrection."

"Because your soul is everlasting, Martin. Remember that. I know that for a fact."

"Yes, ma'am."

"Have you heard from the boy yet?"

"No. I don't think so."

"You must help him. He's lost."

Suddenly I heard Aunt Elizabeth's voice on the line. "Who is this?"

Nana didn't speak, so I did. "It's Martin, Aunt Elizabeth."

"Martin? What time is it?"

"I don't know."

She paused, and then answered, "It's five a.m. I'm very sorry, Martin. I should be keeping a better eye on her. Mother! You can't call people at this hour. Remember? We talked about that? You can't call people when it's dark." I

22

heard the sound of my grandmother hanging up. "Mother?" Aunt Elizabeth turned her attention back to me. "I'm sorry, Martin. She has you set up on speed dial. I'll deprogram the phone so she doesn't do this again."

"That's okay. I don't mind."

"Well, I mind. And I'm sure a lot of other people would mind. Let's all go back to sleep now."

"Okay." I hung up and shuddered. Aunt Elizabeth was my mother's only sibling. She had never married; she had never really left the house where she grew up with my mother, my grandmother, and my grandfather. As the family story went, Aunt Elizabeth had entered the convent to become a nun, but she changed her mind at the last minute. Now she was the administrator of a big Catholic hospital in Boston by day, and she took care of Nana by night.

I did not go back to sleep. I sat thinking about Nana's words until I heard sounds from Mom and Margaret upstairs. Mom still went to work at All Souls every weekday to run the office during the summer session. Margaret went to work every day, too. She had just graduated from intern to temporary employee at an encyclopedia company in Princeton.

I walked up to the kitchen and got some orange juice. Mom said, "I put a grocery list on the refrigerator, Martin. Please go to the Acme for me today and get those things."

I muttered, "Okay."

When I joined them at the kitchen table, Mom started in on me in earnest. "Why don't you invite someone over today, Martin? How about Timothy Connelly?"

"No. I don't think so."

"He seems like a very nice boy. He's from an All Souls family."

"That's right. He's a legacy. That means he doesn't hang out with scholarship kids."

"Martin. I'm sure that's not true. I'm at that school every day. I see all the students getting along together."

I thought, *Right. Did you see him in Lowery's wolf pack? Surrounding the three trembling geeks? Yelping for their blood?* But I just answered, "No, I don't think so. Not today."

"And what are you going to do today instead?"

"I'll read one of those books on the list, I guess."

"How many have you read so far?"

"None so far, but I'm working on it."

"The summer is halfway over, Martin, and you have a total of eight books to read." She looked over at Margaret, trying to enlist her help. "Remember when you did the Newbery project? You read every Newbery Medal winner from 1922 to the present?"

Margaret smiled slyly. "Yes. And l lived to tell about it."

Mom frowned. "Please, Margaret. I'm trying to encourage reading."

"Martin should start by reading things that he likes."

"No, he should start by reading the books on his list. He'll be tested on them in September."

I spoke up. "No. I won't."

"I believe there will be a test on them."

"I believe there will be, too. But I won't be taking it. I won't be at the school."

Mom shook her head, exasperated. She looked at

Margaret. "See if you can talk to him. I don't have time to argue this morning. I'm doing the work of three people at that place."

Mom left shortly afterward, but Margaret hung around. She followed me down to the computer room, where I pretended to log on for an early-morning chat. She stood by the rows of family photos, studying them while asking me casually, "So, Martin, what do you do all day?"

"Nothing."

"That can be good. Sometimes."

I glanced at Margaret's face while she wasn't looking. It was eerie. If you could take them out of time, Margaret, Mom, and Nana could all be the same girl. They are all on the small side (as opposed to Aunt Elizabeth, who is large). They all, at one point, had curly dark hair, blue eyes, and light freckles. And they all flatly refused to smile in photographs, no matter if it was 1940, 1960, 1980, 2000 . . . not a smile from any one of them at any time.

Margaret wasn't smiling now, either. She had a job to do, with me. She took a step forward, folded her arms, and looked me in the eye. "Why do you think you stay in this basement all day, every day?"

I answered carefully. "I don't know. I guess because I'm still too young to get a summer job?"

"Really? Is that it?"

Of course that wasn't it, but I wasn't going to tell her. I changed the subject. "How is your job at the encyclopedia?"

Margaret took a slow step back. "It's really good. It's excellent."

"What do you do there?"

"I do research—fact checking."

"About what?"

Margaret smiled openly at my brazenness. "So you're asking the questions now?"

"Yeah. I want to know."

"Well, I check facts for the new entries in the encyclopedia. Every year they add people and places and things. They drop stuff, too."

"Uh-huh. So who are they adding this year?"

She pointed to one of our grandfather's photos. "Someone I'm sure you've heard all about at All Souls, General Henry M. Lowery."

I felt a flash of humiliation, but I answered lightly, "Really? Hollerin' Hank?"

"That's the guy."

"Why him?"

Margaret thought for a moment. "I don't know. Mr. Wissler handed me a file from an attorney's office. It was full of papers about General Lowery. He said, 'See if any of this is true.' "

"He thought some things were *not* true?"

"I'd say so. Yeah. Mr. Wissler didn't like getting that file sent to him. He likes to collect his own facts."

"And he's your boss?"

"Yes."

"Who else works there?"

Margaret stepped toward the door. "Two permanent staff people, two interns, the IT guy, and me. That's about it." She fixed me with a stare. "Martin, is there anything you want to talk about? It doesn't need to be with me. It could be with a therapist. It could even be with Dad."

"You're kidding. Dad?"

"Yes. He'd do that for you, if we gave him enough notice. You need to talk to someone."

"I do talk to someone. I talk to friends online. I talk to Nana."

"Nana?" Margaret sputtered. "Are you serious?"

"Yes."

"Does she understand you? Do you understand her?"

"Yeah. We understand each other."

"What does she say?"

I thought about that morning's wake-up call. "Today she asked me if I had gone to communion for nine First Fridays."

Margaret mulled that over. "Interesting. That's what's on her mind?"

"Yeah. She seemed really worried about it."

Margaret clenched her jaw and looked down. Then she continued in a confidential tone. "There's a family story about that. Have you ever heard it?"

I held out my arms. "Who would have told me?"

Margaret shrugged. "Dad, maybe. In an indiscreet moment."

"No. I haven't heard it. What happened?"

Margaret pulled over a chair and sat. "This is Mom's version. She calls it 'the short version.' It seems that Nana used to tell a long story about meeting an angel, but Grandfather made her stop because he thought it sounded crazy."

I looked up at the photo of Martin Mehan. "And we can't have that."

"Oh no. That might jeopardize his status as a prominent Catholic layman."

"So what did Nana say?"

Margaret stole a glance at the doorway to ensure that we were alone. "This happened the night Mom was born. Nana was rushed to the emergency room, fearful of losing the baby."

"The baby? Meaning Mom? Meaning we wouldn't be here now?"

"Correct. Nana's heart actually stopped beating during the delivery. The doctors managed to save the baby—Mom—but they concluded that they couldn't save Nana. After doing the crash cart thing and the chest-pounding, she was officially pronounced dead. They covered her with a white sheet and everything."

I felt a sudden chill that made my head and shoulders shake.

Margaret went on, "Nana said that she remembered, clearly, floating up and away into an ether."

"A what?"

"Like a white cloud. Then she found herself in the presence of an angel." Margaret paused for effect. "According to Nana, she had the nerve to speak to the angel, although no sound came from her lips. She said, 'Wait a minute. I was promised by the church that if I went to mass and communion on the first Friday of the month for nine consecutive months that a priest would be there to give me the last rites at my death, guaranteed. Well, I made my nine First Fridays, but I saw no priest before my death.' The angel made no sound, either, but obviously agreed with her. She immediately found herself floating through the ether again, and then she came back to life on that table. She threw off the white sheet, causing one doctor to shout out an expletive and another to fall on his knees in prayer."

I sat with my mouth open. I finally managed to say, "But she only asked me about the nine First Fridays. Why wouldn't she tell me the rest of the story?"

Margaret shrugged. "Maybe Grandfather Mehan still has a hold on her. Who knows?"

"Or," I suggested, "maybe she was going to, and Aunt Elizabeth cut her off."

"Aunt Elizabeth?"

"Yeah. She got on the line and started yelling at Nana about calling people in the middle of the night."

"That's not bad advice, I suppose." Margaret looked at her watch. "I'm going to be late." She reached over, touched my hand once, and pulled it away. "I meant what I said about talking to someone. Someone other than Nana."

I nodded noncommittally.

"Mom asked me to ask you to read a book."

"Okay."

"And to go to the store."

"Okay."

"Okay. I'll see you tonight."

I stayed in the computer room, thinking about Nana's frail voice and Margaret's death story. At about nine, I heard a *ding* on my instant message board. It was Pinak. He was on with Manetti, so I joined them:

JMARTINC: What's up?

PINAKC: Please help us to discuss something other than girls.

MANETTITHEMAN: What do you have against girls?

PINAKC: I have nothing against girls. I like girls. I don't want to discuss girls and nothing but girls, that is all.

MANETTITHEMAN: Homo.

PINAKC: Stop that. Help me, Martin.

JMARTINC: The girls at All Souls are all like my sister. They're not interested in anything but grades. That's why they're there.

MANETTITHEMAN: Your sister is hot.

JMARTINC: What?

MANETTITHEMAN: Is she dating anyone?

PINAKC: Can you not control your libido for one minute?

MANETTITHEMAN: What's that?

PINAKC: Your raging and lustful hormones.

MANETTITHEMAN: Sure. You got it. One minute.

PINAKC: Thank you. Martin, have you emerged from your basement recently?

JMARTINC: No. But I have to go to the super-market today. The sunlight is painful to my eyes. I've gotten to be like a mole down here.

PINAKC: Why don't you move to a sunnier part of the house?

JMARTINC: I belong down here. This is the place of shame. Historically. It was built for my uncle Bob as a place of shame.

PINAKC: You sound depressed.

JMARTINC: Is everybody my psychiatrist today?

PINAKC: My father is a psychiatrist.

JMARTINC: I know. But you're not.

MANETTITHEMAN: Okay, I'm back. Why did your uncle have to live in the basement?

JMARTINC: We couldn't trust him to live upstairs anymore. He was a manic-depressive.

PINAKC: I am not sure you're qualified to make that assessment.

MANETTITHEMAN: Shut up, Pinak.

PINAKC: You shut up.

JMARTINC: Do you guys want to hear this or not?

MANETTITHEMAN: Yeah. Shut up, Pinak.

JMARTINC: Uncle Bob is my dad's brother. He lives in Newark now, and he works at the airport.

MANETTITHEMAN: Is he a pilot?

JMARTINC: No. He's a baggage handler.

PINAKC: Shut up, Manetti.

MANETTITHEMAN: You shut up.

JMARTINC: But about seven years ago, he lived with us. He was really depressed—on medications, under a psychiatrist's care, the whole thing. My dad was trying to help him get

back on his feet. He moved into my bedroom, and I had to double up with Margaret.
I don't remember too much else about him
until this one day, around Halloween. We
were all out front raking leaves. My uncle
took a bunch of pills, jumped out of his bedroom window, and landed headfirst on the
ground.

MANETTITHEMAN: Wow. Was he dead?

JMARTINC: No. Not even close. Just a broken
collarbone. The doctor said he was so heavily medicated that his body became totally
relaxed, too relaxed for anything else to
break.

MANETTITHEMAN: Awesome.

PINAKC: That is terrible. Was he hospitalized?

JMARTINC: No. But he was basement-ized. My
parents had walls put up in the basement to
make a bedroom for him. Uncle Bob stayed
until his collarbone healed, but then he left.
He's up in Newark now. My dad's up there
with him. Before that, my dad lived in the
basement, too. Until he passed out one night
and nearly set it on fire.

I didn't usually write personal family stuff like that, and
I regretted it immediately. A long pause followed. Even
Manetti drew the line at making fun of my dad. I finally
typed in "Gotta go," and the session mercifully ended.

Later, I did my duty and walked up to the Acme super-market. It was about three blocks from our house. The sun really did hurt my eyes. The traffic sounds hurt my ears. The smells in the store hurt my nose. Everything seemed gross and exaggerated to me. Maybe Margaret was right; maybe I was depressed. It was a good thing I lived down in the basement.

The day ended much the way that it began. I went to sleep right after sundown. The phone rang and I answered it, half-awake, half-asleep. It was from the same phone number as before, but a different voice came through the line. "Martin?"

"Yes."

"It's Aunt Elizabeth, Martin. Is your mother there?"

"Yeah. I think so." I waited a moment; then heard the sound of the phone being picked up.

"Hello."

"Mary? It's Elizabeth."

"Elizabeth? Oh no. Is there something wrong?"

"Yes. I'm sorry to say there is. Mother is gone."

"Oh my God! What happened?"

"She died in her sleep sometime this afternoon. I got a call at the hospital. The home health worker checked on her at four and found her dead. She said she looked very peaceful."

"Oh my God."

"It was for the best, though, Mary. She had slipped a lot this month. She had gotten so frail."

"I know. I know she had. It's just . . . so hard to believe."

"It is. But believe me, she is gone." Aunt Elizabeth then added, assuming I would have no idea what she meant, "This time, she is really gone."

A TRAIN INTO THE PAST

Nana's death touched me deeply, though I wouldn't let any-one know it. I had always felt a mystical connection with her, and I had always sensed that Mom and Aunt Elizabeth disapproved of that connection. The long-term effects of Nana's death would remain hidden from me for a time, but the short-term effect was clear and immediate. I would have to leave my basement hideout to travel to her funeral with Mom, Margaret, and Dad.

But first we drove out to the eight a.m. Sunday mass at the All Souls Chapel. Mom fussed at Margaret and me all the way there about what clothes to pack for our trip to Brook-line. She was concerned that if we looked shabby in front of Aunt Elizabeth, she'd think that Mom was a secretary, which she was, and that we lived in poverty, which we did.

I was still half-awake, and half expecting to find out that Nana's death was part of a dream. I didn't come fully to my senses until we sat down in a pew in the Chapel and I saw, to my shock, that Hank Lowery and his family were directly in front of us. I doubt he saw me. The few glances I stole in his direction found him always in the same position—slouching to the left, sound asleep, with his mouth open.

When the mass was over, I led Mom and Margaret out to the parking lot as fast as possible. Once we got inside the car, Margaret did point out, "That Lowery kid's disgusting. A real slug. Can't his parents make him close his mouth, at least?"

Mom shook her head disapprovingly.

I said, "It's Lowery's school. He can do whatever he wants."

This roused Mom. "He cannot do whatever he wants, Martin. He has to follow the school rules like everybody else."

"No. Actually, he *can* do whatever he wants."

Margaret half turned toward the backseat. "What's this about?"

"Mom hasn't told you?"

"Apparently not."

Mom explained, "There was an incident on the last day of school. It involved Martin and some other boys. They damaged the Heroes' Walk in front of the library."

"Really? Martin did that?"

Mom pulled out of the parking lot. "Father Thomas isn't sure exactly what happened. He is still investigating."

Margaret looked at me and raised one eyebrow. "Well, let me investigate, then. Martin, what happened?"

I looked out the window just as we passed the scene of the crime. A string of yellow "Caution" tape still blocked off the area. The entrance to the Lowery Library appeared to be finished, though. All the debris had been cleared away; the marble pedestals were set in place; I couldn't see any chips missing from any of their corners. I finally answered, "I'm not sure. I'd better not say anything until Father Thomas is done checking with the Lowery family to find out what they say happened."

Mom interjected, "Father Thomas has collected statements from everyone who was involved."

"Right. I'm sure he's reading mine very carefully."

Mom slammed to a halt at the entrance and stared at me in the mirror. "We're not going to do this now, Martin. We have had a death in the family, and we have a long trip ahead of us today."

Mom then pulled out with as much acceleration as our little Civic could muster, indicating that the conversation was over. But Margaret looked at me knowingly. She had done her time at All Souls Prep, three years. She knew how things worked there.

Our house was so close to the Princeton Junction train station that we could have walked there, even with suitcases. Mom, however, would have found that far too embarrassing. Instead, we drove our car there and paid ten dollars a day to park in the lot.

My dad had never had a problem with walking. That's how he got to work. He was a relief manager for a restaurant chain called National Steakhouses. Most National Steakhouses were located in airports, so it was a perfect setup for him. He would walk to the train station, ride north for thirty minutes to Newark, and then fly to any airport that had a National Steakhouse and a hotel. As a result, he had more frequent-flyer miles than he could use in a lifetime. He would arrive at some city and manage the National Steakhouse while the real manager went on vacation, then reverse the travel process and come home. No cars; no driving—which was a good thing because his license had been suspended and he had never renewed it.

Following our less-than-one-minute drive to the station, Mom cruised the parking lot for ten minutes trying to find a space. After we fed thirty dollars into the parking meter, we walked for another two minutes to the office and purchased our tickets. Then Mom and Margaret sat on the long wooden benches in the station while I stepped outside, leaned over the tracks, and looked south, hoping to see the train before anybody else.

I had always liked this part. In fact, I liked everything that was to follow. I had been making this trip for as long as I could remember. Mom and Dad, even when Dad had a driver's license, always took us by train to see Nana and Grandfather Mehan. We got on the train here and rode up to Back Bay Station, Boston. Then we walked to the MBTA and took the Green Line trolley out to Brookline.

I felt a low rumble and spied the dim outline of a train approaching, so I hurried back to alert Mom and Margaret. The three of us rolled our suitcases down the platform and climbed aboard a car near the center of the long train. I lifted all three suitcases onto the overhead racks, and we settled into the red leather seats. Mom and Margaret sat in one row, while I flopped into the row in front of them.

I always sat on the right side and looked through the window. I never read or listened to music. Instead, I studied people during the few seconds that it took for the train to pass them by. In that time, I would learn all that I could about them. I would observe their lives briefly; then I would never see them again.

An elderly conductor dressed in dark blue with a brimmed cap entered the car. He collected our tickets, then smiled and touched his finger to his cap. He was what my nana would have called "a colored gentleman." She'd have said that to his face, too, thinking it was a compliment to him. She was very old-fashioned that way. She lived in the past a lot, even when she appeared to be in the present.

After a few stops, I noticed that the taped station announcements were running late. A prerecorded voice would announce that we were about to pull into the station that we had just left. It didn't bother me, but it caused Mom to make an angry comment every time it happened. She wasn't really angry at the recording, though. She was really angry at Dad, and she grew angrier as we got closer to his station.

As planned, Dad was standing on the platform at the Newark Airport station. Mom pointed at the door and told me, "Lean out and wave to him, Martin. He'll never see us."

I did as I was told, actually stepping out of the car to let a stream of passengers in. I spotted Dad standing there in a black funeral suit, staring casually through the windows of the car behind us. I waited until his stare worked its way up to me. Then I waved.

Dad was a thin man with black, wavy hair and sad blue eyes. He smiled his unhappy smile at me. Then he picked up his suitcase and walked forward. "How are you, Martin?"

"Okay."

"Are your mother and Margaret inside?"

"Yes."

He indicated that I should go in first. He followed me into the center of the car, where he made the same polite greetings to Mom and Margaret. No hugs and kisses. No personal greetings. Not in this family.

An elderly woman had taken my seat, so I squeezed in next to Margaret and Mom. Dad stood in the aisle for a moment with his suitcase, looking around. Then he walked to the front of our car and kept on walking, through the sliding doors and out of sight.

Mom spoke through clenched teeth. "He's going to the lounge car. Great. He'll be in great shape when we get to Boston."

Neither Margaret nor I said a thing. We sat there with the assurance, shared by all children of alcoholics, that there was absolutely nothing to say. It had all been said before.

Margaret claims that she can remember many times when Dad was not drinking. I can only remember one. Four years before, we had taken part in a Mehan family reunion in Ireland. As it turned out, it was only a few months before my grandfather Mehan died.

Nana, Grandfather Mehan, and Aunt Elizabeth flew to Ireland out of Boston; Mom, Dad, Margaret, and I flew out of Newark two days later. Mom told her family that we had to wait for Dad to finish a vacation assignment, but the truth was that we couldn't afford to go on their flight. We had to find a deal where we could use Dad's frequent-flyer miles.

Eventually we met up with the others in a two-story thatched cottage in County Wexford. Mom and Dad had made an agreement: He would not take a drink for the five days of the family reunion, but when we returned, he would drink his fill.

As I remember it, we had a stiff but pleasant time. Nana seemed especially tuned in to the Irish mystical stuff—fairies and spirits and the like. She talked to me about those things during the trip, probably because no one else would listen. I remember Grandfather Mehan making comments to her in his thin, sarcastic voice, comments about "seeing little leprechauns."

The grand plan was that we would do one major thing each day. We went to some old churches. We visited Mehans, who didn't really know us but treated us as family. Everywhere we went, though, those Irish people offered my dad drinks. And every time they did, he refused.

However, after we flew back to the United States, and after we got off the train at Princeton Junction, he fulfilled the other side of his agreement with Mom. He never even went home with us. He walked straight to Pete's Tavern, a bar between the train station and our house. He drank so much that he was not able to walk home. He slipped down, dead drunk, and he lay there with his legs on the curb and his head in the roadway. The next car driving past would have crushed his head.

Fortunately, a policeman saw him first, turned on his lights, and blocked traffic while an ambulance came to the rescue. Mom got a call at four a.m. to pick him up at the hospital emergency room. This was not an unusual occurrence at our house. The police, and the ambulance drivers, and more eyewitnesses than I would care to name—all knew about Jack Conway's problem.

Anyway, we finally arrived at Back Bay Station in Boston, stepped off the train, and waited for Dad to do the same. After a tense minute, Mom dispatched me to the lounge car to find him. I started off at a brisk walk, but I stopped still when I spotted him ahead of me. He was swaying slightly on the platform and smiling a silly, wide smile. He called out, too loudly, "Hey, Martin, my boy! There you are! Where's Mom and Margaret?"

Mom and Margaret brushed past me on the left and continued onward, not even looking at him. He winked at me and intoned "Hello, ladies" to them. Then he and I fell in step behind. Some college kids near us on the platform started to laugh—at his silly grin, I suppose.

I didn't.

I don't know why anyone ever laughs at drunks. Especially public ones, with their families cringing nearby.

They're just not funny.

THE HOLY SHRINE

To my surprise, Mom took a seat next to Dad when we boarded the Green Line to Brookline. She muttered at least a few words to him. I couldn't hear them, but I'm sure they were about behaving in front of Aunt Elizabeth and other relatives we might encounter. Dad nodded at her very seriously. It was another agreement.

We rolled our luggage a block and a half from the trolley stop to my grandparents' house, a two-story colonial on a tree-lined street not far from where John F. Kennedy was born. My grandparents had lived in it for over sixty years. The downstairs contained a living room, a formal parlor, a dining room, a kitchen, and my grandparents' bedroom. The upstairs had "the girls' bedrooms," where Mom once slept and Aunt Elizabeth still did, and my grandfather's study.

Aunt Elizabeth greeted us at the door with "Mary and Margaret, you'll be in Mary's old room; Jack and Martin, I've put you in Father's study." Then she added, "Did you all have a good trip?"

Aunt Elizabeth stepped back to give us room to enter. She is a tall, bony woman, similar to younger pictures of Grandfather Mehan. We all congregated in the living room, where we made small talk, mostly about the schedule of events for the funeral. Nana's wake was to be the next evening, from five to seven. Her funeral mass and burial were set for Tuesday morning. After that, we would take the train back home.

Neighbors and church members had been stopping by with food platters that Aunt Elizabeth had categorized at three levels: items for the refrigerator; items for the deep freeze; and items for the trash. Aunt Elizabeth offered us ham sandwiches and potato salad from the refrigerator, which we ate in silence.

The rest of the day dragged on. When the sun finally set, Aunt Elizabeth led us all into my grandfather's study, the room that my dad always referred to as "the holy shrine."

Martin Mehan's study had been preserved by Aunt Elizabeth as if it were just as important as John F. Kennedy's birthplace, around the corner. The room contained a large writing desk, a pair of matching leather couches with end tables, two wing chairs in the Queen Anne style, and two tall, sturdy bookcases containing Martin Mehan's books, photos, and certificates. All had the smell of the past—old paper, dust, a hint of mildew.

Many of the items dated to the year 1940. That year marked the beginning of my grandfather's government career, when he worked for Ambassador Joseph P. Kennedy in London. Other items were from the years he spent at the

Commerce Department in Boston. The most recent photo showed my grandfather on his eightieth birthday, holding a telegram from the White House. To me he looked crazed, like the old man in the Rembrandt painting at All Souls, the one with the long knife.

Aunt Elizabeth began to reminisce aloud about the great Martin Mehan, and his career, and his church work. I could see Dad and Margaret go instantly brain-dead. Even Mom seemed disinterested. Listening to Aunt Elizabeth, I realized how few personal memories I had of my grandfather. Although I had been with him at least once a year for the first nine years of my life, I could honestly say I had no idea what he was really like. After a few minutes, I drifted away from the group and sat on the leather couch that, by tradition, served as my bed.

As soon as I sat down, I noticed a very cool-looking radio on the end table. The radio was made of three different kinds of polished wood. It was about two feet tall and a foot and a half wide; its sides rose upward to a smooth, curved top. The dial was amber, and the control knobs were a deep mahogany. It struck me as one of the most beautiful things I had ever seen. I turned the radio around slightly and looked into its open back. An assortment of tubes and wires filled the bottom half of the dusty space. At the top, inside the curve, I saw some marks on the wood made in black ink.

Suddenly I realized that Aunt Elizabeth was talking to me. "Do you like that radio, Martin?"

"Uh, yeah. I guess I do."

"Good. Because it's yours."

"What? How's that?"

"Mother specifically asked that, upon her death, this radio go to you. She was quite adamant about it, too."

Mom sat next to me and examined the radio. "I've never seen this before. Was it Father's?"

"It was. But he never liked it. He stuck it up in the attic when he came home in 1941, and that's where it stayed. Then, one day, out of nowhere, Mother asked me to go up and find it."

"For Martin?"

"No. For herself. She said she wanted to listen to it. She sat in here for hours, tuning in scratchy stations." She explained to me, "It will only pick up AM stations, and only if they're close by."

Mom leaned closer. "It's a beautiful piece of furniture, though."

Margaret agreed. "It's a fine example of Art Deco." She looked at me. "Art Deco was all the rage in the 1930s." She looked at Aunt Elizabeth. "Is it American?"

"It is. But Father had it with him at the Embassy. It spent at least a year of its life in London."

I moved to head her off before we plunged back into the family story. "I wonder why Nana wanted to listen to it. Maybe she was missing the old days?"

Aunt Elizabeth answered warily, "Maybe."

"Or maybe she was listening for something that was floating in the ether. You know? Nana always had a mystical side to her."

Mom and Aunt Elizabeth exchanged a look. It was Aunt Elizabeth who answered me. "That's a nice way to put it, Martin, but I think there's a more down-to-earth explanation. Mother started doing and saying some crazy things near the end. She did not go out like Father. He was alert and intelligent until the very end."

I looked past Aunt Elizabeth at the wild-eyed old man holding the eightieth-birthday telegram. I thought, *You couldn't tell by that photo.* But I didn't say anything.

On that note, everyone dispersed for their sleeping rooms. It had been an exhausting day for me. I had left the security of my basement, encountered Hank Lowery at mass, traveled for over six hours, and missed my naps. I was soon asleep and dreaming.

It turned out to be a real-place dream. Here is what I remember: I was asleep in the study. I thought I was there alone, but then I heard a noise at the desk. I looked over and saw my grandfather. His hair was disheveled, and his eyes looked weird and blazing. His hands were pawing at the top of the desk, like a blind man's, until he found what he was looking for. It was a silver letter opener, with a curved blade and an ornate handle. He clutched the handle in his right fist and held the weapon high, its blade flashing a beam of light toward my eyes. He turned his head and looked just to my right, at the dull glow of the radio dial. Just then, I heard a voice. I don't think it came from the radio, but it might have. It was a faraway version of Nana's voice, sounding remarkably calm under the circumstances. "Don't worry about him," she assured me. "He's not after you, Martin. He's after Jimmy."

"Why Jimmy?" I asked her.

"Because he's worried."

"Why?"

"You'll find out."

"Tell me who Jimmy is."

She didn't answer, and the dream ended there.

I woke up to the sound of Dad's loud snoring. The sun was already up. I got dressed and started down the hall, but I stopped when I spotted Margaret sitting on her bed, working on her laptop. She looked up and asked, "Did you sleep well in there, Martin?"

I nodded as if I had, but that real-place dream was still on my mind. I just told her, "I'm going down to breakfast."

"Hold on. I'll join you." Margaret logged off. "I've been waiting. I didn't want to sit between Mom and Aunt Elizabeth while they were arguing about silverware and vases and all."

"Is that what they're doing?"

"Yeah. It's stupid. They should let one divide and the other choose. That way, the divider will act fairly. Am I right?"

"Of course you're right."

We entered the kitchen just as Aunt Elizabeth was saying, "So we'll have three categories: things to keep; things to donate to charity; things to throw out. And then we'll divide the things to keep."

Mom agreed quietly. "That sounds fair."

Margaret and I found some small bran muffins. We each took two of them and a glass of orange juice. Aunt Elizabeth and Mom had stopped speaking, so Margaret asked, "How are you going to decide about the things to keep?"

Aunt Elizabeth answered, "I'm sure that won't be a problem."

Margaret directed a nearly imperceptible wink at me. "But isn't that always a problem?"

"It may be a problem if we both want the same thing," Mom said. "Like the Belleek china."

Aunt Elizabeth squirmed. "I shall be staying here in the house; keeping it in the family, so to speak. So it makes sense that I keep anything that is part of the house." She explained, "Like the china collection. It was really chosen to go with this particular dining room. As I recall, you don't even have a dining room."

"Would you say the same thing about the silverware?" Mom asked.

"Yes. I would. These things are part of our lives here. They deserve to stay here."

Margaret took a swig of juice, wiped her mouth, and asked, "Well, what does it say in the will?"

Aunt Elizabeth shot an angry glance at her. "This isn't a legal matter, Margaret. It's a family matter."

"Is it?"

Mom had always been afraid of Aunt Elizabeth, but Margaret had never been. Aunt Elizabeth had once hoped that Margaret would carry on the family tradition of working for the United States government. She had even arranged for an interview for Margaret at Georgetown's Walsh School of Foreign Service, using my grandfather's name as a reference, but Margaret hadn't shown up. To make matters worse, she had bypassed Catholic Georgetown altogether for non-Catholic Princeton. Aunt Elizabeth never forgave her for that.

Aunt Elizabeth took a stab at humor. "Anyway, Margaret,

I thought you went to school to study history, not family law."

"History is full of family squabbles," Margaret replied. "Sometimes they turn into world wars, depending on the families."

"Is that so?"

"World War One was fought by two grandsons of Queen Victoria. Over nine million soldiers died; God knows how many civilians died. No one is sure why."

Aunt Elizabeth had nothing to say to that, so that's where the exchange ended. We all got up and put our glasses and cups in the sink. Aunt Elizabeth asked Mom to accompany her to the funeral home to check on the arrangements. Mom asked Margaret to come along, too. Mercifully, no one invited me, so I stayed at the house. No mention was made of Dad at all.

I dawdled for a while in the kitchen, eating more little muffins. Then I went back up to the study. Dad was awake. He was standing at the wooden shelves, apparently reading book titles. Suddenly he asked me, "Do you like history, Martin?"

"Sure. Why? Do you?"

"Yes. I always have." He plucked a title off the shelf and showed it to me. "Remember this? *Martin Mehan's Memoirs*. He had this published privately. We've got a whole box of them somewhere down in the basement." He handed the leather-bound book to me. "I don't even think your mother's read it. Have you?"

"No. I don't need to. I've heard the live version." I

handed the book back, and Dad restored it to its place. That's when I saw the bottle. Two shelves below the memoirs, right where he was standing, was a bottle of golden brown liquor. I should have known.

I turned away and settled onto the couch. I reached over, instinctively, and stroked the smooth, round top of that Art Deco radio.

"That is a beauty," Dad said. "I'm glad she gave it to you."

"Yeah. Me too."

"She loved listening to the radio. Hated television; loved the radio. She was from a time when women 'listened to their stories' on the radio."

I must have looked puzzled, because he explained. "Soap opera stories. A lot of the big TV soap operas started on radio. But your grandmother wouldn't watch them on TV. You know why?"

"Why?"

"Because of her nasty husband. Old Martin bought a TV, but it was only for the girls to watch cartoons when they were little. Not only wasn't your grandmother allowed to watch it, she wasn't even allowed to touch it. He'd get up and turn it off when the girls were done watching. Your grandmother came to hate that TV. If you remember, she never watched TV at all. Never. Not even after he died. She only listened to the radio. For her, it was a matter of principle."

I had no idea why Dad was talking so much. Then I figured out that he was fixing to steal a drink. Maybe he was talking to me so I wouldn't tell on him. Still, I encouraged him to go on. "That was a terrible way to treat her."

"Sure it was. He was a terrible man."

"He was?"

Dad shrugged. "In my opinion. I never bought into the family story. I guess he went to church a lot, and worked for the government for a long time, and raised two kids, but so what? Lots of people do that. They don't get shrines made to them. Do they?"

"No."

He pointed to the photo of Grandfather Mehan with Joseph P. Kennedy. "Your grandmother was a very nice lady. A little loopy sometimes, but nice. She always dreamed about going to London herself. She had a chance to go with a friend of hers, Mrs. Mercier. This lady needed a traveling companion. It was all expenses paid, but old Martin wouldn't let her go."

"Why not?"

"Because she had to be here to wait on him, to serve him his supper."

"God. When was this?"

"When your mom was in high school and your aunt was studying to become Sister Elizabeth. It wasn't like there were two little babies at home to take care of. He just didn't want his wife going to London. End of story."

Dad reached over, pulled out the bottle, and held it up. "Napoleon brandy. A very genteel drink. Your grandmother used to drink this stuff all the time. Sometimes I'd join her. Martin Mehan never drank anything, not even wine at church. He was a total teetotaler. Anyway, whenever Nana got near the bottom, she'd replace the bottle. The old boy never knew. He was clueless about her drinking. He was clueless about a lot of things."

Dad opened the bottle, sniffed its contents, and took a small sip.

I pointed out, "Aunt Elizabeth said he remained mentally sharp until the end."

"Martin Mehan? No way. He wasn't even mentally sharp in the beginning. He didn't have much to lose. He was clueless at forty, and he was clueless at eighty."

"Then how did he become this famous guy who knew the Kennedys and all?"

"He got assigned to work for Ambassador Kennedy. Pure luck, I guess. How bright could he have been? He didn't even know his wife was an alcoholic."

"An alcoholic? Did she drink that much?"

"She drank every day. You'd have never known it, though. She'd handle herself at family gatherings, except when she'd start to tell that crazy angel story."

I answered knowingly. "About the nine First Fridays."

"Yeah. That's the one. Old Martin would cut her off as soon as he could." Dad took an openmouthed swig from the bottle. He exhaled loudly, then said, "But he got just as crazy at the end—hearing voices, talking out loud to people who weren't there."

This was all news to me. I asked, "How do you know about these things?"

"Your mother," he answered, as if that was obvious.

"She used to tell me all about him, back when we first got together. She was trying to get away from all of this . . . family history stuff."

Dad looked at the wall of portraits, and his lip curled up in anger. "This wonderful family line would be over now if it wasn't for me—your mother and me, obviously. That's what it's all about to them. The family line." He turned away from the wall, pulled out his wallet, and showed me an old photo. It was of a young man in a uniform. "Well, guess what? I've got a family line, too."

I stared hard at the photo. "Grandfather Conway?"

"Right."

"What kind of uniform is that?"

"United States Marine Corps."

"I've never seen that photo before."

"I'm not surprised. It's not hanging on the wall at home, is it?"

Dad seemed to get increasingly embittered after that. He soon stopped talking, but he kept drinking. By eleven o'clock, he had passed out and was snoring loudly. I thought about talking a nap, too, but I was afraid of having another real-place dream, another encounter with a clueless eighty-year-old man armed with a silver letter opener.

At four-thirty, we all drove in Aunt Elizabeth's Maxima to the funeral home. When I got inside, I walked right up to Nana's open casket, knelt down, and prayed. I had done the exact same thing at my grandfather's wake four years before, but this time I felt a physical presence around me. This time I felt that Nana was not lying in the casket; she was

54

hovering around me somehow, in the ether. It was a thrilling feeling, and not at all frightening.

I remember a strong smell of flowers, and a steady stream of elderly people walking past us and shaking hands. We stood in a row to greet them: Aunt Elizabeth, Mom, Dad, Margaret, and me. However, and this bothered me, the people who supposedly came to honor Nana's death weren't even talking about her. They were talking about Grandfather Mehan—how important he was to the church, and to the country, and so on. They actually said stuff like "There's a great woman behind every great man, and she was it."

I kept nodding, shaking hands, and saying thank you for two hours, until the elderly people all started to look alike. Then, near the end, one woman entered who looked different. She was tall and muscular, with rosy brown skin. She was dressed in a work uniform—white pants and a maroon top with the words "Home HealthCare" stitched over the pocket. She came through our line, like everybody else. Then she walked over near the wall, took out a set of rosary beads, and started to pray silently.

When the line finally died out, I approached the woman and stood in front of her until she looked up. Then I grimaced apologetically. "Excuse me. Did you take care of my grandmother?"

The woman smiled a dazzling white smile. She answered "Yes, sir" in an accent I had never heard before. "You must be Jimmy. Your grandmother talked about you all the time."

I recoiled slowly. "Me? No. I'm Martin."

"Yes. I am sorry about your grandmother. She was a real nice lady."

"But you just called me Jimmy."

"Yes, she called you Jimmy."

"She did?"

"I thought so. Maybe not. Maybe I have it wrong."

I leaned closer. "But if she wasn't talking about me all the time, who was she talking about?"

"I don't know, sir."

"I'm her only grandson."

"Yes, sir."

"Was there a boy around named Jimmy? A boy in the neighborhood? Or in church?"

The woman started to get flustered. She looked around until she spotted Aunt Elizabeth a safe distance away. "Miss Elizabeth said she must be talking to her grandson. So I thought that was you, and I thought that your name was Jimmy. That is all. I am sorry."

The woman backed away slowly, but I followed. "So, did she talk to this Jimmy boy a lot? Did she talk to him like he was *really* there? Or was it more . . . delirious-like?"

The woman turned and walked toward the door. "I am not supposed to talk about my clients, sir. I am sorry. Miss Elizabeth would not like that."

When we reached the doorway, I dared to put a hand on her muscular arm. "Please, ma'am. I just want to know what my nana was doing at the end of her life. It's just private information between you and me. It's for nobody else. Certainly not for my aunt Elizabeth."

The woman smiled kindly, but she continued on her way. I walked behind her, out onto the street and through a clump of smokers. When we were past them, she finally stopped and replied, "It was only near the end, sir. The last week of her life. That's when she started talking to Jimmy. It was like he was *really* there. Not like delirium. She never did nothing like that before. Goodbye, now."

I stopped still and watched her as she walked away.

I remained out on that sidewalk for a long time afterward, puzzling over the woman's words. I stared down the dark, unfamiliar street as if looking for a sign. I listened to the noises of the city. And I breathed in the cigarette smell, like the smoke from a distant fire.

THE PHILCO 20 DELUXE

After the funeral, I returned to Princeton Junction and to my life as a basement dweller. For about two months, I emerged only to trudge to the Acme and back and to attend Sunday-morning mass. I insisted that we go to the Resurrection parish church in Princeton instead of to the All Souls Chapel. I was afraid of running into Hank Lowery again.

I continued to sleep a lot, too. I kept expecting my grandfather to appear in another dream, especially right after we got back from Brookline, but he didn't. Still, I remained fearful of him, and of Lowery, and of the dark.

That's where the Philco 20 Deluxe came in. I carried my dad's old TV into the storage area and covered it with a white sheet. I put the Philco on the nightstand in its place. From that night on, I used the radio's round amber dial, glowing as dull and hazy as an ancient moon, as a night-light. And I used its tuner, set between stations, to fill the creepy silence in the basement with the soft rush of static.

It was after I started sleeping with the radio on that I had the weirdest real-place dream of all. I had fallen asleep at nine p.m. to the radio's scratchy whisperings. Sometime around three a.m., though, I woke up. I was lying in bed, looking at the dial, and I heard a voice. I concentrated harder to hear inside the static, thinking that I had picked up a stray channel. Then I noticed a smell. The smell from my grandfather's study. The musty smell of the past.

Suddenly I became aware of another person in the room. I sat upright, totally alert, straining to see in the dark. That's when it happened. A boy—small, thin, dressed in mud-brown clothes—leaned out from behind the radio and whispered, "Johnny, will you help me?"

I remember thinking, *He's got an English accent. A thick one. So I'm definitely dreaming.*

"It's me. It's Jimmy."

The name certainly didn't surprise me. I answered him confidently. "Okay, so you're Jimmy."

"Your gran, did she tell you about me? Did she ask you to help me?"

"Gran? My grandmother?"

"Yeah, that's her."

"She, uh—maybe she did. She did talk about a Jimmy."

"There you go. That's me, then."

"How did you talk to my grandmother?"

He looked over toward the Philco. "Through the radio. I talked to your grandfather, too."

"My grandfather? Martin Mehan?"

"Yeah. That's him. He wouldn't help, though."

"When? When did you talk to him?"

In response, the boy turned his face away, slowly. When he answered, he sounded perplexed. "I don't know."

"Because my grandfather is dead. He has been for four years."

"Yeah? Well, when I talked to him, he was alive."

"My grandmother is dead, too."

He got very still. Then he whispered, "When?"

"Two months ago."

He nodded rapidly. Then he spoke with more confidence. "Right. Okay. That's why I'm here, then. She told me to talk to you."

"To me? Why?"

"She said you would help."

I thought of Nana's distant voice on the phone. "So . . . my grandmother said that I would help you?"

"Yeah." He held up one finger, like he had remembered something. "Yeah. She told me to tell you that your real name isn't Martin at all. It's John. She said I should say that so you'd know she sent me. It's like a letter of introduction."

"Okay. Okay." I leaned toward him to try to get a better look. "That's who I am. But who are you?"

"I told you already. I'm Jimmy."

"Jimmy?" I racked my brain to find a sensible question to ask after that, but all I came up with was "So . . . Jimmy, are you really here? In my room? Or am I dreaming?"

"I don't think it's either one, Johnny. It's something else entirely. We're at a point here, you and me."

I began to feel very confused, and then very scared, like I was losing control of my body. I couldn't look at the boy again. I couldn't talk to him, either. So I spoke aloud, to myself, "I'm going to wake up now."

And I did. I found myself sitting upright in the exact scene of the dream. But there was no boy standing in the corner.

I stared at his spot for about three minutes. Then I started to tremble, like it was freezing cold. I was so shook-up that I forced myself to get out of bed, turn on the lights, and walk upstairs. I walked all the way to Mom's bedroom and placed my hand on the doorknob, ready to confess every frightening, crazy detail.

Then I got ahold of myself and stopped. I was too afraid to go back downstairs, so I retreated to the living room. I turned on the TV and muted the sound. I eventually fell asleep there, in the blue flicker of the screen. When the light of daybreak woke me up, I clicked the TV off and hurried back down to the basement.

I sat on my bed and looked at the radio for a long, long time. Then I walked into the computer room and logged on to the Internet. I got into a search engine and typed "Philco 20 Deluxe."

Over the next few hours, I discovered a whole world of radio repairers and sellers and historians. I found out how to download wiring schemas and how to send for new tubes. I learned that my particular radio was marketed to the wealthiest customers in the 1930s and 1940s. It ranked with other classic Art Deco radios, such as the Atwater Kent 165 and the Zenith tombstone. I learned that the "cathedral" design took its name from the rounded arch of a cathedral. It was meant to discourage people from putting things on top of the radio, which would overheat its tubes and wires.

Aunt Elizabeth had given me the radio in a sturdy cardboard box with a large packing envelope that included the original bill of sale and some other papers. One of the papers was a card from Nana to Grandfather Mehan. It said, in curly blue ink:

> Dearest Martin, I hope this radio arrives safe.
> Like you. The salesman said you need to buy
> an adapter to plug it in in England. Your loving wife, Mary.

The envelope also included a small metal plate with the words MARTIN MEHAN, U.S. EMBASSY engraved on it. The plate was supposed to be screwed into the radio, and it had two holes for that purpose. But a quick check revealed that although the nameplate had once been attached, it had been unscrewed, and removed, and never returned.

The back of the radio was completely open, for cooling purposes. It contained metal boxes, glass vacuum tubes, and assorted old wires. It displayed a list of patents owned by the Philadelphia Storage Battery Company (Philco), and information about voltage (115) and wattage (75). The radio had a number written in ink at the top: USE83040. I double-checked the pile of original papers and, sure enough, saw the same number on the receipt from the U.S. Embassy in London, dated August 30, 1940. Below that number was another, shorter one: 291240. This number was written with black ink in another hand, a sloppier one.

* * *

After my morning nap and a skimpy lunch, I sat down to IM with Pinak and Manetti. We corresponded about once per day, even more often in the days leading up to our meeting at All Souls about the vandalism incident. Pinak, who believed in justice, didn't think anything bad would happen to us. Manetti, who believed only in Manetti, didn't seem to care what happened. Personally, I couldn't see any good coming out of this meeting, for me or for anyone else.

We were usually all online around noon. Sometimes two girls from All Souls checked in, too, through Manetti. Their real names were Penny and Stephanie. Penny was a scholarship kid whose father taught French at All Souls. Stephanie went there the normal way—that is, at great expense to her family.

The best thing about those girls was that they hated Lowery and anyone who would hang around him. I appreciated that more than they could ever know. The subject of Lowery came up often, and they were always happy to trash him with us. Inevitably, that subject came up on the day of our meeting with Father Thomas.

> JERSEYGIRL529: You guys, tell us what happened on the last day of school. Stephanie says she saw you guys fighting by those statues.
> MANETTITHEMAN: We can't talk about it. We're sworn to secrecy, with a sacred oath.
> JERSEYGIRL529: Yeah right. Were you fighting with Lowery?
> MANETTITHEMAN: You'll have to ask Lowery.

JERSEYGIRL529: Gross. I'm not talking to that pus-face. We see him at the mall and we run away.

MANETTITHEMAN: Smooth move. Hey, I'll be at the mall tomorrow. Let's hook up.

JERSEYGIRL529: Let's not.

MANETTITHEMAN: Come on. I'm serious.

JERSEYGIRL529: Where do you want to meet?

MANETTITHEMAN: The food court.

JERSEYGIRL529: No. We're both on diets.

MANETTITHEMAN: You don't need to be on diets. You two are hot.

JERSEYGIRL529: Haha.

MANETTITHEMAN: Meet me at the bookstore. Where the couches are. You can sit on my lap.

JERSEYGIRL529: Right. Both of us?

MANETTITHEMAN: Yeah. Definitely. They got those big couches.

JERSEYGIRL529: Stephanie says she doesn't like books.

MANETTITHEMAN: Me either. So where?

JERSEYGIRL529: She says we'll meet you at the music store.

MANETTITHEMAN: Cool. Much better idea. We can put on the headphones and undulate together.

JERSEYGIRL529: Stephanie wants to know what that means.

MANETTITHEMAN: Tell her she'll find out tomorrow.

64

JERSEYGIRL529: Haha. She wants to know who taught you such a big word.

MANETTITHEMAN: Pinak.

PINAKC: I did no such thing. Leave me out of this foolishness.

JERSEYGIRL529: Seriously though. Lowery and Mayer and Livingstone basically live at that mall. If you guys are fighting with them, it might start up again tomorrow.

MANETTITHEMAN: Whatever. I ain't afraid of Lowery. I'll kick his pimply ass.

JERSEYGIRL529: What about Mayer? And Livingstone?

MANETTITHEMAN: No problem. I'll have my boys with me. Right, boys? You're coming?

PINAKC: I will not be going anywhere with you.

MANETTITHEMAN: Come on, Pinak. You can use that Asian kung fu crap.

PINAKC: First of all, I am an American, of Indian descent. Second of all, Indians do not practice kung fu.

MANETTITHEMAN: Oh no? What do they practice?

PINAKC: Non-violence.

MANETTITHEMAN: Right. What about you, Martin? What's your excuse?

JMARTINC: I don't have an excuse. I AM afraid of Lowery. I won't go anywhere where he is.

MANETTITHEMAN: That's bogus, man. You're bigger than him.

JMARTINC: Forget it.

MANETTITHEMAN: He'll be at All Souls today!
You'll have to see him there.

I felt sick at the thought. I didn't answer. Neither did
anybody else, until Penny typed in:

JERSEYGIRL529: Gotta go. See you at the mall
tomorrow. If you're lucky.

MANETTITHEMAN: I am lucky. I get lucky.

JERSEYGIRL529: Whatever. I'm out.

MANETTITHEMAN: I'm out, too. See you guys at
the big VANDALISM meeting.

When it was just the two of us, I tried, indirectly, to ask
Pinak about my dream.

JMARTINC: Pinak, do you ever wonder if what
seemed to be a dream was actually real?

PINAKC: Are you serious now?

JMARTINC: Yes.

PINAKC: I maybe wonder for a few seconds
when I first wake up. But that's all.

JMARTINC: That's what I was afraid of.

PINAKC: Do you wonder what is real?

JMARTINC: I don't know. I don't know anything.

PINAKC: You sound depressed, Martin.

JMARTINC: Don't start that.

PINAKC: All right. I won't. I have to go now
anyway.

JMARTINC: Me too. I'll see you later at the meeting.

I signed off and trudged into my room for a nap. But I didn't lie down. I was afraid to. I was afraid I'd have another encounter with an English boy who claimed to know my dead grandmother. I had a terrible feeling that I had crossed some sort of line, mentally, with that last dream. In every other dream I'd ever had, real-place or not, I quickly realized that it was only a dream. I woke up, snapped out of it, and felt silly for ever believing it was real.

But that didn't happen with this dream.

Well into the afternoon, I was still wondering if that English boy, that Jimmy, was real.

INDEPENDENT STUDY

I grudgingly changed into my All Souls Prep uniform. I must have grown over the summer, because it no longer fit. I hated the feel of the thing. I stood looking in the mirror for a long minute, trying to figure out a way to never put it on again.

Inside, I was feeling even worse. I was trembling at the thought of sitting in a room with Hank Lowery. Three months' time had not healed the shock or the shame I felt for being slapped in the face by him.

I walked outside at noon to wait for Mom. I was surprised when she pulled up with Margaret in the front seat. I climbed into the back and asked Margaret, "What are you doing here?"

"I'm going with you."

"Why?"

Margaret inclined her head toward Mom. "Because Mom asked me to."

"Oh? What's this about?"

Mom answered simply, "Father Thomas wants her to be there."

The drive to All Souls was predictably tense. I told Mom right off, "I want this to be my last trip to All Souls. Ever. I want you to enroll me at Garden State."

She answered matter-of-factly. "You know that is not an option, Martin. I've worked very hard so you and Margaret could go to All Souls. The only thing you have to do is listen in class and do your work. Is that really so terrible an ordeal?"

I wanted to respond, *Yes. It is.* But I didn't bother. I spent the rest of the ride staring at the passing countryside. Occasionally I saw my own reflection appear in the window. I was surprised to see that I looked a little like Dad. I looked depressed like him, anyway.

As we walked from the parking lot to the Administration Building, my sense of dread rose to the point where I actually thought I might throw up in the hedges. Mom led the way into Father Thomas's office, followed by Margaret. I looked for Lowery right away, but I didn't see him. I even leaned in to look at the corners of the room. Then I assumed he would be coming in behind us, but Father Thomas announced, "Excellent. Everyone is here now."

"Everyone," apparently, did not include Hank Lowery and his parents, or Joey Mayer and Tim Connelly and their parents. Ben Livingstone's father, however, was there. He was a tall, balding man dressed in a blue blazer and gray pants; he wore a bulky Rolex.

Pinak and his father and Manetti and his father were

there, too, sitting in a row of chairs along the left wall. Dr. Chander was dressed impeccably, as always, in a dark blue suit. Manetti's father had a suit on, too, a black one, but it was too small, and he looked uncomfortable in it.

Mom, Margaret, and I sat in three chairs across from them. Father Thomas looked at all the adults in turn and introduced them for the benefit of the others. When he got to Livingstone's father, he said, "Cal Livingstone is the attorney representing the Lowery family and the estate of the late General Lowery. He is also a member of the board of directors of All Souls Preparatory School."

I watched the adults glance at each other and then quickly look away. Mom's face showed surprise, even confusion. She leaned toward Father Thomas and asked him quietly, "Aren't the others coming?"

Father Thomas thought for a moment. "The others? Oh, the other students? No, they have already been here. Some of the families had scheduling conflicts, so I decided to meet with you in shifts. Mr. Connelly brought Timothy, and Mr. Livingstone brought Ben, Joseph Mayer, and Hank Lowery in at noon." He turned to Mr. Livingstone. "Did the boys all get a ride home?"

Cal Livingstone answered, "Yes, with Russ Mayer. I think he was dropping them at the mall."

Mom sat back, blinking, clearly not satisfied with the answer.

Then Father Thomas began to, as he put it, "run down the facts and the repair costs."

Cal Livingstone immediately raised his hand. "The Lowery family is willing to absorb the repair costs. The family is more concerned about the dedication timeline. They have been waiting a long time for the General to be acknowledged by his school, and by his country."

Father Thomas assured him, "We're still on schedule for New Year's Day. The major construction phase of the Heroes' Walk is now over. And that brings us to the reason for today's meetings—the student vandalism at that site."

Father Thomas held up a blue file. "We have collected statements from all of the pertinent parties." He looked at Pinak, Manetti, and me. "As I did with the previous group of boys, I'd like you three to step outside now and take a seat by the Rembrandts. I'll go over the facts with your parents and render my final decision. Then I'll call you back in."

Dr. Chander pointed Pinak toward the door. Pinak walked out quickly. Manetti's father nodded at him, and he exited, too. I got up on my own and followed them both out the door, around the corner, and down to the plastic chairs.

Pinak sat on the right, facing a ghostly painting of a dead man climbing out of his coffin: Rembrandt's *Raising of Lazarus.*

I sat facing *Abraham and Isaac,* the painting of the boy about to be stabbed to death by the crazy old man. The old man looked all too familiar.

Manetti remained standing.

Pinak soon spoke to me. "I don't feel like one of the pertinent parties. How about you?"

I didn't answer, so Manetti did. "I don't even know what 'pertinent' means."

"No. But miraculously, you know what 'undulate' means?"

"Hell yeah. That's a very studly word. I'm surprised you know it."

"I am surprised you could spell it. Amazed, really. You must have had a dictionary on your lap."

"I'll tell you what I'm gonna have on my lap, Pinak. To-morrow, at the mall. Two of 'em."

"Please don't. Please stop."

Manetti laughed and looked around. His attention turned to the painting over Pinak's head. "Look at that knife, man! What's that crazy old dude doing?"

Pinak answered, "He is sacrificing his son to God."

"Yow. That is cold."

"But see how the angel has stopped him, at the last minute. It turned out it was just a test."

Manetti touched the paint on the canvas. "Are these things real? I mean, are they by Rembrandt?"

"Don't be ridiculous," Pinak scoffed. "All Souls Prep can barely pay its bills. They could never afford to own real Rembrandts. They are cheap copies, in cheap frames."

Manetti turned and pointed at the huge historical paintings in the entranceway. "So what about them?"

"Those are two paintings by Emmanuel Leutze: *Washington Crossing the Delaware* and *Westward the Course of Empire Takes Its Way*. No, they are not the originals. Now, please do not embarrass yourself by asking me about the van Goghs."

"Hey. I know *they're* not real."

"Right. You do now."

Manetti looked at the array of art pieces and laughed. "It's like Father Thomas and Father Leonard went out one day to some art flea market and said, 'Okay. Give us two of everything.' "

Pinak actually agreed with him. "Their obsession with symmetry does seem odd. Perhaps it is because they are twins."

We stayed quiet for a minute after that. I listened to the sound of low, indistinguishable voices on the other side of the wall. Manetti, ever brazen, decided to creep to the door and press his ear to it. As he did, Pinak leaned forward and whispered to me, "I think it is pertinent that Father Thomas said all new construction is over. Don't you?" When I didn't reply, he drew the conclusion for me. "I think that means they don't need Manetti Construction around here any-more." After a long pause he added, "Martin, are you all right? You look very pale."

I was not all right. As he was speaking, I had found my-self staring at *Abraham and Isaac*. I had become absolutely transfixed by the boy in the painting. His father had brought him there to *kill* him. And then the angel had intervened to stop it. Still . . . how could he ever forgive his father for that?

Suddenly we heard a loud, sharp "What?" through the wall. It was spoken by Manetti's father. Manetti hurried back to join us.

A few seconds later, Manetti's father threw open the door and looked around. He pointed at his son and said tightly, "Let's go."

Father Thomas, in the doorway, told him gently, "You can, of course, appeal this decision."

"Yeah? To who?"

"To the board of directors."

Mr. Manetti pointed back inside the office. "To him and his buddies?"

"No. Mr. Livingstone is only one member of a five-member board. They are all independent members, I assure you. They will give you a fair hearing."

Mr. Manetti put one hand on his son's shoulder and stood motionless. He sounded more embarrassed than angry when he finally said, "All right. I'll think about that." Then he led his son out the door.

Father Thomas pointed to Pinak and me. "You two can come back in now. The matter is settled."

We took the same seats we had recently vacated. None of the adults looked particularly happy about what had just happened. Father Thomas summarized for us. "The students' statements, and the eyewitness account by Father Leonard, and common sense all lay the blame in one place—on the boy who actually threw the rock that caused the damage. The final result of this investigation, then, is that young Mr. Manetti has been expelled from All Souls Preparatory School. I suggest we all leave this unfortunate incident behind us now and move on. Are we agreed?"

Pinak whispered something to his father. Dr. Chander spoke up. "Before I agree, I would like to ask you about the discrepancies between Pinak's statement and the Lowery boy's statement."

"Yes, Doctor?"

"How did you reconcile these two different views of the same incident?"

"Well, they did disagree on the events leading up to the

incident, but they did *not* disagree on the incident itself, that is, the rock-throwing that damaged the pedestal. I guess I am inclined to let the boys disagree on the peripheral facts as long as they agree on the basic facts."

Pinak whispered to his father again, and Dr. Chander asked, "Wouldn't someone who lied about the peripheral facts also lie about the basic facts?"

"Yes, Doctor, that is an excellent point. That's why I am thankful that we have these other statements to go on." He picked up the blue file for emphasis. This caused an envelope to slip out of it and fall at Mom's feet. We both stared at the handwriting on the envelope. It was Mom's, just as she had addressed it on the last day of school.

Mom picked it up and examined it closely. She asked, "Why is this envelope still sealed?"

Father Thomas reached over and took it back, assuring her, "Because I remembered Martin's verbal statement so clearly. This written version was just a formality. A backup, if you will."

Pinak looked at me and slowly raised his eyebrows.

Dr. Chander took Pinak's arm, stood up, and led him toward the door. He told Father Thomas pointedly, "My son and I must be going now. I rearranged *my* schedule for this meeting, Father. Unlike some others. I agree that you should punish the boy who threw the stone. Perhaps not so severely? But I would also look into punishing the boys who lied to you, whoever they are. Good day."

Father Thomas took a step toward the door with them; he answered grimly, "Good day, Doctor. Thank you." Then he turned back to us. "Perhaps the punishment today was so severe because the implications of this vandalism were so severe."

No one disagreed, so he continued. "The Heroes' Walk is the biggest construction project at All Souls since the Lowery Library went up twenty years ago. As such, it has implications beyond a mere construction project. We all hope that the dedication of the statue of General Lowery will be part of a larger, national tribute to our distinguished alumnus."

He broke off and looked directly at Margaret. "We have received word that a major encyclopedia is about to include General Lowery in its new entries. Let us hope that this inspires other reference books to do the same. And I am delighted to report that another distinguished All Souls alumnus—I should say 'alumna'—is actually working on this important entry. Isn't that right, Margaret?"

Margaret seemed caught off guard. She answered, "Yes. That's right."

Father Thomas was speaking to Margaret, but he was looking at Cal Livingstone. "And your grandfather, Martin Mehan, is another great friend of All Souls Preparatory School, having taught history here for three years following his retirement from the government service." He smiled kindly at Mom. "Martin Mehan served with General Lowery in London, did he not?"

Mom answered. "He did. With Ambassador Kennedy, too."

Cal Livingstone spoke up. "Perhaps Mr. Mehan left memoirs or other papers that could shed more light on General Lowery's contributions to the war effort."

Mom said, "I believe my father did mention him. Didn't he, Margaret?"

Margaret clearly was not pleased to be in this conversation. She answered, "There were one or two mentions of the General."

Cal Livingstone smiled at Margaret. "That is interesting. I was not aware of that. Do you mind if I ask you a few questions?"

"No."

He stood up and approached her. "My understanding is that you work for the Millennium Encyclopedia. Is that correct?"

"It is."

"That is the encyclopedia owned by the Wissler family?"

"That's right."

"You see, my concern, and the Lowery family's concern, is that General Lowery not become the victim of revisionist history. Are you aware of that term?"

"Of course."

Livingstone explained it anyway. "Revisionist history is when the facts of the past get distorted to further someone's agenda in the present. Stalin rewrote the Soviet history books to remove all mention of people he didn't like." He looked back at Margaret. "We just want to make sure no prejudice like that exists here."

Margaret gritted her teeth. "Why does the family think there is prejudice against General Lowery?"

"I did not say the family thought that. The family wants to make sure that none exists."

"But why would it?"

He shrugged theatrically. "Because the world contains prejudiced people."

Margaret continued coolly, "But who could possibly be prejudiced against a hero of two world wars?"

Cal Livingstone sharpened his tone. "Someone who has never been in a war. Someone like your boss, perhaps; your Mr. Wissler."

"I see. Well, to my knowledge, no one has *ever* questioned Mr. Wissler's objectivity before."

"And no one is doing so now. I apologize if it seemed that way."

Margaret's neck and cheeks flushed pink. Now she knew why Father Thomas had wanted her to come. It was to take a message back to her boss from the Lowery family.

The meeting ended on that note, with everyone staring at the face-off between Cal Livingstone and Margaret. Livingstone smiled tightly at her. Then he shook hands with Father Thomas and walked out the door.

Everyone else got up to leave.

I knew I had to do something or I would be back at that place on Monday, ready to start classes, so I spoke directly to Father Thomas. "I don't want to go to this school anymore. I hate it here. I want to withdraw. Right now."

Father Thomas's brow furrowed.

Mom gasped in shock. "Martin! That is ridiculous."

But Father Thomas answered patiently, "Nobody wants summer vacation to end, Martin. You'll feel differently after you see all of your friends."

"No. No, I won't. I only had two friends here, and you just kicked one of them out. Kick me out instead!"

Mom held out her hands in supplication. "I . . . I don't know what to say, Father. I am so sorry. I am so embarrassed."

Father Thomas reassured her. "Don't be embarrassed. Remember, we are dealing with children. They are very temperamental, and they wear their emotions on the outside." He looked at me. "Martin, I know from my own experience, and from my brother's experience, that one day you will feel differently about All Souls."

Margaret spoke over my shoulder. "I don't."

Father Thomas looked at her, puzzled. "What?"

"I've been out for five years and I don't feel differently. I hated All Souls when I was here, and that feeling hasn't changed."

Mom gasped again. "Margaret! That is not true. Why are you saying that?"

Margaret sighed. "Fine. It's not true. I'm lying. But what can we do for Martin? He's not coping the way I coped. As far as I can see, he's not coping, period."

Mom threw up her hands.

Margaret turned to me. "Tell them what's going on, Martin. Don't be afraid to express yourself."

Buoyed by Margaret, I blurted out, "I don't know what I'll do if you make me come back. I might lose it!"

Father Thomas nodded, slowly and deliberately. "I see. All right. Here's the essential question, Martin: Would you commit an act of vandalism, or an act of violence against another student?"

"I might. I really might. I don't know."

Mom was now in tears, so Father Thomas assured her, "Mary, you know how we bend over backwards to help some students. Why wouldn't we do the same for Martin?" He turned to include me. "Perhaps he should pursue an independent study assignment for now. Would you like that, Martin?"

I didn't answer.

"Independent study would give you time to resolve some of these personal issues. You would work on your own, at home, but you would also be keeping pace with your classmates. We've done this in the past for many students."

"What would I study?"

He walked over to a high filing cabinet and pulled out a drawer. "You would have choices. You could study a life cycle, such as the life cycle of a certain pond. You would write about the history of the pond, the science of the animals and plants in it, and so on."

I reached into my pocket and pulled out two folded-up papers. "Can I study this? Can I study the . . . the science of a radio? A classic Art Deco historical radio?"

Father Thomas took the papers. "Hmm. Let me look these over. If the study is cross-curricular, I don't see why not. We need to be able to give you credit in science, history, language arts, and reading."

I pointed at the schema for the Philco 20 Deluxe. "It's all in there—science, history, art. I can research tons of stuff and write papers, and Mom can shuttle them back and forth."

"Father Leonard coordinates all of the independent

studies. I'll have to clear it with him, but I think this looks like a workable plan."

Mom was too stunned to argue, so she quietly agreed. At that point she would have agreed to just about anything to get me out of that office and to keep me, even temporarily, at All Souls.

As we drove home in icy silence, I thought, *I've done it! I've succeeded. I don't have to start school on Monday, because I'm going to do independent study. I don't have to face Hank Lowery, because I won't be at All Souls.*

When we turned in to the driveway, I added: *Now, if only I didn't have to fall asleep again and face that boy named Jimmy.*

LONDON: SEPTEMBER 8, 1940

I'm going to describe this as best I can, just as it happened.

My first experience with time travel still remains a jumble in my mind. Images and words and sounds kept coming at me very quickly. I was disoriented most of the time.

I had just spent two days in the basement. I was doing a lot of Internet research on the workings of radio, the key to my independent study plan—the key to my avoiding All Souls Prep for as long as possible.

I had been up particularly late on Sunday night. I finally fell asleep in my usual position. I had my head next to the Philco 20 Deluxe. I had my eye on its amber dial. I had my ear tuned to its static hiss.

The first thing I remember after that is a damp smell, like the smell of wet wool, and then a sweet smell, like hair cream. I looked for the radio, and I saw it ten feet farther away, sitting atop a small table. It was no longer hissing static; it was broadcasting a voice—a clear, high, British voice. There was a leather chair between me and the radio, and Jimmy was sitting in it, staring at me. I can't say I was surprised to see him again. I was, however, surprised to be out of my basement room. I was, instead, in a dark living room. I knew, as you know in a dream, that I was a long way from home. I knew that I was in London, England.

The boy greeted me happily, in a familiar voice. "You're finally here then, eh, Johnny?"

"I'm where?"

"My house, mate. Where do you think?"

"I have no idea. I can hardly see."

"You'll get used to it in a minute. Everything's darkened for the blackout. Old Canby'll get you if there's a crack of light showing outside."

Jimmy then pointed at the radio. "Lord Haw-Haw said there's terrific looting going on in London, but don't you believe it. It just ain't true. My dad and me are out there every day, and there ain't no looting going on at all. If there were, I expect my dad'd bring home something nice for us, eh?"

I looked around the small room. Aside from Jimmy's chair, a leather wing chair in the Queen Anne style, there was a couch with an ill-fitting cloth thrown over it and a dark wood sideboard with pictures, knickknacks, and military stuff on top.

"Lord Haw-Haw said the King is hiding out in Scotland with the crown jewels, ready to make a run for it. He said that Churchill and Roosevelt take their orders from the Jewish financiers. Do you know if any of that's true, Johnny?"

I had no idea what he was talking about, but I did pick up on one name. "Roosevelt? Do you mean FDR?"

"Yeah. That's him. FDR. There's a song about him: 'Mr. Franklin D. Roosevelt Jones.' Do you know it?"

"No."

The boy reached over and turned the dial. "Do you listen to the radio?"

"I just started."

"How about the news, then? You listen to that, don't you?"

"No. Not really."

Jimmy's face registered surprise. He had a very expressive face—his eyebrows raised and lowered; his eyes winked; his lips smiled or frowned. "Well, at five-forty-two each night, on the BBC, is 'London Calling.' It's special announcements, news, and the like. The BBC's saying that Piccadilly Circus and Leicester Square have surface shelters now. And they've dug trenches for bomb shelters in Hyde Park."

"Bomb shelters?"

"Yeah. And they're crating up the statues all over London for the duration of the war."

"The war?"

"Yeah. Seems like a good idea, don't it? They already crated up Eros and hauled him off. But old Nelson's still in Trafalgar Square, and Richard the Lion Heart's still outside Parliament."

As my eyes adjusted, I could see that the room was so dark because the windows had been taped over with cardboard. That gave the room an eerie feel, like we were sitting inside a box. The front wall had a wood door to the left side and a small window in the middle. The right wall had a sports schedule taped to it with a drawing of a soccer ball and the words *Arsenal Football Club Official Programme, 1938–9.*

I turned to look at the wall behind me. It had a poster taped to it, too, with a drawing of a British soldier. Behind him was a map of Europe that was dotted with white surrender flags. The soldier looked sweaty and beaten up, but very purposeful. The words he spoke were set below him, in large yellow letters: VERY WELL THEN, ALONE!

I pointed to it. "What does that mean?"

"What? The poster?"

"Yeah."

"That's obvious. Look at it. That's a sergeant in the Dukes Regiment, the British regulars. He's saying that we're gonna go it alone against Germany. Don't have much choice, do we? The Dutch, the Norwegians, the Belgians— they've all given up the fight. You see the white flags stuck into their countries?"

I stared at the poster. "Yeah."

"The Frogs only lasted six days against Hitler. Well, we British will last for six years if we have to. That's what my dad says. Hitler will never beat us. We're tougher than he is any day."

Jimmy got up from his chair, full of patriotic enthusiasm. I hadn't noticed before how small he was. He had very thin arms and legs, wavy brown slicked-back hair, and a crooked smile. "Come here, Johnny. Look at this." He led me to the sideboard and held up three military medals. "These are my granddad's. My dad's dad, James Harker. He won them in the Great War, serving with the Dukes."

I walked over to join him, and I took the medals in hand.

"We're from Yorkshire. Three generations of James

Harkers. Yorkshire's where they recruit for the Duke of Wellington's Regiment, the Dukes. Always have. We're the lads that beat Napoleon at Waterloo. Eighteenth of June, 1815."

I laid the medals back on the sideboard, and that's when I saw the book. It was a Bible studies textbook with pictures and stories, and questions answered in black ink. It was opened to a picture that I knew well: Rembrandt's *Abraham and Isaac*. I sputtered, "What? What is that doing here?"

"What? The Bible studies? That's my homework, isn't it? Mrs. Lane will be popping round to make sure I'm doing it."

"Do you know that painting?"

Jimmy studied it for a moment. "I know it now."

"They have this same painting at my school; it's one of the Rembrandts. Do you know Rembrandt?"

"Everybody knows Rembrandt, don't they?"

I stared at the book silently, shaking my head. Then I walked over and sat heavily on the old couch. I finally said, "You don't live here alone, right? Who lives with you? That Mrs. Lane?"

"No. She lives next door with her husband, Bill. He's my dad's mate."

"Your dad? He lives here?"

Jimmy smiled brightly. "Of course he does. Where else would he live?"

"What about your mother?"

His smile faded. "My mum died a year ago, of pneumonia. It's just Dad and me now, but he's like me mum and dad combined. He's really brilliant like that."

Jimmy pulled a metal license from his pocket. He held it out to show me the words engraved on it. "I had a dog named Reg, too, but he got put down."

"What does that mean?"

"Put down? It's, like, killed. Mercy killing."

"No! What for?"

"For the war. What else? They all got put down. All the dogs; all the cats. People figured there'd be no food to feed them and the dogs would start barking when the Germans came, maybe give away a hiding place. They killed all the animals in the zoos, too, didn't they?"

Jimmy pointed at the sports poster. "Dad and me were at the football match today—Arsenal and Fulham. Do you fancy football?"

"Football? British football, right? Soccer?"

"My dad likes the Spurs; I like the Gunners."

"You like who?"

"Arsenal Gunners. They're the best, mate. Do you know them?"

"No. I don't watch sports. I don't play them, either."

"I watch 'em and play 'em. And I listen to them on the radio, but not tonight." Jimmy walked over to the Philco 20 Deluxe and switched the channel. The droning voice faded away and was replaced by big band pop music. He turned toward me. "Do you like Anne Shelton, Johnny?"

"I don't know who she is."

"She was a real favorite of Mum's. Dad and me like Vera Lynn better."

"I don't know who she is, either."

Jimmy's face again registered surprise. "Come on, now.

She sang with Burt Ambrose? Now she's got her own radio show for the soldiers. She sings 'Wishing Will Make It So.' "

"No. Sorry."

Jimmy shrugged. "Your loss, mate."

I heard a soft rap on the front door. Jimmy and I both watched it open slowly, revealing a young woman and a middle-aged man.

The woman stepped into the room first. She was thin and very blond. She pointed at the sideboard and asked, in a high, squeaky voice, "Have you done your Bible lessons, then, Jimmy?"

Jimmy answered quickly. "I have, Mrs. Lane."

She looked at him suspiciously. "You know, if you haven't, your dad'll box your ears."

"Yes, ma'am."

The man was much older than the woman, about twice her age. He wore a helmet over what appeared to be a bald head. His coat bore an armband and a silver badge that said ARP WARDEN. He looked around carefully, with a critical eye.

"Tell your dad for me that I can see light coming through that front door. He'll need to do a proper job of taping that."

"I will, Mr. Canby."

"And he should hang a curtain *inside* the door, from the ceiling, for when you're going in or out. The Wardens' Service calls that a 'light lock.' "

"Yes, Mr. Canby."

"If you don't, you'll have to turn out all lights before you even go near the door."

Mrs. Lane looked at the radio and then at Jimmy. "Who's that playing now?"

Jimmy told her, "That's Geraldo, isn't it?"

"What's the song?"

" 'It's a Lovely Day Tomorrow.' "

Alice Lane turned to the man. "Geraldo's at the Savoy Hotel, Mr. Canby. I'd fancy seeing him someday, but my Bill won't take me."

Canby smiled a discolored smile. "You should join the wardens, Mrs. Lane. I could take you there on an inspection." He took out a small metal flask and handed it to her.

Alice Lane took a long drink from it, grimaced, and laughed. "I bet you could." She walked back to the front door and opened it. "The gossip is that you and the other wardens have a great orgy going on. Is that right?"

She stepped through the door into the utter darkness; Canby followed. "Well, Mrs. Lane, I don't know about the others . . ."

Alice Lane called back from the street, "You stay here now, Jimmy."

Jimmy stared for a moment at the door. "That's Mrs. Alice Lane. She likes her gin and It, don't she?"

"Her what?"

"Gin and It. Her drink. Her liquor."

"What's 'It'?"

"It? It's Italian vermouth, isn't it?"

"I don't know."

Jimmy pulled a rubber-and-canvas contraption out of a drawer in the sideboard. He held it up to me and explained,

"Gas mask, Johnny. Canby'll stop me if I don't have it. He's a real bollocks, that Canby. My dad said being a warden's gone to his head. His bald head. Let's get going."

I thought of the pitch-blackness beyond the door. "Where? Going where?"

"Going out, mate."

"Out in the dark?"

"Yeah, out in the dark, you great girl, you. We got someplace to go."

I didn't move. "Where?"

"The American Embassy."

That got me to stand up. "The American Embassy? In London?"

Jimmy laughed. "That's the one. Yeah."

"Why? Why are we going there?"

Jimmy raised his shoulders and his eyebrows in unison. He held them up comically for a moment. But then he dropped the pose and told me, very seriously, "I'm not sure, Johnny. I know that I have to take you there, and that's all."

I nodded nervously. "Yeah. Okay. And I know that I'm dreaming."

Jimmy answered thoughtfully, "Do you? Did you ever have a dream like this before?"

"No," I admitted.

Then his smile returned. "All right, then. Let's be off. I want to catch my dad before he leaves his post."

I followed him to the door. "Your dad works there?"

"Yeah, for now. Him and Bill Lane. They're with the Auxiliaries."

"Auxiliaries? Like police officers?"

"No. Firefighters."

Jimmy pushed open the door to what could have been the end of the earth, or deepest space. To my eyes it was total blackness, but he walked out into it as if it were midday. I hesitated, but I didn't want to lose him, so I ran out, too.

Jimmy was a mere phantom ahead of me. I hissed, "Wait up!"

He stopped and turned. "Don't worry, Johnny. It's all right. Ain't nothing gonna happen to you."

"How do you know?"

"I know. Don't be afraid of nothing. That's what my dad says to me, so I'm not. I'm not afraid of nothing."

I, however, was afraid of a lot of things, including the dark. But Jimmy spoke calmly, even lightly. "Dad'll get a laugh out of that. Canby said he didn't black out the door properly. He'll say that old Canby can't do nothin' properly, and he'll be right." We crossed the street. Jimmy pointed through the gloom at a structure barely visible ten feet in front of us. It was a one-story brick building, like a public lavatory. "There's some of his handiwork."

"Whose?"

"Canby's, Johnny. Aren't you listening? That's a surface shelter. The government hired contractors to build them all over London, so Canby figured he'd cash in. He built that one, tore it down, and built it again."

After that, I only remember fleeting images as Jimmy guided me through the blacked-out city. A bus passed us with its headlights covered, throwing a small arc of light in front of it. A big balloon floated overhead, like something out of the Macy's Parade.

I pointed up. "What's that thing?"

Jimmy smiled his crooked smile. "That's old Bessie. She's a barrage balloon. Keeps the German planes from coming in low."

We stumbled along, tripping over sandbags that clogged store entrances, smelling smoke from distant fires, occasionally passing other phantoms.

I looked up, trying to figure out where the rooftops ended and the night sky and the smoke clouds began. I said, "This is London, right?"

"Right."

"What year is it?"

"It's 1940, Johnny. The eighth of September, to be exact."

"So this is World War Two?"

"It's war, all right. Us against the Gerries."

"The Gerries. The Germans?"

"Right."

"The United States is not at war?"

"The Yanks? Not hardly. They're too afraid to fight, aren't they?"

I couldn't believe what I was hearing. "What?"

"My dad says you're all playboys over there. You won't fight for nothing. And it ain't just him says it, either."

"That's not true!"

"I'm afraid it is, Johnny. It's just us against Gerry." Jimmy jerked his thumb skyward. "Gerry came at us during the Arsenal match today, up in White Hart Lane. Don't that beat all? We was all watching the match, and Arsenal was beating Fulham: beating 'em soundly, mate." He broke off to laugh. "Bill Lane already got throwed out of the stadium. You know why?"

I had no idea what he was talking about, but I asked, "Why?"

Jimmy sniggered. "He threw a dart at a linesman. For making a bad call, you know? Hit 'im right in the arse."

"That's your dad's mate?"

"Right. Bill was a footballer himself. He's a big bloke. My dad says he's a good fellow most of the time, but he's all talk and no action. My dad's just the opposite. He's not much talk, but he'll have a go at anyone, anytime. You'll meet him soon."

My eyes were finally adjusting to the dark. I could make out some of the city buildings around us. I was even getting less scared.

Jimmy picked up the story. "So! Suddenly, twenty minutes into the second half, the air-raid sirens went off! Dad and me, and all of us, had to run for cover. They even let Bill Lane back in, for safety reasons, but they never did resume play. They called the rest of the match on account of bombing! But the Gunners got the win, five–nil, so I didn't mind."

Soon we turned in to a park, and I saw a large, familiar building looming ahead of us. I knew it from photos in our basement and in Grandfather Mehan's study. I cried out, "That's the American Embassy!"

"Right you are, Johnny." Jimmy pointed to two men standing like sentinels. They wore helmets like Canby's, but theirs had LONDON AFS written on the front. They both wore high rubber boots and uniform jackets with buttons running up the middle. Some sort of telephone box stood behind them, a simple wooden cabinet wired into the ground. Jimmy waved happily, though we were too far away for them to see. "There's my dad! And Bill."

When we got close enough, the smaller man spotted Jimmy, and his face fell into a disapproving frown. "Jimmy Harker, what are you doing out here?" He was a short, fit man with bright blue eyes and sandy hair. He seemed very young: younger-looking than Margaret. The man with him was tall and powerfully built. He had a square jaw and angry, troubled eyes. I figured, correctly, that he was Bill Lane.

The smaller man spoke again, with anger in his voice. "You're supposed to be at home, Jimmy, doing your Bible studies. It's dangerous being out here."

"But you're out here, Dad."

"I got to be." Jimmy and I stopped in front of them. "It's my job to keep you safe. So you get back to Mrs. Lane. You hear?"

Bill Lane expressed his opinion. "I expect if he catches a bomb, James, he's better off being outside than in some brick-and-mortar house. You don't stand a chance in one of those. You're better off in the street."

"Don't scare the boy, Bill."

"I ain't scaring him. You ain't afraid of bombs, are you, Jimmy?"

"No, Bill, I ain't afraid of nothing."

"Good lad."

Jimmy pointed to me. "And neither's my mate here."

94

"Your mate?" Bill Lane looked at me. "Oh? Right. Who's your mate, then?"

"Johnny. Johnny's his name. He's a Yank."

"Is that right? A Yank? Is he paying your way round the nightclubs, then? Spending all his American dollars?"

"Yeah, that's it, Bill."

Bill Lane smiled at me. "How do you do, Johnny? You two will be stepping out with the Brylcreem boys, then?"

Jimmy answered for us. "Yeah. I think we'll go to the Savoy and hear Geraldo."

"You do that. Yeah. Take Alice with you. That'll shut her up."

Jimmy turned to his father. "Dad, I was telling Johnny about Canby and the directions for building a surface shelter."

James laughed quickly, followed by Bill.

Jimmy turned to include me. "The first surface shelter that Canby built was so dodgy it fell down before anyone ever got in it. Turns out he didn't put no cement between the bricks. Know what Canby said?"

I looked from James to Bill to Jimmy. I answered, "No."

"Canby said, serious as you please, 'Why, the plans didn't call for none.' Then he pulled out the plans and showed them round, and it was true. They had forgot to tell the builders to use cement to hold the bricks together. But anybody with a brain was gonna. Right?"

I answered, "Right."

Jimmy assured me, "Not Canby."

James smiled, showing a set of sharp, straight teeth. He turned to Bill and picked up the story. "So then *I* said to him, 'Tell me, Mr. Canby, if you walked into a public lavatory and there was no directions written out telling you to unzip your trousers, would you just go ahead and piss right in them?' " Bill Lane expelled a short, mirthless laugh. James added, "He didn't like that too much."

Bill spat on the grass behind him. "Canby's a bloody spiv. Profiting from the war, from everybody's misery." Bill Lane's face and voice hardened. "If you ask me, there's no reason to fight this bloody war. Hitler don't want nothin' to do with Britain. He never did. Churchill's stirring all this up for his own cause."

James winked at Jimmy and me, as if to say *Here he goes again,* but he asked, "And what's that, Bill?"

"Redemption, mate. Personal redemption for Gallipoli. Churchill sent our men ashore at Gallipoli in 1915, and they was massacred. One of the greatest military blunders in history. So now you and me and everybody else has got to go to war with Germany again so Churchill can have his rematch. That's it in a nutshell, James.

"And his buddy Franklin D. Roosevelt's happy to do it. If there's a war on, he gets to stay president, and everybody has to listen to him." He shook his head in disgust. "I'm no friend of Hitler's, mind you. He's a bloody madman. But think about it, James. Who do you have more in common with? The son of a civil servant, like Hitler—a poor man who made his own way up from the gutter? Or Lord Churchill and Lord Roosevelt, who grew up with silver spoons in their mouths and had tea with the King and Queen? Who, James?"

James gestured subtly toward the Embassy. "Heads up now, Bill. Here comes the Ambassador."

I turned and looked. I saw a well-dressed man with glasses and a big smile. I knew who he was from the most cherished photo in my grandfather's study—Ambassador Joseph P. Kennedy. He was walking with a hulking man in uniform. To my astonishment, the man had Hank Lowery's face.

They stood on the pavement about twenty yards away from us and talked. Then a car drove around from behind the Embassy, with its headlights half covered. Ambassador Kennedy got into the car, but General Henry M. "Hollerin' Hank" Lowery did not. He watched it pull away and waited.

After a moment, Bill Lane continued, with his voice slightly lower. "Look at them two. Not a care in the world except what nightclub to pick for their carousing. The working man's fighting to keep the likes of them in power."

James winked at us again and whispered, "Stop it, Bill. They'll think you're a German spy."

Bill was not amused. "I'm not pro-German. I'm pro–Bill Lane. Your Duke of Windsor, your abdicated king, is pro-German. Bring him back, I say. Let him have his American girlfriend. He'll make a deal with Hitler right quick, him and Joe Kennedy. Get them three together and this war will be over in an hour, and you and me won't be any worse off." He spit again. "Canby, though, will have to turn in his tin helmet and armpatch."

I stopped listening to Bill Lane when I saw a thin, somber-looking young man and a beautiful young woman emerge from the Embassy. It took me about one second to realize who I was looking at—my grandfather, Martin Mehan, the young attaché to the American Embassy. I moved closer to them, as close as I dared, hoping I wouldn't be seen.

General Lowery spoke first, in a loud and angry voice. "Come on, Mehan. I'm standing here waiting for a god-damn bomb to fall on my head."

Martin Mehan laughed as if Lowery had just said something pleasant, which he clearly hadn't. "Sorry, General. Daisy was just putting on her face. She wanted to look her best for you."

Lowery ran his eyes up and down the young woman. She was tall and athletic-looking, with long brown hair and a dazzling smile. Lowery's voice dropped down. "Well, I'd say she succeeded in doing that. Unless she gets even better-looking than this."

My grandfather smiled through thin lips. "You'll have to wait and see." He turned and gestured. "This is Miss Traynor, from the secretarial pool." He gestured toward the big man. "This is General Lowery."

The young woman extended a gloved hand. "Daisy, General. Call me Daisy."

The General took her hand and held it. "I will, Daisy. Tell me, Mehan, can you arrange for me to go for a swim in that secretarial pool?"

Martin Mehan laughed loudly again. Another car with dimmed lights pulled around from behind the Embassy. Martin Mehan held the door as Daisy slipped gracefully into the backseat.

General Lowery waited a moment. He said, "Good

work, Mehan. Now, how is your work going on that . . . other matter?"

Martin Mehan checked to see if anyone was listening. He did not notice me in the darkness. He confided, "Miss Traynor, your date this evening, is in a unique position to help you. She is free to go wherever she likes in the Embassy. Everyone knows her and trusts her. She is also free to go wherever she likes in London. No one would think to follow her."

Lowery nodded thoughtfully. He leaned into the car to take another look at Daisy Traynor. Her long arm reached out and grabbed him playfully by the lapel. He let himself be pulled inside, and then the car drove quickly away. Martin Mehan watched it go without expression. Then he walked back into the Embassy.

Jimmy popped up at my side, startling me. "We'd best be going, Johnny. My dad'll get mad if we stay any longer."

Jimmy took off immediately. I looked around for the two firefighters so I could say goodbye. But I was too afraid of losing Jimmy to wait long, so I just waved in their direction and took off, too. We ran at a fast pace through the dark streets. The trip back seemed to take half as much time as the trip there. I don't remember much about it except that I was frightened at every new turn. Even the moon seemed to be blacked out, shrouded in dark, evil smoke.

We only made one stop, at that surface shelter near Jimmy's house. Jimmy had spotted an old lady and a young boy in the doorway. The old lady's face scared me. I hated to admit it, but she looked a little like Nana. Jimmy asked her, "So, is Gerry coming tonight, then?"

The old woman did not answer. She pulled the boy closer to her and led him into the shelter.

Jimmy leaned toward me and whispered, "I guess it's not tonight. Listen, Johnny, I have to tell you something very, very important."

"What?"

"We're at a point here. A crucial point."

I said, "Yeah? A point? What's that?"

"That's where we are. Isn't it?"

"No. No, we're in a dream."

"You can call it what you like, mate. Just as long as you help me."

"Help you what?"

Jimmy's face got that perplexed look again. "I don't know exactly."

"How can you not know exactly?"

"Johnny, please, I'm just doing what I was told."

"Told by who?"

He muttered, "I don't know that, either."

I stepped forward so he would have to look right in my eyes. "Okay. Just tell me what you do know."

When Jimmy looked up, his eyes were glistening. "It's all a muddle, isn't it? But I know this—you can do something to help, Johnny. Something to help me and my dad; maybe something to help yourself, too." Jimmy stared at me intensely for another moment. When I didn't respond, he spun around and walked rapidly away into the darkness, leaving me alone in another time and place.

But not for long.

I suddenly felt myself falling down, as if the London

street had opened up beneath me. I flailed my arms outward, in a panic, trying to stop my fall.

Then I woke up. I was in my own bed, with the radio back where it had been, right next to me. And I was totally drenched with sweat.

DREAM WORLD

It was a dream. It was a dream. But as long as I lay there, the details refused to fade like they always do with a dream. I bolted out of bed and hurried across to the computer room. I opened a Word document and started typing what I could remember—all the names, all the places. After fifteen minutes, I was finished. I printed out the page, folded it twice, and put it in my pocket.

I placed my hands against my temples and pressed hard, trying to decide what to do next. Could I handle this myself? No. Who was I kidding? I couldn't handle anything myself. But who could I talk to? Who could I trust? I came up with a very short list, two or three people. But I'd have to be very careful or they'd think I was crazy.

I got online and searched for an image that I had seen the night before. I found it on an art museum Web site. There was no question about it; the painting that I saw in Jimmy's Bible studies book was exactly the same as the one in the All Souls Administration Building—Rembrandt's

Abraham and Isaac. Had I simply had a nightmare about the painting? Was that the cause of it all?

I studied the painting like I never had before. A psycho old man was about to stab his own son with a long knife. An angel was interfering with the murderous plan, stopping his arm on its downward swing. The old man looked bewildered—like he had Alzheimer's, like he was hearing voices that no one else could hear, and seeing sights that no one else could see.

I studied the painting for several minutes, until I heard a *ding.* It was Pinak, IM-ing me.

> PINAKC: Martin? Are you awake, you lazy goat?
>
> JMARTINC: Yes. Are you getting ready for All Souls?
>
> PINAKC: Yes. Have you heard from Manetti?
>
> JMARTINC: No. Have you?
>
> PINAKC: No. I tried to IM him, but I think he has me blocked.
>
> JMARTINC: He's gotta be mad. I can't believe what they did to him.
>
> PINAKC: Yes. And to his father.
>
> JMARTINC: Unbelievable. Manetti gets all the blame, and Lowery gets none.
>
> PINAKC: Are you surprised?
>
> JMARTINC: No. Father Thomas isn't going to mess with a legacy. He needs the money too much.

Neither of us had anything else to say about Manetti. Pinak changed the subject.

> PINAKC: What are you doing? Studying old radios?
>
> JMARTINC: No. I'm looking at Rembrandts right now, paintings from the All Souls Two-for-the-Price-of-One Collection.
>
> PINAKC: LOL. *The Raising of Lazarus?*
>
> JMARTINC: Uh-huh. Yeah. And that other one.
>
> PINAKC: *Abraham and Isaac?* Yes. That's a very powerful one.
>
> JMARTINC: Isaac is the kid, right?
>
> PINAKC: Right.
>
> JMARTINC: Tell me, did Isaac know he was going to get murdered? Or sacrificed to God?
>
> PINAKC: Oh no. He didn't. In fact, Abraham made Isaac carry the wood up the mountain, telling him all along that they would be working together to sacrifice an animal.
>
> JMARTINC: That's so sick.
>
> PINAKC: Yes, it is. So what does this have to do with radios?
>
> JMARTINC: Nothing.

I decided to tell him the truth. Or part of it.

> JMARTINC: I saw the painting in a dream. What do you think of that?
>
> PINAKC: I think it must have been a disturbing dream.

JMARTINC: It was. Tell me, how could I dream about things that I've never heard of before?

PINAKC: But you have heard of that painting. You have seen it many times.

JMARTINC: I know. I'm talking about other things in the dream. Some of them were things, like historic facts, that I could never have known about.

PINAKC: Like what?

I unfolded my sheet of paper.

JMARTINC: Like the fact that the Arsenal Football Club won a match at White Hart Lane in September 1940.

PINAKC: The Arsenal Football Club?

JMARTINC: British football. Soccer.

PINAKC: Yes. I am aware of football/soccer. It is the biggest sport in the world. Of course I have heard of it, and you have heard of it, too.

JMARTINC: A little. But I've never heard of Arsenal.

PINAKC: You have. You just don't remember. Arsenal is a very popular team, like the New York Yankees in baseball.

JMARTINC: No. I've heard about the New York Yankees. I know they wear pinstripe uniforms, and they play in Yankee Stadium in the Bronx. But there is no way I could know any details about this Arsenal club. Especially not in 1940.

PINAKC: All right. So what is your alternate explanation?

JMARTINC: Time travel.

PINAKC: LOL.

I typed: "I'm not kidding," but I did not send it. I erased it and sent:

JMARTINC: Do you know anything about time travel?

PINAKC: Only this: Einstein theorized that you could look back in time. You could look, but you could not touch. You could hear and see people, but they couldn't hear or see you.

JMARTINC: That's what Einstein thought, but what do you think?

PINAKC: I do not believe that time travel is possible. But who knows? Who would have thought that right after breakfast, I'd be online playing backgammon with a man in Australia? For him, it was already tomorrow. He was in another time.

JMARTINC: That's just a time zone.

PINAKC: Ah! Here we go! Listen, Martin: While we have been chatting, I was also doing a Web search for the Arsenal Football

Club. Here is the club history: Their home field, beginning in 1913 and until very recently, was a place called Highbury.

JMARTINC: Highbury? Not White Hart Lane?

PINAKC: No. It was clearly Highbury in the year 1940. I'll send you the link if you like.

I heard a tread on the stair, so I typed in:

JMARTINC: No. I believe you. I have to go.

PINAKC: So go.

Margaret rapped on the door and entered. "Martin? I'm sorry. Am I interrupting you?"

"No. I was just doing some research."

Margaret's blue eyes lit up. "Really? About what?"

I glanced down at my sheet of paper. "Gallipoli."

She nodded approvingly. "Is this part of that independent study? I thought it was about old radios."

"It is. It was. I'm already thinking about the next one. And the next. I'm never going back to All Souls."

Margaret settled into a chair and opened her arms. "So . . . what can I tell you about Gallipoli?"

"You can tell me how I know that word at all."

Margaret cocked her head, like a confused dog.

"I've never heard that word before. I don't even know where it is."

"It's in Turkey."

"I don't really know where Turkey is, either."

Margaret answered patiently. "Turkey is in eastern Europe. In fact, part of it's in Asia."

"And Gallipoli?"

"Gallipoli was the site of a very famous battle of World War One. It's a famous movie, too, about an Australian boy who went to his death there."

I shook my head. "I never saw it."

"It was really sad. The British soldiers were slaughtered."

"Was it Prime Minister Churchill's fault?"

Margaret straightened in her chair. "Churchill wasn't the prime minister then. He was First Lord of the Admiralty, the equivalent to our Secretary of the Navy. But yes, he did push for the invasion through Turkey, and yes, the defeat was blamed on him."

"But he was the Prime Minister in World War Two, right?"

"Shortly after the war began, yes." Margaret's eyes shifted to my list, and then back to me. "Why this sudden interest in the world wars?"

"I'm trying to keep out of All Souls, that's all. The more independent study topics I find, the better."

"Well, you know I can help you a little with that. I can help you a lot with World War Two history, especially where it intersects our family's history. Remember when my All Souls class went to London?"

"No. Not really."

Margaret frowned. "It was a pretty big deal, Martin. Mom and I saved for a year so I could go."

I did remember. "Oh yeah."

"We visited all the sacred places of the Mehan family: the American Embassy in Grosvenor Square, the Britain at War Experience, the Cabinet War Rooms." Margaret's eyes lit up. "Those rooms were incredible, Martin. Everything has been kept exactly as it was during the war. Not a paper has been moved; not a thing has been changed. Time has stopped still."

"Yeah? Do you think time can stop still? Or move forward or back?"

"Do you mean scientifically?"

"Yeah."

"No. But you can still get the . . . the spirit of a time by being in the place. I have felt that spirit. I felt it at the Cabinet War Rooms. It was like I was actually living in that time. I saw the telephones that the secretaries talked on; the mirrors where they checked their hairdos; the radios that they listened to. There was nothing of great historical importance, but it all added up to the real history of that time."

I waited a moment, for dramatic effect, then said, "Can I ask you a stupid question?"

"Sure."

"Who decides what 'the real history of a time' is?"

"Martin, that is a brilliant question. And the simple answer is—the winners decide. If Germany had won World War Two, the history books would be very different. What you have read is the American-British version, because they won."

"Uh-huh. And who, exactly, decides what goes into that version?"

"At the Millennium Encyclopedia, it's decided by Mr. Wissler. He and his wife own the encyclopedia, and he's the publisher." Margaret stood up and pointed at the door. "I have to go see him soon, for a meeting. Come with me, and I'll show you how it all works."

I fingered my sheet of paper. "I don't know. I have all this research to do."

"There is no better place in the world to do research, Martin. We subscribe to the best databases, premium government sites, and you'd be free to use them while I'm in my meeting. I'll get Steve to help you."

"Who's Steve?"

"Our IT guy."

I quickly scanned my list of names and places. Were they real? Or parts of a dream? Or something else? I said, "I'll need to get ready."

"Sure. We have a little time. Take a shower. Put on clean clothes. Do you want me to toast you a bagel?"

I refolded the paper and got up. "How about a Pop-Tart for the road? Give me ten minutes."

I stepped out the kitchen door and walked, averting my eyes from the morning glare, to Margaret's old Camry. I was now out of my environment, a subterranean mole exposed to the sun, but I knew I had to do this.

Margaret took a right turn on Hightstown Road and headed toward Route 1. I waited until we crossed the railroad bridge before asking her, "Do you really think our grandfather was friends with Joseph P. Kennedy and General Lowery?"

Margaret feigned shock. "Martin! You're talking about your namesake! How could you doubt that? We have the photos to prove it."

"Yeah. But people pose with celebrities all the time; that doesn't mean they know them. There's a photo of you with some president, right?"

"Right. Bill Clinton."

"Did you know him?"

"No. He spoke at Princeton, and I got to pose with him."

"Yeah. See what I mean? What if Martin Mehan just posed with those guys?"

"Well, there is more evidence, corroborating evidence. Martin Mehan is part of the official records of the U.S. Embassy staff during Ambassador Kennedy's time there. General Lowery was an official visitor, sent by President Roosevelt. There is a lot of paperwork to place them all there at the same time. However, I see your point. That doesn't describe what kind of relationships they had."

"What does Grandfather Mehan say in his memoirs?"

"He describes himself as indispensable to all of them— from Ambassador Kennedy to General Lowery to FDR himself. Remember those passages he would read aloud at Thanksgiving?"

"I remember him reading something. It could have been the Bible, for all I knew. But isn't it possible that, in fact, those guys treated him like crap?"

Margaret sputtered and laughed. "Like what?"

"Crap. I mean, who was Martin Mehan? He wasn't a rich ambassador, or a famous general, or a president of the

United States. He was just a government clerk, right? Some little guy who did what he was told?"

Margaret turned right, into an industrial park, and followed the road around a row of blue glass buildings. "Okay. Yeah, you're right. Back in 1940, he was pretty low on the ladder in government service. That's very insightful of you, Martin."

"And why was General Lowery such a hero, anyway?"

"Hmm. Well, as Colonel Lowery, back in World War One, he earned several medals for bravery." She pulled in to a space and turned off the engine. "He lost a lot of men, but he gained a lot of ground. So he got promoted to General. He was famous for urging his troops forward with a loud voice."

"Hollerin' Hank."

"Right. The U.S. Commander, General Pershing, called him that. Then the newspapers picked up on it. They liked the colorful nickname, so he became a national celebrity."

Margaret and I climbed out of the car and walked to the building entrance. She inserted an ID card into a slot and the dark blue glass door clicked open. I followed her across a small lobby into an elevator, where she pressed number three and continued: "Lowery turned his celebrity into a personal fortune. He sat on the boards of big corporations; he bought and sold companies; he endorsed products. Near the end of his life, he even had his name on a line of hearing aids."

"No!"

"Yes. We have a copy of the TV commercial. He's sitting

with some other old guy, in an army uniform, hollerin' at him that he needs a hearing aid."

The elevator opened onto a short hallway and another set of glass doors with the words MILLENNIUM ENCYCLOPEDIA stenciled on them. Margaret slid her card again, and we entered a row of cubicles and offices. A guy in a plaid shirt with unruly hair was working on a computer in the first cubicle. He stopped and looked up as we passed him.

Margaret led me into a cubicle that had her nameplate attached to the wall. As she powered up her computer, I asked in a hushed voice, "So, does everybody think Lowery was a hero?"

Margaret answered at a normal volume. "That is not a unanimous opinion."

"But some people do?"

Margaret smiled. "People in his family do. And his family lawyer does."

I added, "And Father Thomas? And Father Leonard? And the board of directors at All Souls?"

Margaret stopped smiling. "The people at All Souls Preparatory School can believe what they want to about General Hank Lowery. But I can tell you, the Millennium Encyclopedia is not going to print a fictional version of his wartime deeds. We're not for sale. We're going to print the truth, whatever that may turn out to be."

"Really? Your boss would let you print bad things about Lowery?"

"If I have the proof, yes. Mr. Wissler has his own family money. He doesn't need the Lowerys'."

Margaret clicked an icon on her computer screen. I watched as it filled up with blue hypertext links. She indicated that I should sit in her seat. "You can poke around in these while I'm gone."

The guy in the plaid shirt appeared in the entrance. He glanced at me and said, "Hi, Margaret. Is this your brother?"

Margaret smiled. "Yes, this is Martin, the one you've heard me talk so much about." I had a flash of fear. What did she tell him? That I hide in the basement? She added, "Martin, this is Steve. He's our IT guy. And a very good one."

Steve waved hello. I responded awkwardly, something between grunting and waving.

Margaret spoke to both of us. "I have to leave in a few minutes for a meeting. Steve can help you with any technical difficulties."

Steve pointed toward that first cubicle. "I'll be right over here, for another hour at least."

Margaret asked me, "Did you bring your research questions?"

I patted my shirt pocket. "Yeah. Can I get into these sites and search for names and stuff?"

"Sure. Most of them have search capabilities. But why don't you ask me a couple of them first? Maybe I can point you in the right direction."

Steve spoke up. "Your sister's like a walking database."

Margaret fluttered her eyelids. I took out my list and pointed to the first line. "Okay. Here's my first item. Was there ever a guy named something like Lord Haw-Haw?"

"Yes," Margaret assured me.

"Was he, like, a TV clown?"

"They didn't have TV during World War Two."

"Oh yeah. Right."

"Lord Haw-Haw, a fictional name of course, was a British traitor. He made radio broadcasts full of Nazi propaganda. Actually, he was half British and half American. After the war, they hanged the British half." She looked at the IT guy. "Although all of him died."

Steve laughed. Then he waved at me again and stepped away.

"Incidentally," Margaret continued, "Churchill was half American, too, on his mother's side. He was determined to show the U.S. that the British could take it. That they could stand up to Hitler and, with our help, rid the world of him and his Nazis."

"So . . . this Lord Haw-Haw told the British to give up or the Nazis would bomb them?"

Margaret's eyes bulged. "Martin, the Nazis did bomb them! For years. Thousands of innocent people were killed; thousands more were made homeless; millions were terrorized. But the British did what Churchill said—they showed the world that they could take it. And they did change the course of history, didn't they?"

I laughed. " 'Didn't they?' That's how they talked."

"Who?"

"The people in London. They put 'didn't they?' and 'didn't I?' at the end of everything."

Margaret smiled quizzically. "They did?"

I told her, "They did, didn't they?" I pointed to the list. "Okay. Here's another name. How could I find out if someone named Daisy Traynor worked for our grandfather?"

Margaret looked at the name. "We can probably access payroll records." She quickly showed me how to look for information about the U.S. Foreign Service and the U.S. Embassy staff, but neither site contained the name Daisy Traynor or any spelling variation of it. Margaret checked her watch. "Sorry. We're meeting right now. See what you can find while I'm gone."

For the next forty-five minutes, I clicked through a mass of information about World War II, and London, and the Auxiliary Fire Service. I searched for names from my list, and I learned the following: There was a James Harker in the Auxiliary Fire Service. He was from Yorkshire. There were two Bill Lanes in the Auxiliary Fire Service. One died in action in January 1941. The other one emigrated to Australia and died there in 1971. There was no record of an Alice Lane.

I used a red pen to categorize the items from my dream. I wrote *Wrong* next to Daisy Traynor and White Hart Lane; I wrote *Right* next to Gallipoli and Lord Haw-Haw; I wrote *Maybe* next to James Harker, Bill Lane, and Alice Lane. It was inconclusive. So far it was basically a tie, a tie between me being crazy or not. I hated to admit it to myself, but there wasn't enough information. Not yet. And there was only one way to get what I wanted.

I would have to have another dream.

LONDON: SEPTEMBER 15, 1940

Exactly one week later, I had a second dream.

I worked on the radio that Sunday afternoon, testing a new theory—that the numbers 291240 actually described another sequence for the glass tubes in the back. At present, the tubes in the back were numbered 24, 27, 71A, and 80. I tried to determine where other tubes might go, what they might replace, and so on. It passed some time and gave me material for another independent study paper. Then I lay down for my nap.

Again I turned my face toward the radio and listened to the static hissing through the damp basement air. The dream followed the same pattern as before, too, except this one took place in daytime.

I became aware of the musty sweet scents, and of the wallpaper. I could see it clearly now—the paper was light brown, with a vertical pattern of yellow flowers. Then I saw Jimmy. He was once again sitting in the leather chair, listening to the Philco 20. An announcer, not Lord Haw-Haw, was reading the news about a disaster at sea, a disaster involving children. Jimmy turned and spoke to me. "Ships with evacuees get sunk, don't they?"

I took a seat on the covered sofa, feeling strangely at home. "What are evacuees?"

"They're kids that get evacuated, aren't they?"

"Why did they get evacuated?"

"Are you daft? So they wouldn't get killed by the bombs."

"Uh-huh. So most of the kids left?"

"Yeah. Most of 'em. So many that they had to close my school."

I thought about my list of facts. I asked him, "Tell me more about your school."

Jimmy's lip twisted up, and his blue eyes narrowed. "My school was horrible. I hated it. And I hated my schoolmaster, Master Portefoy. We called him Master Putrefy because he smelled so bad. He cuffed me once, on the ear." Jimmy's eyes widened. "Then my dad went in to see him. He sorted him out right quick! He dared Master Portefoy to cuff *him* on the ear; told him he'd bust him in the nose if he did. Old Putrefy got the message, and he never touched me after that."

I made a mental note of the name. Jimmy continued, "Anyway, most of the kids got shipped out of London, but now some are coming back."

"Why?"

"It ain't no holiday out there, Johnny. Just listen to the news. That boat that went down was full of London kids. Their parents thought they were sending them to safety, but they were sending them to their deaths."

The news was soon replaced by music, big band music. I asked him, "Why didn't you get evacuated?"

"Me? I did! Mum and me both. But then Mum died, and I came back home. Dad said he wasn't sending me away again. Not after losing Mum and all."

Suddenly a horrible whirring, whining sound began outside. It went right through my bones like a jolt of electricity. I shrieked, "What's that?"

Jimmy laughed. "It's an air-raid siren, Johnny. A false alarm, most likely. We get a lot of those."

"We're in an air raid? What do we do?"

"Nothin'. We just wait for the all clear."

"What's that? Another siren?"

"Yeah. If we don't hear it, then we head for a shelter."

"Okay. We head where?"

Jimmy leaned forward and explained, "Well, most people've got an Anderson shelter. It's dug into the dirt in the backyard."

"Do you have one of those?"

"Not exactly. Landlord mucked up on ours, I'm afraid. Nobody uses it. Dad always tells me to run to Mrs. Lane's house and use hers."

"So is that what you do?"

"Hardly, mate. That thing's all muddy, and full of bugs. No, if I ever need a shelter, I pop into the nearest Underground station."

"What's that?"

"Don't you know nothing? It's like, a train underground that takes people places."

"A subway?"

"Yeah. There ya go." Jimmy's eyes opened wide. "Or"—he raised a skinny arm and pointed toward the street out front—"you could take your chances in the surface shelter."

"The one that Canby built?"

"Right."

"Without the cement?"

Jimmy laughed. "You remember that, eh? Well done. No, this time it has cement."

Jimmy turned toward the radio. I hadn't realized it, but the music had drifted away and only static was coming out of it. He suddenly got very quiet and whispered, "You know, sometimes when I'm tuning the radio, and listening . . . I think I hear Mum talking to me."

"Really? What does she say?"

"She says, 'Do your bit, Jimmy.' I think it's *really* her voice saying that. Daft, isn't it?"

"Hey, I'm the last person to call somebody daft."

Jimmy fixed me with a look. "What? Do you think you're daft, Johnny?"

I held out my arms to encompass the room. "This is all pretty crazy, you must admit."

Jimmy shook his head. "No. It's not craziness, I can tell you that much."

"Then what is it?"

His voice dropped down. "Answer me this: Do you believe in ghosts, Johnny?"

I thought, *Not until I met you*, but I shrugged and said, "I don't know. I have no idea."

"What about haunted houses, then? Do you believe a house could be haunted?"

"I guess it's possible. I don't know."

"My mum and dad believe in haunted houses and ghosts because they're from York. York's a haunted city because it's had so many wars, and plagues, and executions and all. It's full of ghosts."

Jimmy turned back to the radio and fiddled with it until he found a pop song. "Do you like this one, Johnny—'We'll Meet Again'?"

"I don't know it."

"Don't know nothing, do you?" Jimmy pulled a small black-and-red tube and a comb out of his pocket. "Time to use my Brylcreem. It's what the RAF pilots use, you know. That's what they call them on the BBC, the Brylcreem boys." Jimmy squeezed out a dab and combed it into his hair. When he was finished, he scooped up his gas mask and attached it to his belt. Then he gestured toward the door.

"Come on. I want to tell Dad what I heard today. Arsenal's playing Spurs on twelve October. I got to know if he's on or off."

"What does that mean?"

"If he's on duty or off. The Auxiliaries go forty-eight hours on and twenty-four hours off. If he can get off, we can go. Maybe Bill, too."

"With his darts?"

"Oh yeah. I expect so."

I thought of my list. I asked him, "Is Arsenal playing at Highbury?"

He looked at me curiously. "No, mate. White Hart Lane."

"Are you sure?"

"I'm sure, Johnny."

I thought, *Then I'm sure I'm dreaming.* I walked over to the sideboard and picked up the medals. "Wait a minute. I want to hear more about these."

"What? My granddad's medals?"

"Yeah."

"His Pip, Squeak, and Wilfred, he called them." He stepped closer, took the medals from me, and held them up one by one. "If you're going to join the Dukes, it helps if you're Yorkshire born, like Dad and me. My dad said he'd have joined if it weren't for Mum. My dad wanted to fight the Germans, but my mum made him join the Auxiliaries." Jimmy laid the medals down. "All right, then? Let's be off."

I stayed on the sofa. "No. I'm not going out there."

"Just to have a look, Johnny. Come on, now. We have to." He smiled and gestured toward the wall behind me. I turned and saw what he was pointing at, the VERY WELL THEN, ALONE! poster.

I told him, "Very well, then. You can go alone."

"No. You've got to come with me, Johnny. It's your bit. You've got to help."

"Says who?"

"I told you before. I don't know."

"You know more than you're saying, though. And I'm not going anywhere until you tell me."

Before my eyes, Jimmy turned from fearless into frightened, like a lost little boy. I smiled as reassuringly as I could,

122

and I told him, "Just talk about it, Jimmy. Just say anything and everything that you remember."

Jimmy closed his eyes. He whispered, "I remember being asked the question."

"The question?"

"Yeah. *What did you do to help?*"

"That's the question?"

"Yeah."

"*What did you do to help?* Help who?"

"I dunno for sure." Jimmy looked at the floor. "But . . . I felt like they meant everybody. Like, the human race."

"Did someone ask you this question? Was it a person?"

Jimmy struggled to remember. "Maybe. It could've been."

"Was it Jesus?"

"No, I don't think so."

I tried to make him focus on that moment. "So . . . was someone's mouth moving? Did words come out?"

He looked like he was going to burst into tears. "I dunno, I told you!" Jimmy walked over to the door and then back. He held out his hands and asked me plaintively, "Now you need to answer something for me, Johnny. One question: Will you do your bit when the time comes? Yes or no?"

"I don't know. When will the time come? When is that?"

He answered with certainty. "On the day of reckoning, whenever that may be. But for now, let's just say that your bit is to follow me out that door—to look, and to listen, and to learn."

We stared at each other for a long moment, and then I

agreed. Without saying a word, or signing anything, or shaking hands, I agreed to follow this strange boy into those bombed-out streets, for a purpose even he did not understand.

Jimmy led me outside to the front stoop. In the harsh light of day, things seemed much worse than they had a week before. People were struggling with cardboard suitcases and paper bags full of possessions. The street next to us was roped off; its houses and shops had been thoroughly smashed by bombs. Several men were shoveling broken glass into trucks.

Alice Lane soon emerged and stood on the stoop to our left, dressed very nicely in a small fur and a large hat. She said, "You stay close to the house, now, Jimmy."

He answered, "Yes, Mrs. Lane." Right after she walked around the corner, though, he whispered, "All right, Johnny. We're just about free to leave. She'll be off with Canby, I expect."

Sure enough, within a minute a small car turned onto the street. Canby was driving; seated to his left was Alice Lane.

As soon as the car pulled out of sight, Jimmy took off at a slow run. In spite of all my fears, I started running with him.

"Don't worry, Johnny," he called. "We're safe. The Gerries done us once today already, didn't they?"

"Did they?"

"Yeah. They hit the East End again. The East End catches most of it because it's along the river. But you never know.

Buckingham Palace caught it on Friday. Bounced the King right out of bed, it did."

We ran for a long way; then we turned onto a rubble-strewn road full of firefighters and firefighting equipment. Jimmy said, "Look up there, mate."

I looked up at an enormous domed church.

"That's St. Paul's. Hitler tried to destroy it. Dropped an eight-hundred-pound bomb on her, but it didn't go off. The hand of God saved it."

We stared at the cathedral for a while longer. Then we continued on our way through the streets of the battered city. It was bizarre; people still went about their business amid the ruins. I said, "Aren't they afraid of getting killed?"

"No. We're not afraid. We've got God on our side."

"How do you know that?"

"I feel that. Every day. Don't you?"

"No."

After another long run, we reached a place that I recognized, Grosvenor Square. When we got close to the American Embassy, Jimmy grabbed me by the shoulder and pulled me down.

"Uh-oh. There's another row going on with the warden."

I peeked out. Bill Lane was standing toe-to-toe with a heavyset man wearing a warden's patch on his sleeve. Jimmy whispered, "That warden's assigned to the Embassy. Him, Bill, and my dad don't get along. They're always arguing. Bad luck that they're at it now. My dad'll be mad at him afterward, but he'll take it out on me." He looked around, as if for an escape route. "Maybe we should bugger off."

"Are you afraid of your father?"

"Sure."

"Why?"

"Because sometimes he gives me a licking."

"He hits you?"

"Yeah. If I deserve it." Jimmy explained, "He has to. He has to be my dad and mum. Doesn't yours hit you?"

"My father?" I thought about Jack Conway and his sad face. "No. Never."

I looked back at the confrontation. Bill Lane was squared off, facing the warden, with James Harker right behind him. The showdown had obviously been going on for a while, as a small crowd had formed.

The warden spat out, "You Auxiliaries, you're just afraid to fight. You're all bloody conchies, aren't you?"

I whispered to Jimmy, "What's that mean?"

"A conchie is a conscientious objector, someone who won't fight."

Bill Lane growled, "Bill Lane's not afraid to fight. Not anybody."

"Yeah. Yeah. You been saying that for ten minutes, but you ain't done nothing."

James stepped forward, elbowing Bill out of the way. "That's enough." To everyone's surprise, especially the warden's, he pulled back his fist and delivered a short, sharp jab right to the center of the warden's nose.

The big man stepped backward, with his right hand covering his face. In seconds, a red trickle of blood showed through his fingers.

James turned around. "You talk things to death, Bill."

"I was getting to it right then."

"Yeah, well, enough is enough. Now it's done with."

The warden scurried away toward the Embassy. Bill went back to his post by the telephone box, but James suddenly paused and looked right at us.

I hissed, "I think he spotted me!"

James strode over toward the bushes. "Oh? What's this, now? A lost boy?" He stood right over us and shouted, "Jimmy Harker! You get out here!"

Jimmy stood up slowly. I stood up with him. Both of us bowed our heads.

James demanded to know, "What are you doing outside during a bloody air raid?"

Jimmy answered timidly. "I heard about a match, Dad. Spurs and Gunners. I wanted to see if you was off duty for it."

"It's bloody dangerous out here. Do you know what happened last night?"

"Yes, Dad. But I figured it'd be safer during the day."

James's face remained hard as granite. "You figured wrong."

"Dad, it's on twelve October. The match, I mean. Do you have the day off?"

Bill Lane joined us, demanding to know, "Why isn't Alice watching you? Where is she?"

Jimmy started backing up, so I backed up with him. "I don't know, Bill. I expect she's at home."

"Is Canby around?"

"I don't know."

James reached out and grabbed Jimmy by the collar. "You'll need to be punished for this, Jimmy. It was a bad thing to do." He hesitated for just a moment, then slapped him across his ears, once left and once right. Jimmy shriveled up like a dying flower. James shook his head. Then he pointed to a spot near the telephone box. "You stand next to me now, and think about what you done wrong."

Tears filled Jimmy's eyes. He walked dutifully to the phone box and attempted to stand up straight. I watched him for several agonizing seconds as he struggled not to cry. James took his post next to him, staring straight ahead. He finally looked down at him, so Jimmy whimpered, "I just wanted to see you, you know, to tell you about Spurs and Gunners."

James's face softened. "It's too early to say, Jimmy. I don't have my work schedule yet."

They remained in those positions for a few more minutes, but the worst part was over. Bill Lane's voice filled the silence. "Do what you can to stay out of this bloody war, Jimmy. The more lads who sign up, the less they care about losing them. It's 'the more the merrier' to them. Give Churchill an extra thousand lads and he'll do another Gallipoli. What does he care? He ain't wading ashore into the machine guns.

"Here's a just war, according to Bill Lane: When the royals are running into the machine-gun fire, and sleeping in the mud, and fighting to the death in order to save this bloody empire, then I'll be fighting with them. I'll be a few meters behind them, maybe, because I don't have quite so much to lose as they do. Let them make the sacrifice first. Then ask the poor people to help."

As I watched, Joseph P. Kennedy emerged from the

Embassy with two well-dressed young men. I knew who they were from Father Leonard's class—the Ambassador's sons Joe and Jack. The three of them walked into the shade of Grosvenor Square, deep in conversation.

Bill commented, "Look at them three. They've already thrown in the towel, haven't they? Off to a party at Cliveden tonight to celebrate the German victory and the end of the British Empire."

James clearly shared Bill's contempt. "They say Joe Kennedy leaves every night for safe lodgings outside London. He stocked his air-raid shelter there with all kinds of cheeses and chocolates."

"Yeah. He'd bugger off altogether if he could. But he ducked out of one war already, didn't he? This'd make it two."

James added, "Do you know what I heard him say, Jimmy? To that General Lowery fella?"

Jimmy was greatly relieved to be included. He finally smiled. "What's that, Dad?"

"That Hitler and his gang will be at Buckingham Palace in two weeks."

"Go on!"

"Two weeks. That's what he said. But let me tell you something else, lad. He made that brilliant statement *three* weeks ago."

James, Jimmy, and Bill shared a patriotic laugh over that. I took the opportunity to drift closer to the Embassy, because I had a feeling what was coming next. The door opened, and I saw my grandfather and Daisy Traynor emerge. They hurried toward me so quickly that I shrank back,

hoping to make myself too small to notice. Both of them reacted to a loud voice from somewhere behind me. I turned
and saw the hulking figure of General Lowery standing by
the curb.

Ambassador Kennedy reacted, too, because he stopped
and called across the square, "Are you hollerin' again,
Hank?"

Lowery turned stiffly. When he saw who was speaking to
him, he smiled. "I'm hollerin' at this girl to slow down, Joe.
So I can catch her."

Joe Kennedy and his sons laughed and walked on.

Martin Mehan escorted Miss Daisy Traynor right up to
General Lowery.

Daisy turned back to my grandfather and poked him
playfully. "Thanks, Mickey!" She told the General, "Martin
Mehan's initials are MM, just like Mickey Mouse. So that's
what I call him: Mickey Mouse."

My grandfather smiled faintly. Lowery ignored the comment. He spoke to him harshly. "What's going on, Mehan?
Do you have anything for me or not?"

Martin Mehan answered softly. "Not today, General.
Nothing has come in."

The General looked at Daisy but spoke to my grandfather. "Nothing through her?"

Daisy arched an eyebrow. "Well, gentlemen, why don't
you ask *her*?" She looked from the General to my grandfather. "You act like I have no idea what I'm doing, or who
Herr Von Dirksen is."

Both the General and my grandfather looked around to

see who had heard that remark, but neither spotted me. Martin Mehan hissed at her, "Do not use names like that in public, Miss Traynor."

Daisy's hand shot up to her mouth. "Oh, forgive me. That was stupid, wasn't it?"

General Lowery smiled benevolently. "Just don't do it again."

"I won't."

"You're lucky I like brunettes."

Daisy beamed. "Yes, I am so lucky."

"Answer the question, though. When you dropped off my message, did they give you anything back for me?"

"No, mein Herr," Daisy purred. "There was nothing to add to all those secret messages that I copy onto lovely scented paper, tie up with pink ribbons, and hide in my hat-box."

"What?"

"Oh yes. It's a red hatbox. I keep it hidden under my bed." She smiled devilishly. "Perhaps you should check under there."

The General stared at her dumbly. Then he smiled back, slowly, acknowledging the joke. "Uh-huh. Sounds like I'd better."

Daisy saluted. "Yes, General."

Lowery turned to my grandfather. "All right, Mehan. Alert me as soon as you get a reply. No matter where I am. That's all."

Martin Mehan looked relieved that he could go back inside.

Daisy cooed, "Goodbye, Mickey Mouse. Say hello to Minnie for me." She laughed gaily and ducked into the car ahead of the General.

I watched Martin Mehan, looking very mouselike, walk into the Embassy. Then I went back to Jimmy's side. I had no sooner reached him when the shrill whine of another air-raid alarm started. Bill Lane announced immediately, "False alarm. Got to be."

James turned to us. "I'm not taking any chances. You get home, Jimmy. Get running."

"Right, Dad. Me and Johnny. We'll have a race."

I interrupted. "No. I'm not running through the streets! Not if they're dropping bombs on us!"

The telephone rang, so Bill Lane crossed over to it. James grabbed Jimmy by the arm. "No playing games now, lad. You get home and stay there. If any planes come, you run to Mrs. Lane's and get straight into the shelter."

"All right, Dad. I will. I'm sorry."

"You'll be sorrier if you do this again, Jimmy. I mean it."

Jimmy took off running, but I remained standing where I was.

Bill slammed down the phone. "Bloody hell. Planes *are* coming."

"How far away?"

Bill gestured contemptuously at the phone. "He didn't know. The bloody twit."

That was all I had to hear. I finally spoke up. "Please, sir, Mr. Harker. I want to go to a shelter close by. There has to be one at the Embassy. Right?"

He didn't answer me.

"Please, Mr. Harker, Mr. Lane. I'm an American. My grandfather works in the Embassy."

James Harker and Bill Lane both looked right at me, but they didn't respond.

I backed away in confusion, and rising panic.

Jimmy's voice called to me from behind the hedge. "They can't hear you, Johnny."

"What? Of course they can."

"No. They can't see you, either."

"But . . . they can. They talked to me last time!"

"Not really, mate. They was just playing along with me, pretending they saw you."

Alarms now whined all around us, rising and falling. I screamed, "Get me someplace safe!"

Jimmy yelled, "All right! Come on!" and took off running.

I leaped over the hedge and caught up with him. "Are we going to a shelter?"

"Shelters stink, don't they? They got one bucket for a thousand people to do their business in. Not nice. Not nice at all."

"I don't care about nice. I'm not running out in the open, with bombs falling on me."

"Here's all you got to do if they get close, Johnny: Lie flat on the ground, facedown, with your mouth open and your hands over your ears."

I couldn't argue anymore; I could only run. The planes were a lot closer than anyone had thought. I could actually see them in the distance, coming in waves of ten and twelve across, heading right toward us. I ran behind Jimmy as fast as I could, jumping over sandbags and lines of fire hoses that crisscrossed the streets.

The incendiary bombs fell first. I saw one crash onto a roof to our right and burst into flame. Then dozens of incendiaries were falling all around us. They let off choking black clouds of smoke and a strong smell of gasoline. Suddenly my eardrums nearly popped open with the thundering ack-ack noise of cannons. The anti-aircraft guns had roared to life on the streets. As they fired at the planes above, shrapnel from their cannons fell back down, landing dangerously all around us with loud, metallic clangs.

Jimmy bounded ahead of me like a deer. I struggled to keep pace, but I had to yell out, "I need to stop, Jimmy. Please! Where can we stop?"

He skidded to a halt. "One place is as good as another, mate."

I leaned over and gasped for air amid the deafening noise and smoke. I looked up at what remained of a building across the street. Only its front wall was still standing. Its windows had exploded outward, and now it blazed with a fierce light.

We took off again. By now, a black-smoke canopy covered the entire city, and the sun was dimmed to blood-red from the many fires. The drone of the German planes continued, but the incendiary bombs were now replaced with high explosives. Buildings imploded to my left and right, blowing chunks of concrete and metal right across the road. To my amazement, the defenders of London—the firemen and ambulance drivers and anti-aircraft gunners—still went calmly about their business.

I saw a man lying in the street ahead of me. I watched as two nurses in white rolled him onto a stretcher. But his arm stayed behind him on the street, a bloody stump still wrapped in a gray coat sleeve. I wanted to stop and throw up at the sight, but my legs kept pumping in terror, following Jimmy. He did not stop until we reached the surface shelter across from his house. Again I saw the old woman and the boy standing in the doorway.

Jimmy stopped and talked to them. "Is this it, Gran? Is this the one?"

The woman did not answer. She once again turned and led the little boy into the shelter.

Jimmy told me, "All right. We'll stop here."

"Aren't we almost at your house?"

"Yeah. But this'll do."

"Aren't we going in the shelter?"

"Everything in its time, Johnny. For now, just listen. Listen to me."

I searched the deadly skies. "All right. Talk, then. Talk!"

"We're at a point here, Johnny. A crucial point. Your gran—"

"My grandmother again?"

"That's right. You know what happened to your gran. You know she's on the other side now."

"Gran? Nana? She's dead."

"Yes. And on the other side. My dad should be there, too, but he needs your help. Will you help him?"

The sound of the bombs got terrifyingly close. Then one

135

exploded right across from us. It hit me fully, like a slap in the face. I fell to the pavement, clutching at my throat, choking on the black smoke and the flying dust.

"Will you help him, Johnny? Will you help?" Jimmy was standing over me and talking, as if nothing had touched him. But his voice turned weirdly flat, and then crackly, and then it blended into the static of the radio. Everything around me—the buildings, the people, the droning airplanes—suddenly disappeared. I was back on my bed, in the basement, all alone and feeling like I was about to die.

I struggled for many minutes to slow down my heartbeat and get control of my breathing. I felt like I was climbing, hand over hand, out of my own grave. Finally, mercifully, my body slowed itself down. I got control of my heart, and my lungs, and I vowed I would never lose control of them again.

I rolled off the bed and fell to the floor next to the Philco 20. I yanked the fraying plug out of the wall. Then I set to work methodically, with my hands trembling, and I removed every glass tube from inside.

Whatever had happened to me, I swore, was never going to happen again.

I was never going back.

MAKING IT
THROUGH
THE HOLIDAYS

When I unplugged the radio, I figured I had unplugged my-self from the world of Jimmy Harker once and for all.

I carried the Philco 20 Deluxe and its tubes to the stor-age area of the basement. I put the tubes in a small plastic bag and stuffed them inside the back of the radio, like a bag of giblets inside a turkey. I slid the radio into its box, cov-ered it with a white sheet, and stuck it in a dark corner. Walking away, I believed I had left the craziness of time travel behind me forever.

But first I stopped in the computer room. I pulled out my original list of facts and added Pip, Squeak, and Wilfred, Mickey Mouse, and Von Dirksen to it. Then I pulled up my online encyclopedia. I couldn't find anything for the first item, so I gave it a *Wrong*. To my surprise, I learned that Mickey Mouse was created in 1928, in plenty of time for Daisy Traynor to know about him, so I gave that a *Right*. Von Dirksen got a *Right*, too, a very disturbing one. His name came up as Chancellor Adolf Hitler's special envoy to London. The list was maddening; it didn't add up to anything: four *Rights*, three *Wrongs*, and three *Maybes*. I decided that the *Maybes* had won: Maybe I was crazy, maybe I wasn't. I folded the list up, stuck it in a drawer under the computer, and tried to forget all about it.

Then I plunged headlong into the world of independent study. I generated four five-page papers per week on radio-related topics in science, social studies, math, and language arts. Sometimes, in the course of my research, I found myself back in the era of World War II. This made me a little uncomfortable, but not enough to make me stop. Everything about that time was still fascinating to me.

Mom dutifully transported the research papers to Father Leonard, my faculty adviser, and then she transported them home marked with A-plusses and many favorable comments. She also lugged books from the Lowery Library back and forth for me. There seemed to be an unspoken understanding that we would all continue this way until January. I believe that Father Thomas wanted to keep me at home, away from Hank Lowery, until they had their dedication of the Heroes' Walk on New Year's Day.

Psychologically, the fact that I was able to crank out top-notch papers at an amazing rate worked in my favor. It made me look less crazy. But I was no more inclined to leave the basement than I had been in September, so the family remained worried.

One morning in October, I overheard Margaret telling Mom, "There are things we could do, you know. There are social services for people who can't afford them."

"We're not a charity case," Mom replied. "We're a

prominent family. A family that believes in turning to God, not to some psychiatrist."

"We're a family that's too proud to ask for help."

"If Martin needs help, we will get it for him. I promise you."

"Really?" Margaret told her, "Well, guess what? Martin needs help."

But neither of them said anything to me.

It wasn't until late November, after I had been in the basement for two and a half months, that Mom finally approached me at breakfast with the awkward question "Martin, do you feel like you need to talk to someone?" She gestured toward Margaret, who seemed surprised at this sudden overture. "I mean, someone other than Margaret and me? Maybe Father Paul at Resurrection?"

"I don't even know him."

"Then how about one of the priests at All Souls?"

My look must have told her that that was never going to happen. She tried another tack. "Well, everyone thinks it is a good idea for you to talk about your feelings."

"Wait a minute. Who is 'everyone'?"

Mom seemed confused. "What do you mean?"

"I mean, who exactly is on my mental health advisory team?"

"Just . . . people in the family. People who care about you."

"Dad?"

Mom frowned. "No. I have not talked to your father about this." Then a thought occurred to her. "Why? Have you?"

"No."

"I have spoken to Aunt Elizabeth, though. And she came up with an idea."

I exchanged a doubtful look with Margaret.

"Aunt Elizabeth thinks you should take the train up to Boston next week. She knows a priest there who is also a psychologist. He specializes in working with teenagers." Mom looked back at me. "It would all be strictly confidential. You wouldn't even have to use your real name."

I told Mom with finality, "I'm not going to do that."

"What? You won't even think about it?"

"No. There's no need to. The truth is, I'm feeling pretty good about things. I think I can finish up this term at home and then go to Garden State."

Mom explained to me once again, "Martin, you have a destiny in life. All Souls will help you to fulfill that destiny. Garden State is not where you go to become someone important in life, someone like your grandfather."

I was ready for her. "Mom, I don't want to become someone like my grandfather. I want to become someone better than that."

I braced myself for an angry reaction, but it didn't come. Mom seemed genuinely surprised by my comment, like such a thought had never occurred to her before. She just shrugged and concluded, "All right. I told you about Aunt Elizabeth's plan and you declined, so that's that. Honestly, I didn't think it was such a great idea myself. We'll just have to see what the new year brings." Then she got up and left immediately for work.

Margaret just stared at me intensely.

* * *

To add to the general mess, Dad came home the weekend before Christmas. The plan, as worked out by Mom, was for us all to go to Sunday mass together, then open gifts; then Dad would leave the next day to relieve a restaurant manager in Toronto.

None of us had much to say to Dad through the first steps of that plan except thank you for some gift certificates. Later in the day, however, while I was finishing up my nap, he surprised me by rapping on my door and asking, "Martin? Do you mind if I come in?"

I sat up against the headboard. "No. I don't mind."

"Were you sleeping?"

"I'm not now. It's okay."

Dad looked around. "This used to be my room, you know."

"I know. Until that, uh, fire thing."

"Yeah. I was smoking then. Fell asleep. Stupid, stupid thing."

"And it was Uncle Bob's room before that."

He smiled sadly. "Yeah. You remember that? He stayed down here, too."

He didn't say anything else, so I asked, "What's going on upstairs?"

"Oh. I have a deal worked out with your mom. No drinking until five o'clock. Then I'll go have a couple of beers."

"Uh-huh." I decided to ask him outright, "Do you think you will ever stop?"

"Drinking?"

141

"Yeah."

"Maybe."

"When?"

"Do you know what they tell you in Alcoholics Anonymous?"

"What?"

"You can stop once you find a higher power to turn to."

"A higher power than what?"

"Than yourself. Than the bottle. When you find that higher power, you find the key to stopping."

I looked at the clock. It was four-thirty. "If you're serious about stopping, why do you work in a place that sells alcohol?"

I expected him to blow my question off, but he answered it at some length. "I guess I work there because I've always worked in that kind of place. It's easy for me. I can make money doing it. That's why a lot of people do things—simply because they've done them before. They get into ruts and keep chugging along in them."

Dad started sliding his back down the wall, intending to sit on the floor, so I told him, "You can sit here on the bed. Prop a pillow up against the headboard."

Dad smiled gratefully. When he was positioned, he said, "What else shall we talk about?"

I answered immediately, "My grandfather."

"Which one?"

I must have looked confused, because he added, "You have two, you know."

"Yes, of course. I'm sorry. I meant Grandfather Mehan, if you don't mind."

"No. I don't mind. What about him?"

"I want to know what he was really like. I want to get past the family story, you know? Past the official memoirs."

"Okay. What do you want to know?"

"Tell me about when you first met him."

Dad thought for a moment; then he spoke very articulately, like a professor giving a lecture. "After he retired from the government, and before he became a full-time Catholic layman, your grandfather Mehan took up teaching for a while. I guess he had his reasons. Maybe he wanted to share his great expertise in United States history. Anyway, he called his old friend General Lowery, and, to make a long story short—something your grandfather would never do— he got offered a one-year teaching chair at All Souls Prep. Did you know about that?"

"Kind of. I didn't know it was a chair. What's that? Like, furniture?"

He laughed. "No. It's a position. They have them at colleges. They used to have them at All Souls Prep, too. It's a teaching position that comes with great benefits, like your own house, and a cook, and a maid."

"So you get a lot more than a chair."

"A lot more. So one summer a quarter of a century ago, your grandfather moved into one of the houses that All Souls used to own, right across the street from the front gate. Do you know that big brick one?"

"They owned that house?"

"They owned the whole street, I believe. But they've had to sell them all off."

"Did Nana move in, too?"

"No. She stayed in Brookline to be close to Elizabeth, who was living in a convent at the time. Your mother had just graduated from high school, and they were looking to get her into that nun thing, too. But she wanted no part of that." Dad formed his index fingers into a cross. "Your mom had come to a crossroads in her life, and she had to make a choice. She took the train down here and stayed with your grandfather in the All Souls house." Dad cocked one eyebrow at me. "Then, to have some spending money and to have something to do, she took a job as a hostess at a restaurant, the same restaurant where I worked as a bartender. Your grandfather came to see the place one night, and that's when I first met him."

"I thought you met Mom and Grandfather Mehan at All Souls. At some religious retreat or something."

Dad smiled, but not happily. "No. I guess the bar story didn't fit in too well with the Mehan family history. But that's how it really happened."

"You were a bartender?"

"Yes. Part-time. I was in college, too."

"Princeton?"

"No. The College of New Jersey."

"Taking what?"

"Education. I wanted to teach history."

"Really? But you never taught?"

"No. We got married, and Margaret was born a couple of years after that. We needed money, and the path of least resistance was for me to work as a bartender and then as a bar manager. We had to pay for a baby, and we had to keep up with the Mehans, you know. We had to show the Mehans that we could make it on our own."

Dad's eyes shifted to the stack of books on my dresser. He changed the subject. "What are all those books about, Martin?"

"I'm doing a paper on radio broadcasts during World War Two. Speeches by Winston Churchill and FDR."

Dad nodded rapidly. "Churchill was a drunk, you know. He drank all day long. FDR waited until cocktail hour. Like me. But he never had a day without a cocktail hour. And he never stopped after an hour. Yep, they were both drunks."

"But didn't everybody drink back then?"

"No. Your grandfather, Martin Mehan, did not." Dad stared at me pointedly. "But you had another grandfather, you know. He did drink, and I guess that was a bad thing, but he also did some good things in his life. He fought for his country in World War Two. He *really* fought, on Japanese-held islands in the Pacific; he didn't just push papers in some embassy in London."

We sat in silence for a minute. Then Dad held up his watch. It was four-forty-five. "Okay," he announced, "it's just about cocktail hour. Remember, Martin: It's always five o'clock somewhere in the world." He slid off the bed.

I did, too, and followed him to the door. I didn't want him to walk out with a stupid joke like that, so I asked him one more time, "Do you really want to stop?"

Dad exhaled loudly. "This is not a good time to be asking

me that, Martin. I can stop more easily next month, after the holidays. And I will."

"Because I really want you to stop. I want you to know that. I pray for it."

"I understand, Martin. I used to do the same thing. I was on my knees every night for many years, praying for one thing: that my father would stop drinking. But it never happened." Dad opened the door and started up the stairs. "Just think where I'd be today if I had spent that praying time learning a foreign language, or playing the violin, or studying European history."

"So I should stop praying for you?"

He stopped and shook his head. "No. I'm not saying that. I'm just saying that . . . life is complicated. You don't only have two simple choices: drunk or teetotaler; saint or sinner. It's more complicated than that."

He opened the kitchen door and found himself staring right at Mom. She took a glance at the clock and then muttered, "You never could make it through the holidays, could you?"

"Merry Christmas to you, too. Do you want to come join me?"

Mom looked at him with undisguised contempt. "You're a disgrace." Then she walked into the living room.

Dad took his coat off a hook by the kitchen door and put it on. He said, "I am not a disgrace, Martin. However, I am someone who understands disgrace." He looked into the living room. "There's a difference." Then he headed out to Pete's Tavern.

* * *

146

I went back downstairs and sat down wearily in the computer room. Manetti had blocked me, too, leaving only Pinak on my buddy list. I saw that he was online, so I checked in.

> JMARTINC: I'm here, Pinak.
> PINAKC: What are you doing?
> JMARTINC: Having a family Christmas, Conway-style.
> PINAKC: Yes? Who is there?
> JMARTINC: Mom, Dad, Sis, and me. Just like on the TV shows.
> PINAKC: Really? Your father is there now?
> JMARTINC: Yes. And no.
> PINAKC: He's around, though?

Pinak did not usually ask this much. Perhaps he had forgotten the rules. I wrote back:

> JMARTINC: Yes. He's around. If you are driving near the railroad bridge, or anywhere around Pete's Tavern, try not to hit him.

After a long pause, he wrote:

> PINAKC: Sorry.
> JMARTINC: Forget it. Let's talk about something else.
> PINAKC: Yes, that is why I messaged you. I found out that a football club DID play at White Hart Lane.

JMARTINC: Yeah? Who?

PINAKC: White Hart Lane was, and is, the home
  of the Tottenham Hotspur Football Club.

JMARTINC: I've heard of them. The Spurs.

PINAKC: Yes.

JMARTINC: Definitely not Arsenal?

PINAKC: No. I told you: Arsenal is at Highbury.
  Do you want to see the sites?

JMARTINC: No.

During a pause with no messaging, I considered asking Pinak a direct question about my mental health. Something like *Am I crazy if I think I've traveled through time?* But I knew what he would say. He would try to steer me to his father's office. So I typed "Goodbye" and logged off.

After the first time travel, I had made a list of people I might be able to talk to about the experience. Pinak was one of them. But since he came from a psychiatrist's family, I doubted he could ever accept it. Margaret was another. But she was so tied up in facts, she was so logical, that I didn't think she could accept it, either. Dad was the third person on that list. I still didn't know what was possible with him.

A LOGICAL PARADOX

On Monday morning, Mom, Margaret, and I sat at breakfast and listened through the walls to the sounds of Dad throwing up. We stared glumly at our food until he walked in, pale and sweating, and said, with as much dignity as someone could under the circumstances, "All right, Mary. I'll be leaving now."

Mom did not look up.

Margaret did. "Goodbye, Dad. Have a safe trip."

"Thank you, Margaret. Have a merry Christmas."

He turned to me with red, watery eyes. "You, too, Martin. Don't spend too much time in that room down there." He glanced at the basement door. "You should get out as soon as you can. You don't want to wind up like me."

He carried his travel suitcase to the kitchen door. I told him, "Have a good trip, Dad, and a merry Christmas." He turned and looked at me with such gratitude that I was glad I had said something.

Margaret offered to take me to the Millennium Encyclopedia after breakfast. Usually she had to coax and coerce me. Today I was eager to get out of the house, and I quickly agreed. We rode there in virtual silence, both of us thinking, I guess, about the latest parental spat and the latest holiday disaster.

When we got into the building, Margaret sat down with Steve in the first cubicle to learn how to use some new super software. I hung out in Margaret's cubicle, surfing for new information about early radio. At one point, I sensed someone in the cubicle's doorway behind me. A short man was standing there. He was about forty, with slicked-back hair and wire-rimmed glasses. He was dressed in a dark blue suit with a red bow tie. "Hello. I'm Dave Wissler," he said. "And you must be Martin Conway."

"Yes, sir."

"Call me Dave. I hear you have a keen interest in the Battle of Britain."

I didn't know what he meant. I answered, "Sir?" and then, foolishly, changed that to "Dave?"

He smiled. "The bombing of London between 1940 and 1944."

"Yes. Yes. Especially 1940."

"Ah. The Blitz."

"Yes. How did you know that?"

He turned toward the first cubicle. "Your sister mentioned it. I hope you don't mind."

"No. Not at all."

"Is there anything I can help you with? I've read a lot about that era."

I thought about the *Wrong* items on my list. The

silliest one came to mind. I grinned and asked him, "You never heard of something called Pip, Squeak, and Wilfred, did you?"

Mr. Wissler's eyes registered surprise. "I don't think anyone has ever asked me that before, and I've always been ready to answer it. Yes, Martin, I have heard of it, or of them. 'Pip, Squeak, and Wilfred' refers to a set of medals awarded to World War One veterans in England—the 1914 Star, the British War Medal, and the Victory Medal. It was a popular nickname, taken from three comic book characters of that time."

I stopped grinning. "I see. Did a lot of the medals go to men from Yorkshire?"

He took a step inside. "I am sure they did. Yorkshire has quite a military tradition, you know. The Duke—"

I finished the sentence for him: "—of Wellington's Regiment was raised there."

He smiled and said, "Yes. That regiment alone lost over eight thousand men in World War One, 'the war to end all wars.' Their names are all recorded in the York Minster."

All I could do was shake my head and repeat, "The York Minster." I tried to think of another question. I raced through my last conversation with Jimmy. I asked him, "What about the kids in London? Did they get evacuated?"

"Oh yes. In June of 1940, for a week straight, one hundred thousand kids got sent out of London to the countryside. There were other, smaller evacuations, too."

"Uh-huh." I thought about Jimmy's mother. "And did a lot of people die of pneumonia around that time?"

"Oh yes. Pneumonia, and scarlet fever, and mumps, and measles, and chicken pox. There were a lot of different ways to die back then."

Margaret suddenly appeared in the cubicle entrance. She looked surprised to see Mr. Wissler. He immediately put her at ease. "Come in, Margaret, and join us. We are having a delightful talk about one of my favorite times in history, the London Blitz."

Margaret held up one finger, stepped into the next cubicle, and returned with a chair. Then the three of us sat and talked about my obsession, my dream, my time-travel destination—whatever it was. I asked Mr. Wissler straight-out, "Do you think time travel is possible?"

He answered seriously. "No. Time only moves in one direction, forward, so travel to the past is impossible. You are here, in this year, so you can't be simultaneously in another year. It's a logical paradox."

"Okay, but knowing all you do about that year and that place, can you imagine what it felt like to be there? What it really felt like?"

He adjusted his glasses. "Certainly. I can draw parallels, which is something that historians always try to do. For example, the destruction that the Londoners experienced was massive. One German bomb could destroy twenty to thirty houses. The only thing I could compare it to, as an American today, is the destruction that occurred in New York on September 11, 2001. Now, imagine if you lived in Manhattan and you experienced that kind of destruction, and then you had to wait for more planes to come back the next day, and the next night, and the next day, and so on for months.

That's what it would feel like. Numbing. Horrifying. I don't know how those poor people did it."

I said, "Well, they didn't have any choice, did they? They couldn't leave." Mr. Wissler nodded thoughtfully; Margaret looked at me, impressed; so I went on: "Unless they were the Kennedys. *They* could leave."

Mr. Wissler confirmed, "That's right. Ambassador Kennedy sent his wife and children home before the Blitz started."

I heard myself talking like Bill Lane. "And he didn't even stick it out in London himself. He hightailed it out of there every night. That's why the Londoners hated him so much. Right?"

Mr. Wissler smiled at my intensity. "I think there was a little more to it than that. But yes, certainly, that's a part of it. It's more like the Londoners hated the things that he was telling them. They had Prime Minister Churchill on the radio telling them that they would definitely defeat Hitler, no question about it. Then they had Kennedy telling them that Britain would fall to Hitler, just like France had, just like every other country had."

"So who was telling the truth?"

Mr. Wissler looked at Margaret. "I'm sorry. I'm monopolizing this conversation, and I know your sister is also an expert on this."

Margaret smiled to acknowledge the compliment. Then she said, "We will never know who was telling the truth, because something unexpected happened: Hitler never invaded Britain."

"Why not?"

"The bombing was supposed to take the place of an invasion. Hitler assumed the British people would surrender, but they never did. They took everything that the Germans threw at them. That's why they call it their finest hour."

"So Kennedy was wrong?"

"I'd say Kennedy was wrong in the short run but right in the long run. Kennedy said the only way Britain could defeat Germany was with American men and material, and that turned out to be true. Once we entered the war, Detroit started pumping out more tanks in one month than Britain could produce in one year. And tens of thousands of American men went over there to fight and die, including Joe Kennedy's sons. He lost Joe Junior, and he nearly lost Jack."

I knew I shouldn't, but I asked, "And what about General 'Hollerin' Hank' Lowery? Did he think the British could win? Wasn't he there on a mission from FDR or something?"

Mr. Wissler glanced at Margaret. "There's . . . a legal matter involved with him. We can't discuss him." He seemed annoyed, but not at me. "I will say that his encyclopedia entry is still under review."

Margaret said, "I don't think Lowery really matters. The heroes, clearly, were the people of London, who took such a beating and yet wouldn't surrender."

Mr. Wissler picked up on her theme. "Indeed. History turns on certain key moments. If London had surrendered during the Blitz, then the war would have gone in a very different direction. I think any historian would give his right arm to travel to one of those key moments in time."

I looked right at him. "If you could pick one day, Mr. Wissler, to travel back to, what would it be?"

He answered without hesitation: "December twenty-ninth, 1940."

"Why?"

"That was the biggest raid of all. FDR delivered one of his fireside chats on December twenty-ninth, 1940, which became known as the Arsenal of Democracy speech. There was great hope in Britain that Roosevelt would come out in favor of sending weapons to help them, and he did. He devised a program called Lend-Lease."

"What did that mean?"

"That we'd lend them weapons and they'd lease us naval bases. Hitler was furious. He ordered a massive bomber assault on the heart of London.

"Six hundred people were killed in that attack. Hundreds of buildings were reduced to rubble, including some of London's most historic churches and halls. St. Paul's Cathedral took another terrific pounding and everything around it was destroyed, but the cathedral itself survived. That great dome, still standing in a hellish scene of fire and smoke, became a powerful symbol of hope for the British. They took it as a sign that God was on their side."

He ran one finger under each eyeglass rim. "I'm not embarrassed to say I find that time, and those people, very moving."

I sat forward. "I do, too. It's like *everything* mattered to them. Life really mattered. Every minute mattered."

"That's true."

"Not like us."

Mr. Wissler nodded sadly. Then he glanced at his watch. "I'm sorry. I didn't realize it was this late. I have to be going. But I'd be happy to talk to you about this anytime, Martin. I mean that. All right?"

"All right, Mr. Wissler. Thank you."

He pointed at his chest. "Dave."

Margaret laughed.

I said, "All right, Dave."

Mr. Wissler added, "Merry Christmas." But then he paused. "I'm sorry. I should ask: Do you celebrate that holiday?"

I thought of Mom and Dad and our angry Christmases past, but I answered, "Yes, we do celebrate it. In our own way. Merry Christmas to you, too."

NEW HOPE

Margaret carefully watched Mr. Wissler go, as if she were waiting for him to get out of earshot. Then she leaned toward me. "Steve showed me some new software that is amazing. I've just been in sites that we've never heard of before. Anyway, I was thinking of you when I was using it. I looked up that name, Daisy Traynor. And Martin, I established that she *was* in London in 1940." She looked at me curiously. "So how did you know about her?"

I lied easily. "I found her name in one of my independent studies."

"Really? As what?"

I blanked for a moment. Then I came up with "As someone who might have worked at the U.S. Embassy, with our grandfather."

Margaret held up an index card. "Well, you're right. At first she worked as a secretary for *Life* magazine in New York, from 1935 to 1939. Then she transferred to the U.S. Embassy in London in 1940."

"Did it say why?"

Margaret lowered her voice even more. "Kind of. It was at the request of a member of Ambassador Kennedy's staff. No official reason is given for it. However, we do know that Ambassador Kennedy really liked the ladies. And we know that he was friends with the owner of *Life* magazine, Henry Luce."

"Uh-huh. So is Daisy still alive?"

"No. She died about ten years ago."

"Did she have a husband? Or kids?"

"No. She never married; she had no children. Listen to this, though: Her next of kin, her brother's daughter, got all of her property. And the daughter lives near here, in New Hope."

"Where's that?"

"In Pennsylvania, but right across the Delaware. Her name is Joan Traynor-Kurtz."

I pointed at the screen. "Can we pull her up?"

"Sure. You go ahead."

I typed in Joan Traynor-Kurtz's name and hometown. I found two listings—a home address with a phone number and a business address with a phone number, both in New Hope, Pennsylvania. I pointed at the business name and read it aloud. "Seraphim. What does that mean?"

"It's a kind of angel. Scroll down. Let's see if there's a Web site."

There was. I clicked on the link, which opened up onto a beautiful screen. It showed a pair of billowing white wings that parted to reveal the inside of a gift shop.

Margaret examined the store items. "Wow. That stuff looks very arty. And very expensive."

"Is it religious stuff?"

"Yeah. Most of it." Margaret pulled her chair closer. "We have her phone numbers. Do you want to call her?"

I froze. "I don't know." I turned to Margaret. "Do you think you could call her for me?"

"Sure. No problem. What should I say, though? That we want to come up there? That you want to find out about Daisy Traynor?"

I gulped audibly. "Yeah. That we both do, for the encyclopedia."

Margaret smiled. "You know, Martin, it's great to see you so interested in . . . something. Anything."

I smiled back weakly.

Margaret checked once more to make sure Mr. Wissler was gone. Then she picked up her phone and dialed. "Hello? Is this Joan Traynor-Kurtz? Yes? Ms. Kurtz, this is Margaret Conway from the Millennium Encyclopedia. How are you?" Margaret gave me a thumbs-up sign. "Let me get right to the point, Ms. Kurtz. We're researching people who survived the London Blitz in 1940, and I see that your aunt, a Ms. Daisy Traynor, was one such person." Margaret's thumb rose up again, higher, and then higher. "Yes, ma'am. Yes, ma'am, I would love to see that photo album. Yes, I know where that is. In the Premiere Gallery. Got it."

Margaret hung up and held out her hand for me to slap, which I did. "Totally cooperative. Eager to help. Daisy Traynor made a photo album of her time in London. Ms. Kurtz said to come to her store and she'll show it to us. She's going home to get it now."

All I could think of to say was "Awesome job."

* * *

Twenty minutes later, we were driving in Margaret's Camry with the Delaware River on our left and walls of dark rocks on our right.

Margaret pointed at the scenery. "Do you know what we're doing? Right now?"

"Going to New Hope, Pennsylvania?"

"No, I mean historically. Do you know what road we're on?"

"The River Road?"

"Right. This is the exact road that General George Washington took on Christmas 1776, on his way to attack the Hessians at Trenton. It was a turning point of the Revolutionary War."

I stared at the road and tried to picture it back then.

"Everything was crumbling around him: His soldiers were deserting; the Continental Congress wanted to replace him. Washington knew that he had to do something. So he got up and he did it." Margaret pulled in to the parking lot of a convenience store. She turned the car back toward the river, and we sat looking at a two-lane bridge with a steel roadway. "This is it. This is the actual spot where Washington crossed the Delaware. He had known nothing but defeat. But on that night, at this very place, he knew victory. Can you imagine being here that night?"

I told her, "Yes, I can." Then I went further. "I think people can travel back into the past."

"Really?"

"Really."

"Like in that book *The Time Machine*?"

160

"I haven't read it."

"Did you ever see the movie *Back to the Future?*"

"Yeah."

"Like that?"

"That's the one where the kid goes back and meets his own parents when they were kids?"

"Yeah. He helps the dad to change his life by standing up to the bully."

"Then no, not like that. I don't think people can change things. All they can do is observe them."

Margaret never even looked at me. She just replied, "Okay." But I could tell she thought I was being stupid, or crazy.

We soon reached Lambertville and turned left, driving over a bridge made of bumpy wooden boards to New Hope, Pennsylvania. We saw rows of small shops ahead. Margaret rolled down the window and asked a woman with a huge dog where the Premiere Gallery was. The woman pointed across the street and up the hill.

Seraphim was a colorful, crowded store on the lower level of the Premiere Gallery. Two huge angels stood in the plate-glass window. The stuff inside seemed to be all angel-oriented, too—books, CDs, and lots of artwork. A tall woman with long gray hair sat behind the counter. She guessed who we were right away. "Margaret Conway?"

"Yes. Are you Joan Traynor-Kurtz?"

"That's right. You can just call me Joan." Joan smiled kindly at me. Margaret added, "This is my brother, Martin. He's interning at the encyclopedia over the holidays."

I was surprised at how well Margaret lied. The woman

said, "That's nice." She pulled an old leather photo album from under the counter. "It's still early for customers. I think we can look at this in my office. All right?"

Margaret answered, "That'd be great," and we all walked into a small back room.

"My aunt Daisy left this album to me in her will. I love it for its sentimental value, but I'm excited that it might have some historical value, too." Joan opened the pages, and Margaret and I leaned over, scouring the faded black-and-white images for faces we knew. There were many photos, and most were captioned in a light, feminine hand: "Vera Lynn at the Mayfair Hotel"; "Edward R. Murrow at the BBC"; "General Henry M. Lowery at Cliveden."

Margaret commented, "This is fascinating. And extremely valuable. History is built, piece by piece, with primary sources just like this."

"I know some of the photos are of famous people. Daisy knew lots of famous people. She was a personal secretary to Henry Luce."

Margaret turned the page to a formal portrait of Daisy and commented, "She was a beautiful woman."

I looked at the picture and nearly gasped. There was Daisy Traynor, just as I had seen her, ready for a night out on the town. I muttered, "Yeah. She was really beautiful."

Joan smiled. "That she was. She knew it, too. But don't get me started on that."

Margaret turned the page again, and Joan pointed out, "There's Joseph Kennedy, with his sons Joe and Jack, and his daughter Kick."

Margaret turned many pages, and she and Joan made comments about many people, but one remained missing. There was no photo of Mickey Mouse—Martin Mehan.

"What did your aunt do after the war?" Margaret asked.

Joan answered proudly, "Daisy remained a strong and independent woman. She moved back to New York City and worked at Time-Life. She loved the city."

As soon as Margaret reached the last page, I wondered out loud, "Is it possible that Daisy wrote memoirs, like Grandfather Mehan's?"

Margaret picked up on that thought. "Oh yes! A lot of people who lived through historic times, people like your aunt, published their memoirs, even if it was just for the family. Did Daisy ever do that?"

"No. No memoirs. She was a terrific letter writer—" Joan seemed to catch herself. She completed the thought hurriedly. "But none of those got saved."

"What about diaries?"

"No. Not that I've ever seen. Or heard about."

Margaret pressed her. "Is it possible that someone else in the family received memoirs or a diary or letters?"

Joan looked out toward the store. Then she looked back and told us, in a voice that was suddenly weary, "All right. If you dig a little further, you'll find this out, so I'll just tell you. There was a minor scandal late in her life. She needed money, I guess. She tried to sell love letters to a tabloid magazine called *The Recorder*."

"I see. Love letters from whom?"

Joan pointed at the photo album. "That general in there. Lowery. He wrote her some letters—some pretty hot ones, apparently—while they were both serving in England. The Lowery family got wind of it and sued the tabloid to stop publication. My understanding is that they got possession of the letters and burned them."

I asked, "Were there any other things, like official memos or telegrams or dispatches?"

"No. Nothing like that."

"Nothing in German, or from a German guy?"

"Nothing."

Margaret waited to see if I was through. Then she dug out a card. "Okay. Thanks so much. Here's my number, in case you think of anything else."

Joan took the card and then fished around for one of her own. "Here. In case you have any questions about Daisy, you can call me at home. I do want to keep the facts straight about her. She deserves that."

Margaret held up the book reverently. "Might we possibly take this with us and study it at the encyclopedia's offices? I promise you we will return it unharmed."

Joan shook her head. "Sorry. No. Those photos are priceless to me, as you can imagine."

"Of course. Well, can we possibly copy some?"

Joan thought for a moment. Then she pointed to her computer, nearly covered by a white, detached angel's wing. "Okay. If you want, you can scan them here and e-mail them to your office."

"Excellent. That'd be excellent. Thank you so much."

Margaret walked quickly over to the scanner, leaving me with Joan. After an awkward pause, I made the hopelessly stupid observation "So, you're interested in angels?"

Joan rolled her eyes, but she answered with patience. "That's what this store is all about. That's what I'm all about. Do you know anything about angels?"

"Me? No. Not really."

"Well, do you believe in them, at least?"

I glanced over at Margaret, wishing she would hurry. I answered, "I'm not sure."

Joan fluttered her hand in the small space between us. "Have you ever felt a presence, a benevolent presence, right next to you? Like this?"

A shiver went up my spine. I mumbled, "No. Never."

Just then, Margaret turned toward us and announced, "Okay. That's it. I just sent about a dozen photos to the Millennium Encyclopedia offices." She handed the photo album back. "Thank you, Joan. Thank you so much."

"You're very welcome." Joan led us to the front, where she stashed the album under the counter. We waved a final goodbye to her and exited past the bright displays of angel cards, crystals, and candles.

We located our car and were soon driving back, retracing General George Washington's path toward Trenton. Margaret looked at me and did a double take. "Martin! You're actually smiling. From ear to ear."

"I am?"

"Yes."

"Sorry."

Margaret poked at me playfully. "Come on, tell me. Why are you so happy?"

I looked at the river passing by. I thought about the photos of Daisy Traynor, young and alive, and I smiled even wider. "Well, everything was crumbling, and I had to do something, and I did it. With your help, of course. I did it."

"Did what?"

"I just crossed the Delaware."

After a pause, Margaret admitted, "I don't get it."

"Let's just say, after many defeats, I've just known victory."

And we left it at that.

When we got back home, I went down to the basement and checked for messages. There was an urgent one from Pinak that just said, "Read this, Martin! Right away!" I clicked on it, and saw:

> PINAKC: Martin, I was troubled by your complete assurance about that Arsenal Football Club location. You're never completely sure about anything. So I checked further. The team has a website and a team historian. I wrote to the team historian three days ago, and I heard back tonight. I have attached his message.

I clicked on the attachment:

> Sir—Your question addresses an unusual time in Arsenal's history. While Arsenal did indeed call Highbury its home throughout the 20th century, the club was forced to move home fields during World War II. Highbury

was taken over and used as a First Aid Post and an Air Raid Precautions Centre. Arsenal matches in 1940 took place at White Hart Lane in Tottenham, where the club shared the field with its arch-rivals, the Spurs.

I thrust my fist up in the air. Then I pulled my list out of the drawer. I quickly changed the status of Daisy Traynor and White Hart Lane. I pounded my fist on the desk. Then I typed in furiously:

JMARTINC: Thanks, Pinak! You bloody spiv.

I was startled when he wrote right back.

PINAKC: What is a bloody spiv? And why am I one?

JMARTINC: I don't even know. I'm sure you're not one. Thanks for the information, Pinak. Thanks for everything!

PINAKC: Martin, tell me, how could you possibly have known about Arsenal, and World War II, and White Hart Lane?

JMARTINC: I know because I was there.

PINAKC: No. You weren't.

JMARTINC: Okay, then because I know someone who was there.

PINAKC: No. You don't.

JMARTINC: Then it's a logical paradox. But it's still true.

I logged off and tallied up the list. James Harker, Bill Lane, and Alice Lane were no longer *Maybes* to me, they were *Rights*. So the score for Jimmy Harker was now ten *Rights*, no *Wrongs*, and no *Maybes*. It was a clean sweep. What more proof did I need?

I hopped to my feet and paced back and forth. I absolutely could not keep still. I burst into my bedroom, walked up to the dresser mirror, and looked hard into my own eyes. I asked myself aloud, "Will you help? Will you do your bit?" And I answered myself, slowly and solemnly, "Yes. Yes, I will."

I had a destiny, all right. But it sure wasn't to go back to All Souls Prep. It was to go back to London.

I walked out of my room and into the dark, damp storage area. I resurrected the Philco from its box, pulling it up slowly, like raising Lazarus from the dead. I returned to my room and carefully replaced the glass tubes—the three 24s, the 27, the two 71As, and the 80.

I placed the radio back on its nightstand, plugged it in, and lay down to face its orange glow and its distant crackling.

LONDON: DECEMBER 29, 1940

I went to bed each night with the possibility that I would travel through time, but I had to wait until Sunday for it to happen.

I had spent the week in a state of rising anticipation. I don't know when I have ever felt more alive. I actually caught myself singing on the way up to breakfast one morning. I started working out every day, too—push-ups, sit-ups, jumping jacks—the entire Garden State Elementary School PE routine. And I did them over and over. I took to running to the Acme and back; I even took to running through the hilly streets behind our house for no reason at all. My energy, so long dormant, was now coursing through my veins.

I stopped napping entirely, preferring to go to bed as exhausted as possible and to fall asleep as quickly and as deeply as possible. I was physically tired but mentally alert when I finally lay down on Sunday night.

Ironically, for the first time in months I could not sleep. Eventually I got up and walked to the computer room. I looked up cures for insomnia and learned that fresh, cold air could induce sleep. I pulled on a coat and slipped upstairs, quietly opening the kitchen door and stepping out into a freezing, starlit night.

I filled my lungs with cold air for a long time, breathing in and out, storing up oxygen for what I suspected might be a dangerous ordeal ahead. When I finally returned to my room and assumed my sleeping position with my face toward the radio dial, I didn't have long to wait.

I found myself transported almost immediately to that place of musty scents and gloomy darkness. I looked around the familiar room and saw Jimmy Harker in his wing chair, seated next to the radio and staring right at me.

He sounded relieved. "I was afraid I'd never see you again, Johnny."

He reached over and turned the dial until he found a bouncy tune. Then he broke into a delighted smile. "Here it is! I knew I'd find it. Listen, Johnny. It's 'Mr. Franklin D. Roosevelt Jones.' "

I listened to the words and smiled along with him.

He added, "That FDR. He's all right, ain't he?"

"Yeah. I guess."

"Gonna sell us the arms we need to fight Hitler. Gonna tell us about it tonight."

We listened to the song all the way through. Jimmy stood behind the radio, singing along, running his fingers across the smooth, curved surface of the Philco 20 Deluxe.

When it was over, I asked him, "Do you know what they call this kind of radio? The kind with a curved top?"

"What?"

"A cathedral radio."

"Oh yeah? Why?"

I shrugged. "Because it looks like a cathedral?"

"It don't look nothin' like the York Minster. Maybe a little like St. Paul's." Jimmy looked up at me with his eyes ablaze. "The BBC said that St. Paul's caught a pocket earlier. Gerry blasted everything around it, but the great cathedral still stands. Imagine that, Johnny. Hitler hurls his bombs at it and God just swats them away."

He walked over to the sideboard and looked at his grandfather's medals. "Gerry's in for it now. We'll have the guns to beat him, with or without you Yanks."

I was puzzled. "Without the Yanks?"

"Yeah. Everybody knows how it is: Old FDR wants to fight, but Joe Kennedy don't. That's because them Kennedys is all playboys. They just want to have it off with all the movie stars, don't they?"

I shrugged. "I don't know."

"They say there's two yellow races now—the Japs and the Americans."

I thought of Margaret's words—that Joe Kennedy lost one son and nearly lost a second in the war. I thought of my grandfather Conway, too. I told Jimmy, "The Americans aren't afraid to fight."

"No? Then where are they?"

"In America. Where do you think?"

"Lotta good they're doing there."

I had heard enough. "What are you talking about? It was American men, and American weapons, that won the war."

Jimmy looked at me, puzzled. "American?"

Suddenly I realized that Jimmy had no idea how this war

would spread, or how it would end. He had no knowledge beyond 1940. Perhaps he had no knowledge beyond this night. I conceded, "Okay. You're doing a brave thing, standing up to Hitler like this. The whole world knows that."

"That's right."

I wandered over to the radio and looked at it closely. It was my Philco 20 Deluxe, definitely, but it looked newer and shinier. "This is a real beauty."

"I'll say. Best on the block."

"Where did you get it?"

"My dad brought it home."

"I have one just like it. My nana gave it to me. Look at the wood on the front. It's like three different kinds of wood. And look at the back here. Mine had a nameplate that said 'Martin Mehan.' On this one, there's two little screw holes but no plate."

I watched Jimmy as he squeezed out a dab of Brylcreem, combed it through his hair, and lay the tube down on the table. Then he smiled, like he knew the jig was up. "You're right, Johnny. Of course you're right. I know it's not our radio. Not really. I expect that Bill Lane pinched it."

"Bill Lane?"

"Yeah. He gave it to my dad so we'd have a good radio for the war news, and the football matches, and the music. My dad said he thought Bill pinched it from the Embassy's storeroom."

"But . . . how could he do that?"

"He goes in there whenever he wants. So does my dad. They're firefighters, mate. They gotta check on things." Jimmy stopped and looked up, as if listening for a sound outside. "Don't worry. My dad's gonna return it tomorrow. They've got year-end inventory comin' up."

I walked around, behind the radio, and looked inside. I saw the number from the Embassy's storeroom, but that was all. Something was missing.

Jimmy came up beside me. "You hear that sound outside?"

I listened, and I did hear some voices and some car horns.

"People are celebrating. It's a night to remember, Johnny. And here's what I'm doing to remember it." He bent over in front of me and wrote, with a black fountain pen: "291240."

I sputtered, "What? It was you who wrote that?"

"Yeah."

"What does it mean?"

"Mean? It's the date, isn't it?"

"No. It isn't."

"Twenty-nine December, 1940: 29.12.40."

"No. That would be 12-29-40."

"Hardly, mate."

"That's how we write December twenty-ninth: 12-29."

"Then you write it wrong, don't you?"

The mood changed right after that. Jimmy stared, fixated, into the back of the radio for a long time. His good spirits faded away completely, and a great burden seemed to descend on him.

When he spoke again, it was dreamily, like he was remembering a scene from long ago. "I shouldn't have wrote the date in there. But it was a great night, wasn't it? And I

173

wanted to celebrate. People were celebrating all around. I heard car horns beeping outside, and . . ."

Jimmy sighed. Then he dropped the black pen to the floor. I watched it roll until it stopped next to his gas mask. He said softly, "So let's get started then, Johnny."

I didn't like his actions, or the tone of his voice. "Started where?"

"Where I have to go. And you have to follow."

Jimmy turned toward the door. I pressed my hands to my temples, trying to think fast. "Wait, Jimmy! Listen: 29.12.40. December twenty-ninth, 1940. I know what happens."

"I'm not so sure you do."

"We . . . we can't go outside. We have to find shelter."

Jimmy told me calmly, "We will, mate. You'll see." He opened the door and we stared out at the black emptiness, like looking into a grave. Jimmy turned. "What's the matter? Are you still afraid of the dark?"

I was. I was terrified. But I followed him out. As I waited, trying to get my eyes to adjust to the blackout, a lone man brushed past us. He stopped and exchanged polite greetings with Jimmy. Both of them muttered, "Goodbye and good luck."

Jimmy told me, "Watch your step. There's a big bomb crater to your right. I expect there's still a bit of shrapnel in the road, too."

I followed Jimmy across the street. Another person passed and exchanged the same greeting. Jimmy explained, "That's what we say instead of 'Merry Christmas' this year, Johnny. We say 'Goodbye and good luck.' "

The next thing he said made me freeze with fear. "Listen to that, now. Here comes Gerry."

The first sound I heard was the air-raid sirens as they cranked up.

Then I heard the droning of engines high above. German bombers. Hundreds of them. The incendiaries hit us just seconds later, bursting into flame, marking the way for the high explosives to follow.

I saw the outline of the surface shelter ahead. Two people, the old woman and the boy, were standing by the doorway. Jimmy walked up to them at the entrance. "This is it, then, Gran?" As before, the woman and the boy didn't reply, except by turning and walking inside.

I ran up and tried to go inside, too, but Jimmy blocked my way. "You can't go in there."

"What? Why?"

Jimmy pointed to a spot on the sidewalk. "You're to wait over there and watch."

"Are you crazy? You have to let me in. I'll get killed out here!"

"Don't be a bloody fool, Johnny! You can't get killed. You never could. This isn't your time."

I stared into his eyes. In the dark, I couldn't tell if Jimmy was sweating or crying, but his face was wet. His voice softened. "I shouldn't have gone out tonight, Johnny. I was wrong to. I should have stayed home, like Dad said."

I could hear a wave of horrible booming noises racing toward us through the dark streets. One by one, nearby buildings began to explode under the massive barrage.

Jimmy's hands shot up to cover his ears. Then he

lowered them and shouted over the din, "But some good can come of this! I believe that. If you'll do your bit. If you'll just watch. Some good can come."

Jimmy's resolve suddenly started to melt. I saw a fat tear roll down his face as he struggled to speak, like a condemned prisoner delivering his last words. "Do you remember the question they ask you when you die?"

"Yeah. *What did you do to help?*"

"That's right. Well, this could be what you answer, then. You did this, to help me. And my dad."

"What?"

"You and my dad, you're both still alive, so you can still change things. All you've got to do is tell my dad what you saw here tonight, and that I'm sorry. Okay, Johnny?"

All I could do was nod, up and down. He pointed again. "You stand right there. And you watch. Then do what you can for us, eh?"

I kept nodding.

"Goodbye, then, Johnny. Goodbye and good luck." Jimmy's face was illuminated one last time in the flash of an exploding bomb. He turned quickly and ducked into the surface shelter.

I did what he told me to do.

I took a spot on the sidewalk, exactly where he had said.

I stared at the surface shelter.

I heard the thudding of the German bombs all around.

The explosion that followed was tremendous. It slapped me in the face so hard that I flew backward onto the pavement. I looked up at the shelter just in time to see the force of the blast blow out all four of its walls. The concrete roof hovered for one horrible second, and then crashed down on the three people inside.

I screamed "No!" and struggled to my feet. I scrambled across the road, picking my way over the hot, jagged rocks, and stared into the pile of debris. I ran around the perimeter and tried to find a way inside, but there was none. Not that it mattered. It was too late. No one in that rubble could still be alive.

All I could do was stand there, helplessly, and watch.

Within two minutes, and seemingly out of nowhere, a crew of firefighters arrived. I backed out of the way as they went about their business, doing what they could. They used iron crowbars to move aside massive pieces of concrete. As I watched, two big men searched for the bodies of an old woman, a little boy, and Jimmy Harker.

That's when my heart broke open. I twisted myself away from the horrible sight and stood hunched over as hot, dirty tears poured down my face.

As I stared down at the street, I expected to find myself transported immediately back to my own bed, in my own time, but that didn't happen. I was still in London, in 1940, in the middle of an air raid, and I had no idea what to do next.

I finally straightened up and stumbled back across the street, dazed. I had always had Jimmy as my guide; now I was alone. What could I do now? What would he want me to do?

The scene around me was horrifying. The bombers had

wreaked massive destruction, and the bombs were continuing to fall. Between the shattering bursts of the explosions, I could hear voices crying out in the dark, in pain and terror.

I took off running, blindly, hoping something familiar would appear to guide me through the hellish streets. My lungs were burning and my legs were sore when I finally stopped to rest. I looked up and found myself in front of a large, ornate building with the words RITZ HOTEL written across the doors.

A car was idling in front, and a big man was running toward it. A woman in high heels was trying to follow him, but she could not keep up. As the man opened the car door, I could see that it was General Lowery. He dove into the backseat and hollered at the driver, "Don't wait for her. Go! Get out of here now!"

The woman was Daisy Traynor. She screamed after him, "Wait! Wait!" She reached the car just as it was pulling away. In a fury, she yelled after it, "You bastard! You big coward!" She shook her fist to the sky. "Listen to me! I *do* have your precious memos! Every one of them! You traitor! You coward!" When her fury was finally spent, she muttered, "You'll be hearing from me again. Believe that." Then she limped off, right past me, into the night.

I watched her for a moment, dumbly, until the thought hit me: *She's going to the Embassy!* I had a guide now, and a direction.

I gulped in some air and took off again, soon overtaking the tall figure of Daisy Traynor and other fleeing phantoms, running all the way to the telephone box in Grosvenor Square.

I came to a stop directly in front of James Harker. Futilely, I screamed at him, "Mr. Harker! It's Jimmy! He's been killed!"

He looked right through me without a blink.

I heard the ringing of the telephone. I ran up behind Bill Lane as he answered it. He listened for a long moment and hung up. His face looked terribly troubled as he walked over and whispered to James. After ten seconds of talk, they both took off running. And I took off behind them.

We kept up a steady pace all the way back to the remains of the surface shelter. An ambulance was parked there now. So was Canby's car, with Canby in it.

James searched frantically around in the rubble until he spotted a row of three corpses laid out on the street. I watched from afar as he fell to his knees and cradled Jimmy's broken body in his arms. His sobs and his desperate cries of "No! No!" echoed down the walls of that shattered block.

Bill Lane turned away from his friend and spotted Canby's car. He walked over and pointed to Canby to roll down the window. I could hear Bill yell at him, "You built this shelter! You're responsible for them that died in it!"

I could see Canby shaking his bald head emphatically, defending himself.

An ambulance driver and a helper lifted the bodies of the old woman and the boy up on stretchers and slid them inside the back door. They waited for James to let go of his son.

He finally did. Then he stood up, not quite straight, his head flopped over to one side like a hanged man's. The driver and helper said a few last words to him and slid Jimmy into the ambulance, too.

After a moment, James straightened himself and walked heavily through the rubble. I could see that his fists were clenching and unclenching. As he approached Bill Lane, Bill yanked the car door open and pulled Canby out.

"You killed them, Canby!" Bill shouted. "You and your bloody cheap construction!"

Canby tried to squirm away. He protested, "No! No! That's not right!"

James Harker walked quickly up to them, pulled back his fist, and smashed it into Canby's face. Canby snapped out of Bill Lane's grasp and fell hard onto the jagged pile of rocks. James stood over him, panting "You killed my Jimmy! You killed my Jimmy!" over and over until his fury seemed to subside. He left Canby lying there, corpselike, and turned toward Bill.

"James, you must go with your boy now," Bill told him. "Go with him."

James just stared at Bill without expression.

"Who knows, James? Maybe his spirit hasn't left this earth yet. He'll need your prayers. He'll need you to be there with him."

James asked wonderingly, "Yeah?"

"Yeah. Go now." Bill took James by the shoulders and started him walking toward the ambulance.

I watched all this, thinking, *What am I doing here? Why did I need to see this? How did I help anything? Or anybody?*

Still, I stayed in my place amid the smoke and the fire. I struggled to keep control of my heart rate and my breathing, but I couldn't. I was losing it. I realized that I could not move any part of my body. I could only stare straight ahead, feeling the thud of the bombs, smelling the stench of the smoke, sensing the heat of nearby flames.

Suddenly I saw movement up ahead of me, twenty yards away, in the dusty haze. I saw two people, two people I knew. Something horrible was happening between them. I tried to move toward them, to stop them, but I could not budge. All I could do was watch it happen, as helpless as a ghost.

I watched them until I felt myself start to fall downward again, like I was falling through the street. My fear gave way to absolute panic as I fell and fell and fell.

Then everything went black.

I don't remember landing. I just remember being carried by strong arms. And I remember a light. I remember thinking that I might be dead and in the presence of an angel, like Nana had been.

Slowly the light came into focus. It was a large white bulb hanging from a ceiling, directly above me. I thought, *That's a real light, so I can't be dead.* I shifted my eyes. I saw that I was in a small space bordered by blue curtains. I could hear the sound of a machine beeping.

Then two people stood up right next to me and stared down into my face: Mom and Margaret.

I gasped, "Where am I?"

Margaret answered, "You're at Princeton Hospital, Martin, in the emergency room."

Mom looked very pale. She took hold of my hand,

squeezed it lightly, and whispered, "We heard noises downstairs. We . . . we couldn't wake you. You were having some
kind of seizure. We had to call an ambulance."

Margaret peered into my face. "Martin, what happened
to you?"

VERY WELL THEN, ALONE!

The doctor in the emergency room had no idea what was wrong with me, so after seven hours, a skull X-ray, and a CT scan, he sent me home. My diagnosis, as written on the discharge papers, was "petit mal seizure." I was ordered to stay in bed for twenty-four hours.

Mom spent a lot of that time in the basement with me, relieved periodically by Margaret. The emergency room visit turned out to be a crossroads for Mom. She treated me differently at the hospital, on the ride home, during the following day, and from that time on.

During her very first shift in the basement, she pulled the computer chair into my room, sat next to the bed, and announced, "You can go to Garden State Middle School. I'll call them as soon as the holidays are over."

"That's great," I sputtered. "But why? Why did you change your mind?"

"I've been changing my mind for a while now. But this helped me see it clearly. Facing your child's death helps you see things clearly."

I thought of James Harker. "Yes. I'm sure it does."

"I know All Souls is wrong for you. I . . . I thought it was right for Margaret, but maybe that was a mistake, too."

"Really?"

"She would have been just as smart in a public school."

"Yeah. I guess so."

"And I've never liked working there."

"No?"

"No. Father Thomas is very tight with money. He knew I needed more; he knew I deserved more. He took advantage of the fact that I was desperate to get you two an education." She added sadly, "He treats me like a servant." Mom paused, as if looking into the past. "I once lived across the street, you know. With your grandfather. And we really did have servants."

"I know. Dad told me."

Mom seemed mildly surprised. "He did?" She went on, "I always believed in destiny. I guess I got that from your grandmother. When your grandfather got the job at All Souls and I lived there, too, and I met your father there, it just all seemed to say *This place is your destiny*. I even got married on All Souls' Day."

"Really? When's that?"

"November second. It's the day after All Saints' Day."

"That's the day for the souls in purgatory, right?"

"Right. They're on their way to heaven, but they haven't arrived yet."

"So where are they?"

Mom shrugged. "Someplace in between. I don't know." She smiled weakly. "Maybe they're under your bed."

I thought, *Or maybe they're in my radio.* I asked her seriously, "Do you think we can do more than pray for those souls? You know—to get them into heaven faster, do you think we can actually *do* things for them?"

"Things like what?"

"I don't know." I remembered Jimmy's words: *Will you do your bit when the time comes? On the day of reckoning?*

I thought it better to change the subject. "And did you get married at All Souls Chapel?"

"No. You've seen the pictures, Martin. It was up in Brookline. At St. Aidan's. Your grandfather's teaching job was over by then."

"Oh? Somebody else was sitting in his chair?"

Mom smiled. "Your father told you about that, too?"

"Uh-huh."

"I didn't know you two talked so much."

"Just twice. Once at Nana's funeral, and once at Christmas."

Her smiled turned rueful. "Another jolly Christmas. He could never make it through the holidays." She swallowed hard. "How many did he ruin for us?"

"A few. Do you hate Dad for his drinking?"

"No. Certainly not. I might hate what his drinking did to us."

"Do you think there's any hope for him?"

"With the drinking?"

"Yes."

"Well, anything's possible. But I doubt it. Unless he truly hits bottom and gets the help he needs."

"Professional help?"

185

"I was thinking of God's help. But professional help would be good, too." Mom looked down; she struggled to say, "The flesh is weak, Martin, as the Bible says. Maybe I have given up on your father's drinking. But I want you to know, for certain, that I've never given up on his immortal soul." Two quick tears ran down her cheeks. She wiped them away and tried to smile. "Oh my. Here I am, talking your ear off, and you're supposed to be resting. Shut your eyes for a while."

I pretended to nap after that, but I certainly didn't need to. I had never felt better in my life. I had never felt healthier, or more clearheaded, or more sure of my purpose.

My life, which had seemed to be such a waste just a few months ago, was now driven by a force so powerful that I felt I could not resist it even if I wanted to. I created a list in my head of the things that I needed to do, made out in the exact order in which I needed to do them. Two of those things involved people named Henry M. Lowery.

When Margaret relieved Mom, I took advantage of the time to take care of some serious business. The third trip to London had left me with several burning questions, so I passed them on to Margaret. Whether she thought I was crazy or not, she agreed to take my questions to work and to research them on the most advanced sites she could find.

I pretended to sleep through most of Mom's next shift, too. When Margaret returned, Mom went upstairs to make dinner. As soon as she closed the upstairs door, Margaret whispered excitedly, "All the names checked out. They're all real."

I wanted to say *I know they're real,* but I kept quiet. She flipped open a notepad and informed me, "Harold Canby was an Air Raid Protection Warden in London. He died in a raid on December twenty-ninth, 1940. Two William Lanes were members of the London Auxiliary Fire Service. One died in the line of duty, fighting a fire on January tenth, 1941, at a place called Potters Fields. Alice Lane was listed as his widow. She later remarried, to a Sergeant Dennis Hennessey, in 1944. She died from cirrhosis of the liver in 1955."

I stopped her. "How do you get cirrhosis of the liver?"

"From drinking. Alcoholics die of that."

I repeated Jimmy's words. "Mrs. Alice Lane liked her gin and It." Margaret looked at me, puzzled. "It's a drink. What more did you find out about James Harker?"

She checked her notepad. "James Harker was also in the Auxiliary Fire Service."

"I know. Did he die?"

"Not that I could find. He was born in Yorkshire in 1915, but he had no death date listed anywhere."

"Do you know where he is now?

"No."

I looked across the room at the Philco 20 Deluxe and, thinking out loud, said, "I know he once owned a cathedral radio."

"Is that right? Like yours?"

"Exactly like mine. And Jimmy Harker and Mr. Wissler both told me that York has a cathedral."

"That's right. It has one of the oldest and largest in Europe, the York Minster."

"So . . . I have a feeling, a strong feeling, that I know where James Harker is."

"Where?"

I pulled the covers back. "Back home. In York, the haunted city. Tell me—is it ever too late to solve a murder? Is there a statue of limitations?"

Margaret smiled. "You mean a *statute* of limitations?"

"Yeah."

"No. I don't think so. Not for murder. They're always digging up skeletons to test for poison, or DNA, or whatever." Margaret flipped her notepad closed. "How long ago are we talking about?"

"Sixty years."

"Then definitely not. There may even be eyewitnesses to that murder who are still around."

I thought, *Yeah, like me,* but I kept my mouth shut.

Margaret added, "King Tut was dead over three thousand years before they claimed he was murdered." Her eyes shot to the door. She whispered, "Come on, Martin. I did all this work for you. You have to tell me. Whose murder are we talking about?"

I pointed at her notepad. "Harold Canby's."

I slid out of the bed. "Don't tell Mom that I'm up. This will just take a minute."

"Are you sure you're okay to do this?"

"I am as okay as I have ever been in my life." I hurried across to the computer room, bent down in front of the screen, and did a quick search. Then I wrote a short, hopeful e-mail to the General Enquiries address at York Minster.

* * *

My twenty-four hours of bed rest were up on Tuesday morning. By seven a.m., Margaret and I were on the road, the
River Road, retracing the steps of George Washington's
army back to Pennsylvania.

Joan Traynor-Kurtz's home address was within walking
distance of her store. In spite of two wrong turns, Margaret
and I were standing at her glass door just after breakfast. She
seemed a little annoyed, but not enough to tell us to go
away. Margaret said, in a perky voice, "Hello, Joan. Do you
remember us?"

"Yes. From the encyclopedia."

"That's right. You said to come back if we had questions?"

"I said to come back? Or I said to call?"

"To call. I'm sorry. But the questions we have are of the
face-to-face variety. I promise we will not take more than
fifteen minutes of your time. May we please come in and ask
them?"

Joan shifted her tall figure to block the doorway. "No.
Sorry. The place is a mess."

"Then may we ask them right here? Again, I am terribly
sorry for the imposition, but we're facing a deadline."

Joan shrugged. "So, what else can I tell you?"

Margaret did not expect me to speak up, but I had to.
"Please, ma'am, we need to know about Daisy Traynor's secret papers. The ones that deal with General Lowery and
the German attaché."

Joan's face hardened. "I told you, there are no such
papers."

She started to back away, but I stopped her. "Ms. Traynor-Kurtz, I have to talk to you, in private." I turned to Margaret. "You'll have to wait by the curb. What I have to say is for her alone."

Margaret gulped. She whispered, "Okay," and drifted back toward the car.

I waited until Margaret was out of earshot; then I turned to Joan. I extended my hand, as she had done at Seraphim, and fluttered it in the space between us. "Ms. Traynor-Kurtz, you asked me before if I had ever felt a presence. I said no. I acted like I didn't know what you were talking about. But I was lying."

Joan watched my hand until it stopped. When she looked up, I locked eyes with her. "I have recently been contacted by a spirit. He may have been an angel from heaven, or a soul from purgatory, I don't know. But he was real enough to me, and his message was real. Do you believe that things like that happen?"

She answered simply, "Yes, I do."

"I know that you are a spiritual person. And that's why I have to share part of the message with you. I have not shared it with my sister, or with anyone at the encyclopedia, or with anyone, period."

Joan shifted from foot to foot. She couldn't leave now if she tried. I told her, in measured words, "Daisy Traynor did keep copies of the correspondence between General Lowery and the German attaché, Von Dirksen. She wrote the copies out in her own hand, on scented paper. She tied them up with pink ribbon and stored them under her bed in a red

hatbox. She referred to one man as 'mein Herr.' She referred to another as 'MM,' or 'Mickey Mouse.' "

Joan's mouth literally dropped open. "How . . . Where
did you hear all that?"

"I received a message, and I am passing it along to you.
I don't know anything beyond that."

Joan's eyes began to flutter wildly.

I asked her simply, "Is it the truth?"

She whispered softly, "Yes."

"Then maybe it's time for the truth to come out."

Joan's head dropped down to her chest, like she had
passed out. She seemed to look inside herself. Then she
looked back up. "You wait here."

I stole a glance at Margaret. She raised her hands in a
"What's going on?" gesture. Before I could reply, Joan returned.

She had a red hatbox in her hands.

She spoke very deliberately. "I am going to trust you,
young man, because you invoked the spirit world. And because I believe this is the right thing to do. If this is some
trick, for some cheap tabloid story, then your soul is in for a
lot of torment, and I wouldn't want to be you. Do you understand?"

"Yes, ma'am," I assured her. "I understand."

Joan regarded me fiercely. She finally said, "I'll want
these back when you're finished. However long that takes."

"All right." I took the hatbox in my two hands. It felt
solid and round, and it still emitted a light, delicate scent.
Joan closed the door without another word. I turned and

carried the hatbox back toward Margaret reverently, like a chalice. She jumped into the car and opened the door for me. We shot down the steep road and then pulled over. Margaret demanded to know, "What is that?"

"It's a box full of Daisy Traynor's secret papers from London. Copies of messages that she was sent to deliver."

She snapped, "Pass it over here!" Margaret removed the round red top, set it on the backseat, and started to finger, very carefully, through the papers within. As I watched and listened, Margaret came as close to cursing as I had ever heard. She kept muttering "Holy crap!" over and over, in ever-rising excitement.

After a while, I started picking up the papers, too, and reading the curly, feminine handwriting. They weren't really memos, they were more like notes about memos—full of names, and dates, and places.

We must have sat there for twenty minutes. Margaret finally reached back for the lid, covered the letters, and handed the box to me. "Here. You hold this. You're the one who discovered it."

Margaret threw the car in gear. Soon we were on the wooden bridge over the Delaware, bouncing across to New Jersey. I felt giddy with excitement. "How big a deal is this?"

"This? This is as big as King Tut."

"No!"

"Yes. This is primary source material, Martin. Verifiable. Cross-checkable. Incredible. I see why the Lowery family has worked so hard to deny its existence, and to discredit Daisy." Margaret actually took her hands off the wheel and threw them up before regaining control. "Good God! Daisy

Traynor has reached out from the grave! And you, Martin, are her instrument."

"Instrument? For what?"

"For revenge on Lowery. To bring him down."

I thought of Daisy's last, angry words to Lowery during the air raid. I said, "Yeah. Well, maybe he was just using her, you know? And then he abandoned her."

Margaret actually cackled. "Well, no woman scorned has ever taken sweeter revenge."

"What will this do to Lowery's reputation?"

"It will destroy it."

"Really? I don't understand. What did he do that was so bad?"

"According to those papers, he carried a highly detailed plan from the German attaché, Von Dirksen, to President Roosevelt. The plan outlined how the United States could, essentially, stab Britain in the back and make a deal with Hitler. Fortunately, FDR rejected it."

"So Lowery was a traitor?"

Margaret thought about that. When she finally answered, she was more subdued. "No. I wouldn't say that. He was an isolationist. He wanted to keep the United States out of the war. A lot of people did."

"The isolationists were antiwar?"

"They were."

"Was that a bad thing?"

"I guess it depends on your point of view. From our point of view, we can say that it was absolutely essential to stop Hitler. But people back then still thought they could make a deal with him."

"So? That's all that Lowery was doing. Trying to make a deal. Why will that be so damaging?"

"Because he lied about it! He lied about it back when it happened, and he continued to lie about it for the rest of his life. He claimed that he was always solidly behind the brave Londoners and that he suffered through the Blitz with them when the truth was, he got out of there as soon as he could and he tried to sell them out to Hitler."

Margaret's hands flew off the wheel again. "Martin, what on earth did you say to that woman?"

"I appealed to her spiritual side."

"Really?"

"Yeah. Nana and I have a spiritual side, you know."

"I know." Margaret sounded a little envious.

"Oh yes, and I told her the truth."

"That's always good."

"She said she wants the papers back."

"Sure. They're her property. It may be a while, though. My God! Mr. Wissler is going to die when he sees those papers."

"How are you going to give them to him?"

"I'm going to let you do it. You can tell him . . . the truth." She stole a worried glance at me. "Don't be offended by this, but I don't think you should bring up the time-travel stuff again. Okay?"

I wasn't offended, but I told her, "I'm going to tell him the truth."

Thirty minutes later, we used Margaret's ID to enter the offices of the Millennium Encyclopedia. While she waited by the front, I walked back to a large office, where I could see Mr. Wissler working at a desk. I rapped lightly on the door. He looked up and smiled.

"Hello, Martin. What can I do for you?"

I held out the red hatbox. "Here. I got this from . . . the relative of an eyewitness to history. The eyewitness's name was Daisy Traynor. Reading it is a kind of time travel."

He was definitely intrigued. "Time travel? To when?"

"To our favorite time." I held the box out.

He took it in his two hands. "It certainly smells nice."

"Yes. I'll leave you with it now. I think you'll know what to do with it."

I backed out as he continued to stare at the hatbox. He was so fascinated that he didn't even say goodbye.

Mom, Margaret, and I had a pleasant dinner back at home. Then we went to the Acme to pick up snacks for some New Year's Eve TV-watching. I also spotted an item that I had to buy—a tube of Brylcreem in the "original scent," the kind popular with the RAF pilots and the little boys who idolized them.

We ate our snacks, watched the revelers in Times Square, and wished each other a happy New Year at twelve o'clock. Then, sometime after one, I noticed that I had received an e-mail from over three thousand miles away. It said:

Dear Mr. Conway—I am a York Minster volunteer. I am authorized to confirm for you that a James Harker does work part-time at

the Minster. I must leave it to you and Mr.
Harker to work out whether he would like to
participate in your research project. Good
luck to you.

Sincerely, Helen Mills

NEW YEAR'S DAY

New Year's Day is also a holy day of obligation in the Catholic Church, commemorating the circumcision of the infant Jesus. All Souls Chapel was having a special holy day mass prior to the dedication of the Heroes' Walk, but I asked Mom to take us to Resurrection in Princeton instead. She readily agreed, adding, "At Resurrection, we won't have to listen to that Lowery boy snoring."

I spent my time at mass thinking about Hank Lowery anyway. It had been nearly seven months since he had slapped me in the face. Today was the day he was going to pay for that.

I did not realize it at the time, but Mom and Margaret each had a personal agenda for the day, too. After mass, we drove east through the gray snow of the farmland along East Windsor Road. As we drew closer to All Souls Preparatory, we each grew more somber, and focused, and determined.

When Mom pulled in to the All Souls campus, I noticed a long flatbed truck parked just outside the gate. It was a familiar sight to me, but I was surprised to see it today. It had MANETTI CONSTRUCTION written on the cab door. Atop the open bed sat a small bulldozer, a yellow John Deere 350C.

A crowd was gathered at the entranceway to the Lowery Library. I saw a row of bleachers, twenty feet across and five rows high, facing a podium. A new marble statue stood next to the podium. It depicted General Henry M. "Hollerin' Hank" Lowery standing with his right arm raised, pointing his men forward into battle. His mouth was open, presumably in mid-holler. The statues of FDR and JFK were set in a small arc beside him. Embedded in gold in the gray slate of the entranceway were the words THE HEROES' WALK.

We parked down by the Student Center and walked back. I spotted Hank Lowery right away, but he didn't see me. He was standing with Ben Livingstone and Ben's father, the Lowery family's attorney. I kept my eyes focused straight ahead, following Mom and Margaret into the Administration Building. A small group was inside, including Father Thomas and Father Leonard.

Father Leonard approached us and said, "Congratulations, Martin, on those fine research papers. I haven't read papers that good since Margaret was my student."

I said, "Thank you."

Margaret smiled cryptically.

Father Thomas came over as soon as he saw Mom. "Thank goodness you're here, Mary. I've been priest, principal, and master of ceremonies, all mixed together."

Mom didn't reply. She opened the top desk drawer, removed some items, and put them in her purse.

Father Thomas looked at Margaret and me. "Good to

see you again, Margaret. I know Mr. Livingstone wants to talk to you again about your work at the encyclopedia."

Margaret's smile receded. "I'll bet he does."

"And you, too, Martin. How have you been?"

"Very well, Father. Never better."

"I'm glad to hear that. Father Leonard has been very impressed by your reports. I have read some of them, too. Excellent."

Father Leonard added, "Superior research skills, Martin."

"Thank you. I've enjoyed doing the reports. In fact, I'm working on another one now."

"Oh? What's that?"

"It's called 'Their Finest Hour.' It's about survivors of the London Blitz."

Father Leonard looked intrigued. But before he could ask me about it, Hank Lowery's mother tapped him on the shoulder. He turned away, and he never did turn back.

Father Thomas answered for him. "That is interesting. I'll look forward to reading it."

I shook my head. "You won't be reading it."

"Oh? Why not?"

"Because I won't be turning it in." Father Thomas was clearly confused. I added, "I'm not doing it for you. I'm doing it for me. And for . . . someone else."

He shook his head and muttered, "I'm afraid I don't follow you. Perhaps we could talk about it later."

"There is no later. I won't be coming back here."

Father Thomas looked to Mom for support, but he heard instead "Actually, Father, I won't be coming back, either."

His eyes widened. After a stunned pause, he finally managed to say, "I'm sorry to hear that, too, Mary. Very sorry. When will you be leaving us?"

"Right now. Effective immediately."

Father Thomas's eyes shot to the pile of papers on his desk. "Immediately?" His voice sharpened. "But two weeks' notice is customary. In writing."

"Sometimes it is. But as I recall, Martin gave you a statement in writing and you didn't think it was worth reading. Or even opening."

"Mary, I explained that—"

"Yes, you explained to me that a verbal statement alone was enough. So this is yours." She hesitated, then added, "Now you can hire another servant to work for minimum wage."

Father Thomas protested, "That's not fair. You received a wage plus benefits. And tuition at All Souls."

Mom agreed. "Yes, that's right. That was the deal. Now we no longer need the deal. So goodbye."

Before Father Thomas could manage further reply, his brother called out, "It's time to go, everybody!"

Father Leonard took Father Thomas by the arm and guided him to the head of a loose line composed of well-dressed men and women. I recognized some of them from masses at the Chapel—the extended Lowery family. The men had all inherited the large head and broad shoulders. A couple of the women had, too.

Father Thomas led the group past the large painting of Washington crossing the Delaware and into the bright winter light. Mom, Margaret, and I followed at a distance. We heard a smattering of applause to our right as the other invited guests caught sight of the Lowerys. The family members took seats in the first row of the bleachers. Mom and Margaret climbed up to the top row on the left side. But I found my own spot, on the right edge, two rows behind Hank Lowery IV.

Father Thomas began by formally greeting the members of the Lowery family, naming them one by one. He even named their family lawyer and some other important alumni. Then, backed by the life-size statue of the General on its three-foot-high pedestal, he launched into a speech: "The statue that we dedicate today is symbolic—symbolic of history, of heroism, and of honor. We all know the story depicted by this statue. Colonel Henry M. Lowery—while commanding troops in France in World War I; while under withering fire from German machine-gun positions; while losing over half the men in his company—still managed to destroy those positions and win the day, earning himself a field promotion to General. In the process, he also earned the applause of a grateful nation. He continued to serve his country and his community throughout his life. And even in death, he has given most generously to his school, All Souls Preparatory, in the form of this magnificent library."

I watched two rows ahead of me as Hank Lowery IV turned to his mother and announced, "I gotta take a whiz."

She hissed, "Can't this wait?"

"No. I gotta go bad."

The woman moved enough to let him slip by. As he hopped off the bleachers, I knew my own moment had come. I jumped down after him. I stayed ten yards behind until he reached the Administration Building; then I moved quickly to catch the door before it closed.

Lowery turned, startled to see me. But his look of apprehension quickly turned into a familiar snarl. "You, Conway? What do you want?"

I closed the door and walked toward him, like James Harker toward that warden sixty years earlier and three thousand miles away. As I walked, I made a speech of my own. I said, "This is for all the boys Hollerin' Hank led to their deaths so that he could become a big general, and be in all the newspapers, and endorse hearing aids, and build that library." Then I added, "And this is for me, too."

I pulled my fist back and threw one quick punch at Hank Lowery's nose. The punch wasn't that hard, but it struck him dead center, and it caught him completely by surprise. His big head snapped back. Then his whole body followed it, backpedaling wildly down the hallway. I went after him, ready to punch him again if necessary, but it wasn't.

Lowery's left leg hit one of the plastic chairs, throwing him off balance. He waved his arms, fell down, and immediately started grabbing at his ankle like he was in excruciating pain. I didn't believe he was in pain—either from the punch or the fall—but he screamed bloody murder.

I hesitated, not knowing what to do next. I waited until Lowery finally quieted down. He pointed at me and sputtered, "You're gonna pay for this, Conway. Big-time."

"Get up, then. Make me pay for it now. Just you and me."

"I can't get up."

"Yes, you can, you coward."

He snarled, "We'll see how brave you are when school starts."

"I'm not coming back to this school. I'm brave right now. Get up." I stepped forward again, causing Lowery to scurry farther back across the floor. "This is it, Lowery. You and me alone. What are you going to do?"

"You'll find out!"

"I already know what you're going to do. Nothing. You're going to do nothing because you *are* nothing. A big nothing when you're by yourself." Lowery was now crouching against the chairs directly below Rembrandt's *Abraham and Isaac,* and I suddenly knew what to do next. I grabbed the thick wooden frame of the painting, pulled it off its hooks, and held it over Lowery's oversized head.

He yelled, "Are you crazy? That's vandalism! That's a Rembrandt!"

"No, it isn't. It's a cheap imitation. This school doesn't own a Rembrandt."

I let the painting crash of its own weight, right on top of him. The canvas stretched in the middle and then ripped away from the frame. Lowery's head poked through from below. He pretended to fall unconscious to the floor, but I knew he was faking.

I stood over him for several seconds, panting triumphantly, until I became aware of someone standing behind me. I spun around and found myself face to face with Manetti. He looked from me to Lowery and back again. Then he smiled.

I stammered, "What . . . what are you doing here?"

Manetti grinned nonchalantly. "Checking you out. Nice

work." He made a dismissive move with his hand in Lowery's direction. "Forget that punk. Right?"

"Right."

"So? How are you doing?"

"I'm okay."

"Good. That's good. And how's my man Pinak?"

I stole a quick look at Lowery. He still hadn't moved. "He's okay, too. You know—Pinak is Pinak."

"Yeah. I know. I miss busting his balls."

"Yeah. You should let us IM you again. I miss your messages."

"Really? What about Pinak?"

"He misses them, too."

Manetti shrugged. "Yeah. Okay. Maybe I will."

I thought about the day he got expelled. I told him sincerely, "I'm really sorry about what happened to you here."

Manetti actually smiled. "Hey. This place sucks. I'm glad I'm out. It's my dad that's pissed."

"Really? Still?"

"Yeah. More than ever. He's not so good at letting things go."

"Are you at Garden State Middle?"

"Yeah."

"How is it?"

"The chicks are hot, man. Makes this place look like the dog pound."

"I'll see you there soon. Maybe we can hang out."

"Yeah? Cool. We can go to the mall."

"Sure. Why not?"

We finally heard Lowery move. Manetti yelled at him,

"If you come out of there, Lowery, I'll kick your ass next. I'm just waiting for my turn." He winked at me. "And don't let me see you at the mall, either."

Suddenly I was startled by the sound of a diesel engine throttling to life. I tried to imagine what it could be. I looked at Manetti. He wasn't startled at all. I asked him, "Wait a minute, Manetti. What are you and your father doing here?"

He looked toward the outside door. "I'm not sure. But I think something's going to happen. In fact, I'd bet on it."

He led the way to the door and threw it open. The Manetti Construction truck was now inside the gate. Mr. Manetti was sitting in the cab of the small bulldozer, raising up the iron-toothed bucket on the front and then dropping it down again.

I shouted over the engine noise, "What's going on?"

"Like I said," Manetti answered simply, "my dad's pissed."

Mr. Manetti threw the bulldozer into gear and throttled it slowly down the back ramp of the flatbed truck. Then he drove it straight across the road to the slate entranceway of the Heroes' Walk. The group of Lowery family and friends watched, befuddled, as the John Deere 350C rolled like a small yellow tank past the statues of FDR and JFK and bore down quickly on the statue of General Lowery. The dozer must have been traveling at twenty miles per hour when it hit, creating a jagged crack between the pedestal and General Lowery's feet and spewing chunks of Carrara marble all over the slate. Members of the Lowery group screamed and scattered.

Mr. Manetti threw the bulldozer into reverse, lurched

back, and accelerated forward again. This time he raised the bucket in front and struck the statue full in the chest. General Lowery's pointing arm broke off. Then his great marble head tottered slightly forward, then slightly back, and thudded onto the gray slate, further panicking the group of family and friends. Mr. Manetti pulled back, lowered the bucket, pulled forward again, and scooped up the marble head. Then, with an enormous diesel roar, he lurched off toward the river.

Cal Livingstone broke from the group and ran after him. He managed to catch the slow-moving vehicle after twenty yards. He tried to grab the back of the cab and leap on, but he lost his grip and fell to the asphalt roadway, tearing the pants of his blue suit and skinning his right knee.

Mr. Manetti didn't stop the bulldozer until he reached the back wall of the school. There he raised up the bucket to its full height, extended it over the iron railing, and dumped the marble head into the icy Millstone River.

I looked left, toward Manetti, and then right, toward the Heroes' Walk. Every mouth on the campus was hanging open. Father Thomas stood rigidly among the guests, clearly in shock. When he finally snapped out of it, he started shouting to the family members: "This cannot be! We will make repairs immediately! Nothing will prevent this historic dedication to this great American!"

Cal Livingstone's wife and son ran to him, but he angrily pushed them away. He limped back to the first row of the bleachers, his bloody knee showing through his suit, and screamed at Father Thomas, "What are you waiting for? Call the police! Arrest that maniac!"

Father Thomas stammered, "Yes, I will," and took off immediately toward his office.

Meanwhile, Mr. Manetti drove the bulldozer back along the roadway, veered to the right, and rolled slowly up the ramp of the truck. He hopped down and gestured to his son to join him. Then the two of them got into the cab and drove away without so much as a sideways glance.

I caught sight of Mom and Margaret in the crowd, and I ran over to them. Mom looked shocked, too, but Margaret looked elated. I watched her give Mom a gentle shove toward the parking lot, telling her, "Go on and start the car, Mom. Martin and I will be right behind you." She waited until I was next to her to fulfill her own secret purpose. She walked over to Cal Livingstone with a look of great concern on her face. "Mr. Livingstone?"

Mr. Livingstone looked at her with annoyance. He didn't speak, so Margaret continued, "I wanted to talk to you again about that entry. The one at the Millennium Encyclopedia? We are indeed doing an entry on General Henry M. Lowery. It will include some new primary source material that we recently uncovered—some memos copied by a woman named Daisy Traynor."

Mr. Livingstone's eyes bulged.

"The entry will, of course, be meticulously fact-checked and devoid of all prejudice. We *are* giving the General a new nickname, though. I thought I'd preview it for you today. Are you ready? It's 'Hitlerin' Hank' Lowery. How's that sound?"

Margaret spun on her heel and walked off briskly before he could even react. I looked back at the Administration

Building. Hank Lowery still had not emerged, but Father Thomas must have found him by now, along with the ruined Rembrandt. No doubt about it, it was time for the Conway family to leave All Souls. For good. I took off running after her.

We drove home in a wild and giddy mood. Mom articulated the feeling for all of us: "We're free from that place now. And from all of those people."

After a few miles, though, reality started to set in. Margaret asked Mom, "That was cool how you quit. But what are you going to do? Look for a job?"

"No. I don't have to. I won't have to for years if I manage my money right."

Margaret and I exchanged a look. "What? What happened? You sound like you won the lottery."

"No. No lottery. It's my inheritance. Half of the house in Brookline is mine, and it's worth a lot of money. I've directed Elizabeth to sell it."

"You directed Aunt Elizabeth!" I sputtered. "How did that go?"

"Not well. But she has no choice, legally. Now the house is on the market, and it should sell for at least eight hundred thousand dollars, maybe more."

"Whoa!"

"But what about Grandfather Mehan's shrine?" Margaret asked. "Where's that going to go?"

"Elizabeth is buying a condo in Boston, closer to the hospital. It's only two bedrooms. But if she wants to turn one into your grandfather's shrine, that's up to her. Personally, I hope she doesn't." Mom looked in the mirror at me and con-cluded, "Enough is enough."

At home in bed, I lay and thought for a long time about the events of that tumultuous day. Mom's words echoed in my head: *Enough is enough.* Both Lowerys had gotten theirs. That was over, and it was, indeed, enough. I wouldn't give much thought to either one of them ever again. Two items from my list had been accomplished.

But the third one loomed before me. It was a logical paradox—impossible to do; impossible not to do. I would need someone's help to even attempt to accomplish it, someone who hadn't been much help in my life up until now.

I would need Dad.

THE BASEMENT DWELLERS

During the following week, I put some of the steps of my complicated plan in place. Step one was to get Mom to allow me go to England with Dad. Margaret helped me out with that one. She supported my claims that I had talked to Mr. Wissler about an important research project, and I knew exactly what I was doing, and I would be all right. For my part, I made it clear that I was going no matter what, so Mom grudgingly agreed.

Step two was to call Dad. I timed the call for eleven a.m., just to make sure he was sober. He seemed really amazed to hear from me. "Martin? Is anything wrong? Is your mother okay?"

"Everybody's okay. I do need your help, though."

"What can I do for you?"

"Can the vacation manager take a vacation?"

"Sure."

"When?"

"Whenever I want. As long as I don't have an assignment."

"Do you have one now?"

"No."

"Do you have frequent-flyer miles?"

"About ten trillion. Why?"

"I need you to take me to England."

"Where?"

"England. For three nights, more or less."

After a long pause, he came back. "England. Uh, yeah, I have enough miles for that. Can you tell me why?"

"I can. I will. But not now. Okay? I'll tell you on the way over."

He finally answered, "Has your mother agreed to this?"

"Absolutely. Mom is on board."

"She is? Well, what can I say then? It'll be good to take in some of that British history. And it'll be great to see you."

"Can I come up there on the train?"

"Sure. Just call ahead. Either Uncle Bobby or I will pick you up at Penn Station, Newark. Okay?"

"Okay."

By Tuesday morning, I was ready to go. I had packed enough clothes and stuff for three days. I included my tube of Brylcreem for luck. I also included a shirt that I had just purchased over the Internet. It was a vintage Arsenal football jersey, bright red with white sleeves. Then I went into the computer room, accessed my research files, and printed out everything I had ever learned about London and York, present and past.

I said goodbye to Mom and Margaret, promising to e-mail them and assuring them I would be back in a few days. Mom thought I was taking a trip related to one final independent study. She was right, as far as that went. Margaret knew that there was more to the trip, but she did not know exactly what. She gave me a bon voyage present, a small Sony voice recorder, explaining, "It's what real interviewers use. It'll make you look more official."

I turned down an offer from Mom to drive me to the train station. I said that I preferred to walk, and she accepted that.

Things were clearly changing at home.

I left the house at four p.m., carrying a small suitcase in one hand and a large garbage bag in the other. Inside the bag was the Philco 20 Deluxe in its original box. I crossed Hightstown Road and walked through the train station parking lot. Then I climbed up the stairs to the train office, purchased my ticket, and stepped out onto the wooden platform to wait.

The first thing I saw was a short man in a blue suit standing and looking at me. He had on a red bow tie and wore wire-rimmed glasses. I said, "Mr. Wissler? Dave?"

"Hello, Martin. I hope this isn't an unwelcome intrusion, but Margaret told me about your trip. I thought a letter from me might help open some doors."

Mr. Wissler held out a piece of paper, so I set down my bags and took it. It was a very official-looking letter on Millennium Encyclopedia stationery. It said:

> To whom it may concern:
> Martin Conway has traveled to Great Britain to interview surviving members of the

London Auxiliary Fire Service for a *Millennium Encyclopedia* feature titled "Their Finest Hour."

It was signed by David S. Wissler, and it was decorated with a red circle on the lower left that felt bumpy to the touch. He explained, "I added a raised seal to the paper. The British love raised seals. I think they invented them."

I took the letter. "Thank you. Thank you very much."

"That was quite the treasure trove that you left for me, Martin. A historian's dream, really."

"Like time travel?"

"Indeed. Let me tell you what I've done with it since Tuesday." We each took hold of one of my bags and moved them to the side. "I brought Daisy Traynor's materials over to Princeton to have them authenticated by experts. I know many of the historians there. They've already analyzed the chemical compositions of the ink and paper, with some very exciting results. Based on your discovery, I think we will be rewriting an entire chapter of World War Two history. We will certainly be redefining the role of General Henry M. Lowery."

Suddenly I thought about Mom. "Do you think my grandfather's name will be part of it?"

Mr. Wissler looked troubled. "Well, he won't be in the encyclopedia entry. I can promise you that. But perhaps someone at the university will want to write a more in-depth book about what happened." He paused and shook his head. "No. There's no *perhaps* about it. This is explosive stuff. There will definitely be a book, or books, about

General Lowery's secret negotiations with Von Dirksen. And your grandfather, whether he was involved or not, is mentioned in some of the papers. Apparently he helped set up some of the message drops. I'm sorry. I understand that this may be embarrassing to your family."

I spotted the train in the distance. "My grandfather's holy shrine in Brookline was about to get dismantled anyway." I grabbed a bag in each hand. "Enough was enough."

Mr. Wissler nodded his agreement.

"Honestly, Mr. Wissler, my life would have been much easier if Martin Mehan had not been a hero."

"I know what you mean. We have a few heroes in our family, on my side *and* on my wife's." He backed away as the train pulled in. "Good luck on your trip, Martin. And thank you again."

Dad came through admirably, as he always did when he was not drinking. He and Uncle Bob met me at the train station. Dad handed me two tickets. "This is the best I could do. It's coach class, I'm afraid."

I assured him, "I don't care about that."

"We take off in about three hours. We fly all night and land at Gatwick in the morning."

"Great."

"Do you know what to do after that?"

"Yes. I have it all printed out. We take the Gatwick Express train to London, spend a few hours there, and then we take another train up to York."

Dad smiled. "Okay. You're the boss."

My uncle Bob held out his hand, and I shook it. He said, "Good to see you again, Martin. It's been too long."

"Good to see you, too."

Uncle Bob is a burly, hairy guy, with watery eyes. By habit, I suppose, he grabbed my suitcase. Then he asked, "What's in the garbage bag?"

"It's an antique radio. A Philco 20 Deluxe."

"Cool. How valuable is it?"

"To me, it's the most valuable thing on earth."

"Wow. That's pretty valuable. Is it going with you to England?"

"Yes."

"Gatwick Airport?"

"Right. And then up to York. That's where I'll really need it, up in York."

Uncle Bob thought for a moment. "York's closer to Manchester Airport. Listen: If you really don't need this until you get to York, I can have it delivered there directly. Then you won't have to donkey it around."

I looked at Dad. "I won't need any of this stuff until we get to York. Not the radio; not anything in my suitcase. How about you?"

"We're going to be in York the first night, right?"

"Yeah."

"No. I won't need anything, either."

Uncle Bob made a note on an index card. "Then you'll see all this stuff at your hotel. You got the address, Martin?"

I pulled out my sheaf of papers. "We're staying at a

bed-and-breakfast hotel called the Wayfarer. Here's the information."

Uncle Bob copied it carefully. He told me, "I'll walk these through security myself. I'll put 'Lost Luggage' labels on them and the airline will treat them like gold. They'll deliver them right to the door of your final destination, with their apologies."

"Thanks, Uncle Bob."

He smiled humbly. "It's what I do."

Dad suggested, "We have time for dinner, Bob. Come join us. The drinks are on me."

Uncle Bob checked his watch. "Yeah, okay. I'll join you for a little send-off. But no drinks. I gotta work the late shift."

We had dinner at the National Steakhouse in the airport. They treated Dad, and all of us, like VIPs. Uncle Bob took great pains to assure me that my radio would arrive safely and in working order, which I really appreciated. I realized as we sat there that we all had something in common. We were the three basement dwellers. First Uncle Bob, with his depression; then Dad, with his drinking; then me, with my . . . what?

When Uncle Bob left to go to work, Dad pointed after him. "He's a great guy. I didn't know that until the past year or so. He's turned out to be saner than anybody."

"Good for him. How did he do that?"

"He finally got the right combination of medications." Dad smiled. "I guess that's all anybody needs."

I understood what he meant. I wasn't smiling about it. "You mean, your medication is liquor? And all you need is the right amount?"

He shrugged. "Yeah."

"Did your dad drink like you?"

"He was much worse than me. He drank all the time. And he drank himself to death. Cirrhosis of the liver." Dad concluded, "He was a major drunk, all right."

"He was other things, too, though. You've told me that."

"Sure. He was a veteran. He fought in World War Two."

"That was something. He was a soldier?"

"He was a marine. Yeah. He expected Bob and me to join up, too."

At that moment, I realized how little I knew about my father's past. "And did you?"

"No. Bob did. He fought in Vietnam. That was a terrible stretch for all of us. Mom died while he was over there. Two weeks later, Dad checked in to the Veterans Hospital with cirrhosis. He had turned all yellow. He only had about three months left to live. He didn't care if I joined up then or not, so I didn't." He looked at me intensely. "So I never became a marine, like your grandfather Conway, or a representative of the federal government, like your grandfather Mehan. I became an alcoholic restaurant manager instead."

I looked back, just as intensely. "You once told me that you understood disgrace."

"I did?"

"Yeah. At Christmas."

"Okay."

"What do you think makes one man a disgrace and another one a hero?"

"That's a tough question. I don't know. DNA? Fate? Good luck?"

"Do you want to find the answer to that question?"

Dad thought for a long moment. "I do."

I told him, as seriously as I could, "So do I. I can't promise anything, but maybe . . . something will happen to you on this trip. Maybe London is calling you, too."

Dad and I settled into two of four seats in the center aisle of a Boeing 767. Fortunately, no one sat in the other two, so we got to spread out. I was determined to use every minute of this trip. As soon as we took off, I returned to my serious conversation with Dad, starting with "Do you believe in God?"

He answered. "Sure. I'm Catholic, Martin. Like you."

"And do you believe in heaven and hell and purgatory?"

"Yeah, I suppose I believe in all that."

"So what do you think happens when you die?"

He gestured weakly. "You go to one of those places that you just said. Why? What do you think happens?"

I leaned toward him. "I think they ask you one question at the end, on your day of reckoning. They ask you, *What did you do to help?*"

"Yeah? And what are you supposed to say?"

"Well, you'd better have *something* to say, something better than 'I made lots of money' or 'I had expensive cars' or 'I had lots of girls.' "

"Wait a minute. Who's asking you this question?"

"I don't know. I suppose it's whoever sent Nana back that time. You know, the time when she died."

Dad laughed; then he stopped. "Sorry. You're serious?"

"I am. Tell me, did you make your nine First Fridays?"

He laughed again, but in a more subdued way. "Oh yes. When we first got married. Your mother made me do it."

"I think that was a good idea. It was like taking out an insurance policy."

"Yeah," Dad agreed. "That's true. What do you have to lose? Except nine Fridays."

A flight attendant came by holding a bottle of liquor in each hand. She smiled at me, then at Dad. He muttered, "In a little bit." The flight attendant moved on. "It's a long flight, Martin. On a long flight, I usually have a few drinks to put me out. Is that all right with you?"

"I'll make a deal with you, an agreement, like the ones you make with Mom. Here it is: I have a story to tell you. After I'm finished, you can drink all you like."

"All right. That's a deal. But it will only be a few drinks."

Then, for the next hour, I told him the story of Jimmy Harker. The entire story, from the beginning. I told him about the Philco 20 Deluxe, from Grandfather Mehan's office to the basement; I told him about Jimmy's house in London; I told him about the terror of the bombings in 1940. I only left out one part, because somebody else had to hear that first. When I finished, he bowed his head and said, "Wow. That is some story."

"Do you believe it?"

He closed his eyes and squeezed them. "I believe that you believe it."

"That's not good enough. Do you believe that it really happened?"

Reluctantly, he shook his head no.

"Then what do you think it was?"

"A dream?"

"Maybe. Maybe it was a dream. Or maybe I'm crazy."

"No." Dad furrowed his brow. "Your grandmother Mehan had a real spiritual gift. We all laughed about it because we didn't understand it. Maybe you have it, too."

I considered the possibility of that. "Maybe." I told him, "Whatever it turns out to be, I want to thank you for helping me get to England."

Dad placed his hand on my elbow. "I can tell you're serious about this, Martin, so I am, too. You just tell me what to do when we get there."

"All right. At the very least, you'll be able to point to this at the end of your life, on your day of reckoning, and say, 'This is what I did to help.' "

"That sounds good. I need something to say."

The conversation ended there. I settled into my seat. A few minutes later, Dad ordered his first drink.

I slept, on and off, for six hours across the Atlantic. To the best of my recollection, I had no dreams.

ANGLICAN COMMUNION

Sometime the next morning, Dad and I exited the plane at Gatwick Airport. We cleared Immigration and took the Gatwick Express to Victoria Station, London. Dad felt jet-lagged—or hungover—but I felt totally pumped.

Dad followed me out to the taxicab queue. We climbed into a big black taxi with fold-down seats, and I directed the driver to our first destination: "The American Embassy, Grosvenor Square."

It was thrilling beyond belief to actually be there in London, rolling through the streets on the left side of the road. We passed Buckingham Palace and some large, tree-lined parks. I took it all in hungrily. I was sorry that it only took a short while to get to Grosvenor Square.

While Dad paid, I climbed out and looked around.

I didn't like what I saw.

The American Embassy was surrounded by concrete terrorism barriers, and barbed wire, and policemen. I stared at it, completely baffled. This was not the place that I remembered at all! The building had a different façade and a different shape, and it stood in a different spot from the place I had visited with Jimmy. I felt a horrible sense of dread welling up in me. And foolishness. And craziness. I spun around three hundred and sixty degrees, not recognizing one thing.

The taxi pulled away and Dad approached me, smiling slightly. "I couldn't understand a word that guy said, but he sure was friendly." When he saw my face, though, his smile vanished. "What's wrong, Martin? You look pale. Are you feeling sick?"

I pointed at the Embassy and choked out the words, "That's not it."

Dad shook his head. "I don't understand."

"Remember what I told you on the plane? I went to the American Embassy in Grosvenor Square. Three times. But it wasn't anything like this." I felt my voice rising in desperation. "If this is wrong, then maybe it's all wrong. The firemen—James Harker, Bill Lane. Those are common English names. There must be hundreds of people with those names. Some of them would have been in the Fire Service, right? Canby's a common name, too. Some Canby guy could have been an air-raid warden. He could have gotten killed. Thousands of people were getting killed then."

Dad placed his hand on my arm. "Calm down, Martin. Don't work yourself into a state. I'm sure there's an explanation for this."

"Yeah. But what if the explanation is that I'm crazy? That I have been all along?" I sat down right there on the curb, muttering like a lunatic, "My God, what have I done?"

Dad left me sitting in my misery and crossed over to the

Embassy's security gate. He talked to the policeman there for a moment; then he turned and waved for me to come over. I put my head down and pinched my nostrils together, trying to fight off tears. When I got myself under control, I stood up and joined them.

"Here, Martin. Ask this fellow what's what."

The policeman smiled kindly. "What can I tell you, lad?"

I exhaled sharply, trying to find my voice. I pointed around me. "I, uh, I didn't think this was the American Embassy. I didn't think it looked like this, or that it was in this location."

Dad interrupted. "How long has this building been here?"

The policemen answered, "Since 1960, sir."

I pricked up my ears. "Really? Nineteen sixty? Please, where was it before that?"

"How long before that?"

"Nineteen forty."

"Just turn around and walk east, boys, to the other side of the square. You'll see the Canadian High Commission at Number One Grosvenor Square. That was the American Embassy during the war."

"During the war. Yes! Great! Great! Thank you so much." Both the policeman and Dad smiled at my utter relief at hearing that bit of news.

I hurried toward the east end of the square, with Dad right behind me. We passed a memorial to President Franklin D. Roosevelt. I told Dad, "They loved FDR in London. They even wrote pop songs about him."

"Is that right?"

As we drew nearer to the corner, and the Canadian High Commission, my heart started to pound. Yes! That was it! That was it. It was right here that it all happened. Here's where I saw my grandfather come out; here's where James and Bill stood at their telephone stand; here's where I hid with Jimmy Harker, hoping his dad wouldn't see him and give him a licking. I took it all in, remembering every precious second of it, until Dad asked, "So, is everything okay now?"

"Oh yeah. Everything's okay. This is the place. This is where it happened."

"This is the place in your story?"

I objected to the word "story," but not much. Nothing would bother me from here on out. I believed in myself again. "You can call it a story if you like, Dad. All I ask is that you stick with me for three days. Okay?"

Dad nodded. He looked around the vast expanse of the square. "Hey, I saw a pub over there, near where the taxi dropped us off. How about if we go there for a bite?"

"A bite?"

"Yeah. We have to eat."

"To eat, huh?"

"Yeah."

"Not to drink?"

He shook his head, embarrassed. "My understanding is that they go to the pubs for food here. Grown-ups and kids alike. Everybody goes."

I hadn't meant to embarrass him. I felt terrible, and ungrateful, after all he had done for me. I said, "I'm sorry, Dad.

I'm going to stop bothering you about drinking. You go ahead and do what you want. I have some things that I want to do."

"What? By yourself?"

"Sure. I've got a map, and a pretty good idea of how to get around." I could have added, *because I've been here before,* but I didn't. I pointed to the west end of the square. "Why don't you go have lunch over there, and I'll come back and meet you."

"Here?"

"No. Let's meet where we got out of the taxi." I looked at my watch. "It's ten a.m. now. I'll meet you at twelve o'clock."

"Twelve o'clock, where the taxi dropped us off?"

"Yes."

"All right. You be careful." Dad took off walking.

I took off running down the east side of Grosvenor Square, trying to remember the route that I had traveled with Jimmy. I stopped for a moment on New Bond Street, in disbelief, when I saw a bench with two statues. A bronze Franklin D. Roosevelt was sitting and chatting with a bronze Winston Churchill while a group of Japanese tourists posed with them and snapped photos.

After a breather, I took off again, running easily until I turned left on Piccadilly and hit a wall of cars and people. I moved as quickly as I could through them, consulting my map, working my way steadily past Leicester Square toward the great dome of St. Paul's.

When I finally got to the cathedral steps, I paused to rest and to take it all in. St. Paul's was enormous, dark, and powerful. It was surrounded by place-names from my history searches, like Paternoster Square and Ave Maria Lane. This whole area had been a blazing inferno on 29.12.40.

I took my time walking up the long flight of steps to the entrance doors. I paid a fee, received an admission guide and a ticket, and passed inside. I read in the guide that I was in the cathedral's nave. It was an immense space—wide, high, and deep—and it filled me with a sense of awe. I sat in a wooden pew for fifteen minutes, just resting. I gazed up at the dome and thought about life and death, and heaven and hell, and purgatory.

I checked the guide again, got up, and walked to a stair-well. St. Paul's has 530 steps to the top, which I proceeded to climb. At one point I came out of the dark cement stair-well into the Whispering Gallery, a railed walkway that ran around the bottom of the dome. Then I walked outside to another stairway to complete my climb.

When I finally reached the top, I took a quick lap around the viewing area, studying the city of London from every direction. I used my map to pinpoint Grosvenor Square. Then I did my best to calculate how far Jimmy and I had run, and in what direction. I studied the warren of streets below me intently. Somewhere down there, on one of those streets, had stood a surface shelter where Jimmy Harker and an old woman and a little boy had been killed by a German bomber, and where an air-raid warden named Canby had been killed by a distraught man in a moment of rage.

A few minutes later, I worked my way back through the Whispering Gallery and down the worn stone stairs to the cathedral floor. I fell in step with a group heading into the cathedral's sanctuary, which, I learned, was called the Quire. I joined those people, and a priest, in an Anglican communion service. It turned out to be very similar to a Catholic mass. When it came time to give out the host, the priest told us all to get up from our seats and walk to the center of the Quire. Then he passed out the wafers and told us to pray silently. As I swallowed mine, I said prayers for a list of souls—souls who may have been in heaven, or hell, or purgatory. I whispered their names into the immenseness of St. Paul's Cathedral: Jimmy Harker, Harold Canby, Alice Lane, and Bill Lane.

I half walked, half ran all the way back to Grosvenor Square, arriving just after twelve o'clock. Dad was not at our agreed-upon spot. He was not there at twelve-fifteen, either. I finally set out in the direction our taxi had taken until I saw a pub—the Golden Eagle. I stepped inside, through a wall of smoke, and spotted Dad. He was sitting in a booth with a glass of dark beer and what I took to be the remains of a hard-boiled egg and some meat. He looked up. "Martin! Oh no, is it that late?"

"It's almost twelve-thirty."

"Oh man. Sorry."

"Forget it. Are you ready to go?"

"Yeah. If you are. Do you want something, Martin?" He pointed at his plate. "Do you want a Scotch egg?"

I regarded his plate suspiciously, but I was hungry. "Yeah. Okay."

"How about something to drink? You must be thirsty."

"Uh, water, I guess. But can we get it to go?"

"Sure. Are we running late?"

"A little."

Dad went to the bar and negotiated the egg, the water, and a taxi while I went out to the street to escape the smoke. I looked around, trying to imagine these same streets blacked out, packed with sandbags, reverberating to the wail of the air-raid sirens and the anti-aircraft guns.

Soon another big taxi pulled up, and the driver took us through Mayfair, past Russell Square, and up to King's Cross Station. By two p.m., Dad and I had settled into seats on another train. He asked me, "So, did you like London?"

"Yes. Most definitely. I think I could live here."

"Then maybe you will."

"I don't know. Maybe. But I don't want to become Martin Mehan."

Dad seemed genuinely surprised. "Really? You don't?"

"No. Of course not. Did you think I did?"

"Yeah."

"Never. I never did."

After that, Dad turned away and looked out the window. I expected him to fall asleep, but he didn't. He seemed lost in thought as we rode north to our final destination, the haunted city of York.

As advertised on its Web site, the Wayfarer Bed-and-Breakfast Hotel was within walking distance of the York train station. The manager, a skinny man in a short-sleeved white shirt, showed us to a corner room upstairs. Our

228

suitcases and a large box were already waiting for us, lined up against one wall.

"Those arrived from the airline," the manager said, "with their apologies."

The room had a single bed and a cot. I told Dad to take the bed, which he did gratefully. He was snoring loudly within minutes. I had no such intention. It was now nearly five o'clock, too late to talk to most workers at the York Minster, but not too late to go there. I fished out my Map-Quest printout of the city and slipped out of the room quietly. The hotel manager, seeing my printout, handed me a York welcome packet that included a foldout map, a brochure for a Viking museum, and an advertisement for a Haunted City ghost tour.

I hurried through an area called the Shambles, which, the packet claimed, was the oldest street in Europe, dating to medieval times. I looked up and suddenly realized that the Minster, the great cathedral, was looming right before me in the darkening sky. It was huge, completely dominating the city. It was visible from just about anywhere.

I ran up to a high, wide front door and pulled it open. As I had done at St. Paul's, I paid a fee and entered. The York Minster, according to its brochure, was one of the largest Gothic cathedrals ever built. "Gothic" meant that it had two towers instead of a dome. Still, entering the cathedral filled me with that same sense of awe. I walked slowly forward through the nave, past row after row of perfectly straight wooden chairs, taking in the carved artwork on the walls and the ceiling.

Then I saw what I was looking for: the stairs to the top. A volunteer seated at a table took my payment, but she told me, "You'll have to wait ten minutes to go up, son. Passage on the stairs is one way only. For thirty minutes, the traffic climbs only up. Then, for thirty minutes, it climbs only down."

I said, "All right. Thank you," and drifted back against a cold stone wall to wait with some other tourists. After ten minutes, a cluster of people emerged from the stairs; then it was our turn to climb. My group, mostly middle-aged English and German people, allowed me to go first, probably since I looked like the fastest climber. The steps, 275 of them, were very narrow and entirely circular. I took my time climbing them, but I still reached the top far ahead of the rest of the group. Another volunteer, a petite older woman in a blue blazer, was standing in the door of a small office to the right. I waved to her, and she said, "Is there a group coming up now?"

"Yes. I'm the first." I took advantage of the moment to ask, "What do people usually look at from here?"

In reply, she reached under a counter and produced a pair of binoculars. "There is nothing in particular to look at. The cathedral is what most people come to York to see, and you're already in that. But you're welcome to use the binos to look around, if you like. The view is lovely with the lights coming on."

I reached out and took them. "Thank you very much."

The woman left her post and led me across the roof. The top of the cathedral was a windy place with a strong wire cage overhead and on the sides—I guess to keep people from throwing stuff off. The woman stopped and pointed down at the city. "You see that street down there? That's the Shambles, the oldest street in Europe. Have a look."

I trained the binoculars where she had pointed. Then I screwed up my courage and asked her straight-out, "Do you know a man named James Harker?"

"Yes, I do."

"He works here?"

"Part-time. Yes. He's on the stoneyard staff."

"I see. Will he be here tomorrow?"

"I believe he will be. If he isn't, I'll knock him up."

"Is that right? So you're a friend of his?"

"I look out for him. He's at an advanced age, you know. He only puts in a few days a week here, to keep busy." The woman stopped and scrutinized me. "How do you know James Harker?"

"I don't really know him. Not yet. I'm here to interview him for an encyclopedia, though. I e-mailed the Minster a few weeks ago."

"Did you? That does sound familiar. What did you want to ask him about?"

"His experiences in 1940 with the Auxiliary Fire Service."

The woman leaned closer to the wall. "Well, if you know where to look, you can actually see James's place from here."

"You can?"

"Yes." She directed the binoculars to the left. "Do you

see a blue door on Stonegate, next to the streetlight, about halfway up the second block?"

I scanned the street until I did, indeed, spot a blue door. "Yes! I see it."

"There you are, then." She turned as the rest of the group finally arrived on the roof. "Now I must get back to my post. You can return the binos when you're through."

"Yes, ma'am. Thank you very much."

I spent my entire thirty minutes staring at that blue door and the nine windows above it. There appeared to be three apartments in the narrow building, one on each floor, and each apartment had three windows. When the woman finally announced that we could descend the stairs, I led the group back down.

Once outside, I hurried across the dark, narrow streets of York until I was standing before that blue door. The lights of the second-story apartment were on. I stepped onto the stoop and studied the three doorbells on the right—designated as Flat 1, Flat 2, and Flat 3—and I read the names of their inhabitants. I had nearly worked up the courage to press the buzzer for Flat 2 when the lights on the second floor went out.

I stepped back, into the medieval street, and looked up.

I thought about what I had come here to do. James Harker was in this building at this very moment. I would see him and talk to him tomorrow morning.

Our two lives had come to a crossroads.

THE CATHEDRAL

Dad was asleep when I let myself back into our room at the Wayfarer, and he remained asleep for the rest of the night. I was happy to see that he had gotten up to purchase a roast beef sandwich for me and a bottle of apple juice. I wolfed them down, standing by the window and looking out at the dark streets.

I unpacked most of my things before I turned in. Then I opened the box that held the radio. The first thing I saw was a small black square with metal prongs. It had an index card taped to it and a short note from Uncle Bob: "You need an adapter to run American appliances in England. They have different voltage." I took the adapter, turned the prongs away from me, and plugged it into an outlet. Then I turned my attention to the radio.

Uncle Bob had done a great job packing it. The Philco 20 Deluxe was safely surrounded by at least three inches of solid Styrofoam on each side. I pulled it out, trying not to wake Dad with the squeaking of the white foam. I placed the Philco on the floor near the electrical outlet. I sat there for a long time, trying to work up the courage to plug it in. But I couldn't do it. Not yet.

In the morning, I put on my vintage Arsenal jersey, and I combed a dab of Brylcreem into my hair. I waited until Dad went into the bathroom. Then I called through the door, "Go to breakfast without me, Dad. There's something I have to do."

"What? Where are you going?"

"To the York Minster. The cathedral."

After a long pause, he said, "All right. Like I said, let me know what I can do to help."

"Okay." I pulled on my coat and left immediately, barely able to contain myself. I took the steps of the Wayfarer two at a time, ran past the unoccupied front desk, and hit the street. I hurried through the Shambles, past the blue door on Stonegate, and up to the entrance of the cathedral. It was still too early to go inside, so I sat on a bench in a triangular green park next to the church.

Not more than ten minutes had passed when suddenly I heard a rolling, bumping sound to my left. I turned and saw a wiry old man pushing a two-wheeled cart. The cart was painted the same dark green as the man's pants and shirt, and it carried a black trash bin on top. The man proceeded noisily down the stone path until he was close enough for me to see his face.

I had seen that face before.

It was very old, and very wizened. And it belonged to James Harker.

I gasped. My throat got so dry that I could not even swallow. All I could do was turn my head slowly as the man pushed the cart past me and parked it in front of one of the wooden doors of the cathedral. He pulled out a small broom and dustpan, swept up two cigarette butts, and picked a third one up by hand. I was barely in control of my breathing when he came back toward me, without the cart, and sat on a bench to my right.

I knew my time had come.

I reached into my pants pocket and pulled out Margaret's gift, the Sony voice recorder. Then I reached into my coat pocket and pulled out Mr. Wissler's letter. I stood up and took three steps toward him. "Good morning, sir."

He glanced up at me curiously. "What's this, now? A lost boy?"

I recognized his voice. It had barely changed. I took another step and asked him the question that would seal his fate: "Are you, by any chance, Mr. James Harker?"

The old man took a good hard look at me. "I am. Now, who wants to know?"

"Mr. Harker, I am Martin Conway. I am conducting interviews for the Millennium Encyclopedia, interviews that will be part of a feature titled 'Their Finest Hour.' "

He regarded me for a few more seconds without answering, so I held out my letter from Mr. Wissler. "Please, sir, if you could take a look at this letter of introduction, you'll see what I mean."

He pointed to his cart in a self-mocking gesture. "You saw what I just did, lad. I'm a janitor. I'm not part of anybody's magazine article."

I corrected him: "Encyclopedia article."

"Or of anybody's 'finest hour.' " But he reached into his

top pocket and pulled out a pair of glasses. Then he took the letter from me.

I explained, "We're especially interested in any members of the Auxiliary Fire Service who were serving during the London Blitz."

James Harker read the letter. He fingered the raised seal. But he still didn't reply. I went on. "Internet records list your name as a member of the Auxiliary Fire Service in London in 1940."

He finally looked up. "Aye. Me and a thousand others."

"Yes, but you were posted at the American Embassy. Weren't you?"

"That's right. I was. For a bit."

"That would give you, perhaps, a perspective on what the Americans were doing at the time."

James Harker opened his mouth, revealing a set of sharp, stained teeth, and laughed. "They weren't doing bloody much! I can tell you that, lad. Not when I was there." He put his glasses away and conceded, "Later, of course, they got into it proper."

James Harker looked directly at me. He spoke with a hint of challenge in his voice. "Now you tell me, lad. Why was it my 'finest hour'?"

"Well, because you wouldn't give up. Hitler expected you to give up. I guess the whole world did. But you wouldn't."

"I see. And what did I gain by that?"

I pulled out my voice recorder. "Do you mind if I record this?"

"No."

I pressed the button and said into it, "James Harker,

at York Minster. What did you gain from standing up to Hitler?"

I held the recorder out toward him. He smiled a very unfriendly smile and articulated, "Nothing. I lost. I lost my wife. I lost my son. I lost my friends. I wound up alone, a glorified janitor for sixty years."

He reached into another pocket, pulled out a pack of cigarettes, and lit one. I racked my brain for something else to say. I tried, "Your wife, sir. May I ask how she died? Was it in the bombing?"

He lit the cigarette and squinted as a puff of smoke blew into his eyes. "No. She died before that." He paused to take a deep drag on the cigarette and exhale. " 'Finest hour.' They say we all muddled through it together. But some of us muddled a bit harder than others, didn't we? The poor people lived like they always lived, and died like they always died. My Peg died because she waited too long to go to hospital. She didn't want to leave our boy alone." He pointed at my recorder. "I don't recall that happening to Mrs. Churchill. Or Lady Halifax. Or the Queen Mum. Do you?" He took another drag on the cigarette and muttered, "Let's hope nobody catches us over here. Can't sit and have a fag anywhere nowadays. Except the pub."

I followed up on what he'd said. "Your son, sir. Did he die in the bombing?"

Without emotion, he replied, "That's right."

"So who do you live with now?"

"Me? I live by myself."

"Do you live near here?"

"Not far."

237

I tried to sound like I had done several of these interviews, like I was reading from a checklist. "And do you, sir, have any historical items from that period?"

"No. Not really."

I continued, "Like a poster? Or a football program?"

James Harker's suspicious look returned. "I've got nothing that'd interest you."

I held up the letter again, with the seal showing. "The encyclopedia would pay you for any authentic items that I photographed, and that we used."

"Pay, eh? Now you're talking, lad. Let's see. I've got my dad's medals. He won the British War Medal, the Victory Medal, and the 1914 Star." He exhaled a long blue stream of smoke. "But they're from World War One, aren't they?"

I said, "Pip, Squeak, and Wilfred."

"Hey! That's right. You know some things, lad."

I told him sincerely, "I've worked very hard at this, sir. Would it be possible for me to visit you at home, just for a short time, whatever time is good for you, to do a more formal interview?"

"Ah, I don't know. The landlord don't like me having company. Don't like me doing anything, really. He's always popping round to check that I'm not smoking. Or to check that I'm not dead. I'll have to say no to you, my boy. But good luck with the 'Finest Hour' and all."

He got up, stubbed out his cigarette on his heel, and put the butt into his pocket.

Not knowing what else to do, I unbuttoned my coat and blurted out, "Mr. Harker! Take a look at this."

James Harker's blue eyes bored in on my red-and-white

Arsenal football jersey. He looked at me, totally confused. I asked him, "Do you remember the match when Arsenal beat Fulham up at White Hart Lane? I think it was five to nil."

His confusion suddenly turned into anger. He made a dismissive gesture with his hand. "I don't know what you're on about, boy. Get away. Let me get back to work."

I watched in silence as he wheeled his cart off in the opposite direction.

I knew I had gone too far. I turned off the recorder, put my papers away, and sat down. I replayed everything James Harker and I had said to each other, with and without the recorder. Then, when the first visitors of the day arrived, I got up and followed them through the huge doors of the York Minster.

Someone ahead of me in line was arguing loudly with the volunteer from the night before, the small woman with the blue blazer. She was listening patiently as a large woman in an orange coat complained about the admission fee. When the woman finally stopped, the volunteer explained, "But it is a voluntary offering."

The woman in orange shot back, "If it's voluntary, why do you have a price list posted?"

"That's just a suggested fee."

"You shouldn't have to pay at all in the house of God."

I spoke up. "You'd pay more if you went into St. Paul's Cathedral in London." The woman spun around and glared at me. I continued, "And they'd tell you exactly what to pay, too. It's not voluntary at all."

"I'll thank you to keep out of this."

"I was just there yesterday. It cost me three pounds."

The woman in orange sneered at me. But then she plunked down a coin for the suggested amount and entered.

The volunteer woman favored me with a smile. "You're back already?"

I handed her my payment.

"Tell me, did you do your interview with James Harker?"

"I did some of it. The preliminaries."

"I saw you talking to him outside."

Another volunteer stepped up next to her and said, "I'm here now, Helen."

My volunteer said, "Thank you, Sylvia." She stepped away from the desk and joined me in the nave. I asked her, "Would you mind answering some questions?"

"No. Not at all. That's part of what I do."

I started with something neutral. "How many men work outside here, like James Harker?"

"Well, let's see. The stoneyard staff, the custodians and janitors, and the security people . . . I'd say about one hundred. Full- and part-time."

"Do you know how long James Harker has been here?"

"A long time. Since the war."

"He returned home after the war?"

"Yes. He is a Yorkshireman." We reached the area with folding chairs. "Let's sit for a moment," Helen suggested. Then she told me, "James had a wife from Yorkshire, too. She died of diphtheria, I believe."

"It was pneumonia."

She looked at me curiously, adding, "And he had a son. He died in the war, too. In the Blitz."

240

"Yes, he did. Twenty-nine December, 1940. The massive German air raid."

"How do you know all of this?"

"Research. Internet research, mostly."

"Well, I can tell you something that's not on the Internet. Mr. James Harker has a very kind heart. I volunteer at the children's shelter as well, and I know he dedicates a portion of his salary every week to the boys there. The lost boys, he calls them."

We sat in silence for a moment. Then she said something unexpected: "Yes, James Harker is a very nice man, but he's also a troubled man."

I sat up straighter. "Oh? Why is that?"

"He spends half his time in the pub, which is not unusual for a single man, I suppose. But he spends the other half sitting right over there, in the Quire, just . . . looking up."

I followed her gaze to a beautifully carved wooden section of the church. "You told me yesterday that you help him out a little?"

"That's right. It's not much. Sometimes he sleeps in and doesn't show up at work. I pop over and get him. I don't want him to lose his position." Helen stood up. She pointed at me and smiled. "And that's all the news you'll get from me, Mr. Nosy Parker. Thank you for your kind intervention with that lady, but now I must get some work done."

I left the Minster and walked slowly back to the Wayfarer, trying to think. Dad had finished breakfast and was watching a game show in the lobby with the manager. He came upstairs with me and listened carefully as I described everything that had happened that morning. He said, "I don't think you did anything too wrong, Martin."

"I drove him away. He was practically running."

"The old man was overwhelmed, I guess. You ambushed him."

"Yeah. I hit him with a lot of stuff at once."

"The poor guy was just trying to do his job, and smoke his cigarette. Let's see how he is at quitting time."

We waited until three-forty-five and then headed out together through the winding streets of the city. James Harker must have slipped out early, because we ran into him halfway up Stonegate.

I said, "Mr. Harker. It's Martin. I'm sorry if I asked too many questions this morning."

He warned me, "You leave me alone, now."

"Mr. Harker, this is my father, Jack Conway."

Dad stayed behind me, but he called out in a friendly voice, "Very nice to meet you, Mr. Harker."

James walked past us to his stoop. I looked at Dad, pleading with my eyes. He stepped up. "Mr. Harker! I know this is a terrible imposition. You certainly weren't expecting company. But Martin has this assignment, and it's worth a lot to him."

Mr. Harker unlocked the blue door.

"And it's worth a lot to me that he sees it through. So I want to offer you twenty pounds for a quick look at some of your World War Two memorabilia."

James turned around. "Twenty quid?"

"Yes, sir."

We heard the sound of someone clearing his throat behind

us. A man wearing running shoes, gray sweats, and a black leather jacket had stopped to stare at us. He told James, "I'm off to the gym, Harker, to exercise my lungs. Make sure I don't smell any secondhand smoke when I get back, eh?"

James didn't answer him, and the man continued on his way. Once he was out of range, James muttered, "If you go to the gym, why are you so bloody fat?" He looked at Dad. "Make it twenty-five."

"Twenty-five it is."

"I ain't no housekeeper, boys. You can have a quick look, but you're not to touch anything. Understood?"

I assured him, "Yes, sir."

He led Dad and me up one flight of worn wooden stairs. He put his key in the lock and opened the door onto a very dingy living room with a small kitchen area and a side door leading to a bedroom. The place smelled like sweat and cigarettes and stale beer. Everything seemed to have a faded yellow tinge to it. Still, I was thrilled to be in there. I took in the sight of each object hungrily. There, on the wall, was the poster: VERY WELL THEN, ALONE! To the right was a program for a football match: "Arsenal v. Spurs, White Hart Lane, 12 October 1940."

It was all exhilarating, and all heartbreaking. He had a narrow table set up by the front window. On it were the collection of World War I medals and a thick old book: *Illustrated Bible Stories for Children.*

Dad peeled off twenty-five pounds and handed it to James as I walked closer to the table. I pointed to the book and said, "May I just touch this one item, Mr. Harker?"

"Why?"

"I want to see if a certain painting is in there."

"Which one?"

"Abraham and Isaac."

He stared at me for several long seconds. Then he whispered hoarsely, "You know it's in there, don't you?"

"Yes, sir."

"All right, then. Go on. Look at it."

I grasped the heavy cover, opened the book, and turned until I found the page. The grisly picture was the same— crazy and shocking. I looked at the questions on the left side. They were followed by answers, half completed in black ink in a young boy's hand. I thought, *You didn't finish your homework, did you, Jimmy?*

Dad looked over my shoulder. "Do you know that painting, Martin?"

"Yes. It's at All Souls, in the Administration Building."

"Do you know it, Mr. Harker?"

"Aye. I know it bloody well. The son of Abraham gets sacrificed to God." James Harker stuffed Dad's money angrily into his pocket. "But he's not the only one, is he? Even the son of God—Jesus himself—gets it. God the Father was willing to sacrifice Him!"

Dad said, "It sounds like you know your Bible stories."

"It's the same story over and over, isn't it? If you're not willing to sacrifice your son's life, then you're not a man of God. I guess I'm not a man of God, then."

Dad told him, "I guess I'm not, either, Mr. Harker."

"You've paid your money. You can call me James."

"Thank you, James. You had a son, too. I know that."

"I did. But he got sacrificed."

"I'm really sorry."

"Aye. So am I." He told Dad, "Be nice to your boy, Jack Conway. Give him something good to remember you by. I wish to God I had done that."

I had to interrupt. "You did good things for your son. I know you did."

"You do?"

"Yes."

"Then tell me why I can't remember any? Looking back now, all I can remember doing is punishing him. He was all I had! And all I can remember is punishing him!"

Dad tried to console him. "I'm sure you thought you were doing what was right."

James's face twisted in anguish. "How could that be what was right?" He gestured at the medals. "What was I trying to do, turn him into another little soldier? So some politician, or some general, could use up his life to make a big name for himself? Is that what I was doing? My Jimmy already did his bit, standing up to Hitler like he did. Like we all did. He didn't have to do anything else."

James pointed a nicotine-stained finger at Dad. "Be kind to your boy while you can. Talk to him kindly. I can't talk to mine. All I can do is pray, and I never hear anything back."

Dad nodded his solemn agreement. He joined me in looking at Jimmy Harker's Bible book.

I couldn't contain myself any longer. I blurted out, "Maybe you *are* hearing something back."

"What?"

"Maybe that prayer has been answered." James Harker

started getting that agitated look again, but I couldn't stop. I talked faster. "Sure, I could have looked up the score of that Arsenal match and found out that Arsenal had won five–nil. But I could not have learned this: that Bill Lane got kicked out of the stadium because he threw a dart at a linesman." James's eyes bulged wide. " 'Hit 'im right in the arse.' "

James's hands began to shake.

"It seems impossible, Mr. Harker, but it isn't. You have to believe me. I didn't come all this way to lie to a stranger." James put his hands over his ears, but I knew he could still hear me. "I know that you were a good father. You had to be Jimmy's father *and* mother. I know you went into school and stood up for him. You sorted out that Master Portefoy, and he never touched Jimmy again."

James rasped at me, "What are you, a trickster? A mind reader? A bloody teenage con man?"

I tried to placate him. "No, sir—"

"Well, you'll get nothing from me, because I have nothing."

"We don't want—"

"Get out now! I mean it. Or I'll call the coppers."

I crossed to the door and opened it, already kicking myself for what I had done.

Dad put the Bible book down and followed me, saying, "We're very sorry to have upset you, Mr. Harker. We meant no harm. Really—"

Mr. Harker slammed the door behind us. We stared at it for a few seconds more. Then I trudged down the stairs ahead of Dad, feeling totally stupid and totally defeated. Out on the street, I told him, "That's it. It's over. He'll never talk to me again."

Dad tried to console me. "He's a very old man. You don't know what memories you're disturbing."

"Yes, I do."

"Well, then, you don't know what words are going to set him off. Let him sleep on it. Maybe he'll be different in the morning."

Bizarrely, at that very moment a tall man dressed in black with a high-top mortician's hat walked past us. He was followed by about twenty people with cameras, fanny packs, and other tourist trappings. I knew who they were right away. "That must be the ghost tour," I told Dad glumly. "I was hoping we could take that, once all this was over."

Dad answered impulsively, "Then let's take it!" He called after the mortician guy, "Hey! Can we still join the tour?"

The man turned a dark comic visage toward us. "How many souls are in your party?"

"Just my son and me."

The mortician held out a bony hand. "That will be five pounds."

Dad fished out a pocketful of coins and paid him. The tour resumed, with Dad and me now bringing up the rear. I wasn't really listening to the guide, though. All I could think about was my own stupidity. I had sprung things on James Harker too quickly. He would never see me again, not if he could help it.

I looked over at Dad. He wasn't into the tour, either. The mortician's jokes seemed to depress him. Many of them were about drunks. Maybe that hit too close to home. For whatever reason, when the tour passed by the Shambles, he asked me, "Are you enjoying this?"

"No. I'm not even listening."

"We can walk to the hotel from here. How about if we get out now, before we get too far away?"

"Sure. Okay."

So we gave the mortician and his followers the slip. We found a fish-and-chips shop where we stood and ate french fries soaked with vinegar. I was ready to go crash after that, but Dad had one more stop to make. We went into an off-license liquor store, where he purchased a bottle of Napoleon brandy.

Once back in the room, I lay on the cot and tried to go to sleep, but I couldn't. I couldn't stop replaying my two disastrous meetings with James Harker over and over in my mind.

I secretly watched Dad for a long time. He was sitting next to the window and drinking the brandy, swig after swig. He was clearly upset. He kept looking outside longingly, as if he had lost something; as if he was hoping to find it again in the black, ghost-filled streets.

IN THE QUIRE

Dad didn't get up in time for breakfast at the Wayfarer, which consisted of eggs, toast, and sliced tomatoes. He must have consumed half the bottle of Napoleon brandy before going to sleep, because the other half remained on the fireplace mantel in our room. During breakfast, I asked the manager about sending e-mail, and he directed me to an Internet café at the end of our street. I walked down there, paid a fee, and sent this message to Margaret:

> We arrived safely in York. Tell Mom that I
> went to a communion service at St. Paul's in
> London. I met James Harker, the firefighter
> from 1940. I hope to interview him further
> today. Dad is fine. Martin

I went back to the room, keeping as quiet as I could. I screwed up my courage and plugged the radio into the adapter. The Philco 20 Deluxe worked fine, delivering a few seconds of sports talk very clearly. I turned it off right away to avoid tuning to a space between stations. Then I put the radio and the adapter back into the box, minus the packing foam. It would be easy enough to carry for a short distance if and when I had the chance to use it.

I didn't have a clear plan for the day, but I knew that whatever I did would require Dad's help. I waited until he finally got himself together, at about eleven. The manager was kind enough to bring out some coffee and toast for him. Then Dad dutifully followed me through the winding streets to the entrance area of the York Minster.

We found a bench in the triangular park and sat for a long time. I looked down toward Stonegate, waiting to spot James Harker. Dad, I could tell, had his eye on a pub across the street called the Three-Legged Mare.

When I finally caught sight of James Harker's wiry figure approaching, I whispered urgently, "There he is."

Dad placed a firm hand on my elbow and stood up. "Let me handle this." He walked straight toward James Harker and called out, "Mr. Harker! I am truly sorry about yesterday." Mr. Harker detoured enough to walk around him, but Dad turned in pursuit. "Those kids can do amazing things on the Internet now. It seems like hocus-pocus stuff to us, but it's really not."

He reached out and touched the old man on the shoulder.

I froze, wondering whether Mr. Harker would turn to listen to him or to punch him in the nose. Fortunately, he listened. "For example, if you type in a boy's name and a school and a year, you can pull up his teacher's name. Even from sixty years ago. Or if you type in the name of a team and the year, you can find out about every match that team ever played. And what happened in that match."

The old man heard him out. But then he turned back, without reply, and started to walk away. Dad called after him, "Are you working today, James?"

Mr. Harker stopped again. I hadn't known he was aware of me until he pointed in my direction. "Why don't you bloody ask him? He knows everything about me."

"Because, if you're not working," Dad continued, "I would like to buy you a drink."

James's answer to that question was a barely perceptible shrug. However, he did walk ahead of us, straight into the Three-Legged Mare, so Dad and I followed.

James Harker slapped his hand loudly on the bar. He pointed at the bartender and explained to us, "Jocko here won't let me in unless I show him my money." He turned and looked at me. "Ain't that a shame, considering I'm a national hero and all, and being written up in a fine encyclopedia." He told the bartender, "Give me a bitters," and asked Dad, "Do you fancy a bitters, Jack?"

Dad answered, "Sure."

"Make it two, then. And a Squirt for the boy."

As Dad put his money on the bar, James commented, "Jocko here can tell you, I spent some of *my* finest hours right here in this pub."

The bartender set down a green bottle with LEMON SQUIRT on the label and two brown bottles with YORK BIT-TERS on theirs. James collected them all and led us to an ob-long table set on top of two barrels.

As soon as we sat down, Mr. Harker asked Dad, "So, Jack Conway, tell us: Did your father serve in the great World War Two?"

"He did, sir. He served in the Pacific, with the Marines."

"Ah. Nasty business, that. Guadalcanal. Iwo Jima. Fierce fighting."

"Yes, indeed."

"Did he ever talk about it?"

"No. Never."

"Can't say I blame him." James hoisted his bottle. "Here's to the Marines, then." He drank half of the bitters down in one gulp. Dad took a swallow of his, but he did not seem to like it.

I took a swig of my Lemon Squirt, a syrupy, tart soda. I grimaced, then said, "Can I ask some questions, Mr. Harker?"

He growled, "If you must."

I pulled out my Sony voice recorder and my sheaf of papers. James Harker suddenly slapped his hand on the table and pointed at the Sony recorder. "Don't that beat all! Your grandfather, your dad's dad, fought in the Pacific war, and you're standing there with a bloody Jap radio?"

"It's a voice recorder."

"Do you know what they did to your Marines? They chopped their heads off."

I didn't know what to say to that. I looked at Dad. He gestured that I should turn the recorder off, which I did.

"That's right. No prisoner-of-war camps for the Japs. No Geneva Conventions. No. They chopped their heads off. And here you are, buying their bloody products. Isn't that the bloody end?"

I spoke up for myself. "That was a long time ago, Mr. Harker. Two generations ago. You can't blame the grandchildren for what hap—"

"I can and I do! It was yesterday for me, my boy. I blame them all. The Germans. The Japs. I'll hate them till I'm dead. And you should, too, if you have any sense. If they'd do that to your grandfather, what would stop them from doing it to your father? Or to you?"

James pointed at the recorder. "Turn that thing back on. Tell your encyclopedia that World War Two was hell. Tell them that war isn't anybody's 'finest hour.' It's not an hour at all. It's weeks and months and years of a living hell. It's having breakfast with lads in the morning, and talking and smiling with them, then seeing them two hours later, charbroiled and dead, like Egyptian mummies. Burned alive. Looking like they're still smiling, 'cause there's no flesh left to cover their teeth. That's war. It's a bloody, horrible, endless thing. And the poor people of the world fight it, make no mistake about that. The rich people come on the radio and make the speeches."

I let him calm down a little; then I said, "But sometimes you have to defend your country. Right?"

"Oh, that's right enough. Except, as it turned out, not too much of this country belongs to me. Just a little flat, without smoking privileges." He paused. "By the way, do you mind?" Without waiting for an answer, he reached into his pocket, pulled out a cigarette, and lit it.

No one said anything else for a few minutes. Mr. Harker got another bottle of bitters; Dad didn't seem to be drinking his. I knew what I wanted to ask next, but I was afraid to. I opened my Millennium Encyclopedia letter and held it so that he could see the raised seal. Eventually he growled, "Ah, go on. Your dad's paying. Ask away."

"Mr. Harker, did your family stay in London during the war? Or did they evacuate?"

"A bit of both," he answered. "I sent Peg down to Dorset with Jimmy early on. She didn't want to go, but she knew it was best for him. She wasn't feeling well when she left; had a bad cold. I made her promise to have it looked after down there. Turns out she and Jimmy got put with a farm family. They was in an upstairs bedroom with no heat; cold water only. Peg's cough got aggravated. She didn't want to be trouble, so she kept her mouth shut. Finally she asked the family to fetch a doctor. Doctor put her right in hospital, but it was too late. She'd had pneumonia for a week. The medicines they gave her did no good."

He flicked ashes from his cigarette onto the floor. "Stupid bloody farmers. Didn't have proper medical care, if you ask me. Peg died the second day in hospital. I went down and got her and brought her back, with Jimmy. It's ironic, eh? Peg leaves London to be safe, and she dies."

After a somber moment, I went on, "And if I may ask, sir, how did Jimmy die?"

"Jimmy?" He said the name awkwardly. I wondered how long it had been since he had talked about him. "A bomb. An accident. A case of builder's negligence. All of the above." He took another deep swig of York Bitters and then continued. "We had a bloody air-raid warden on our block who fancied himself a builder. Couldn't build a doghouse. He tried it once; built it too big to get it out of the bloody

254

basement. And they let him build bomb shelters! He built one on our street. It caught a bomb, and it caved in. It caved in and crushed my Jimmy."

I couldn't look at him after that. I turned to my list again. "Then . . . what did you do after the war? Did you continue on in the Fire Service?"

"No. They disbanded the Auxiliaries. Didn't need us no more, us being auxiliary and all. I had no job. And let me tell you, there was no jobs to be had."

"You left London?"

"Aye. I took the train up to York. I drank up what money I had left. Then I wandered into the cathedral and sat there."

"In the Quire?"

"That's right."

"Why there?"

"It felt right. It felt like the right place to do my penance."

"Your penance for what?"

"That'd be my business, lad."

"Do you feel like you did something terrible?"

"More mind-reading, my boy?"

"No, sir. I just want to know—"

James swilled down the last of his drink. He hopped to his feet and held up one hand to me, like a traffic cop. "That's it. The interview's over. I ain't telling you nothing else." Before we could even react, he walked quickly to the door and left.

Dad said, "You'd better let him be, Martin."

"No. I know exactly where he's going. I need to go there, too.

255

"Do you want me to come with you?"

I looked at the brown bottles on the table. "No. You stay here."

"You tell me if I can do anything."

"All right. I might need you to do something. I just might."

As soon as I emerged from the smoky pub, I looked toward the Minster. I saw James Harker disappear through the cathedral door, and I ran right after him.

I entered, placed a donation on the desk, and walked through the nave. Moving slowly and quietly, I settled into a seat behind him in the Quire. No one else was around. I spent a few moments looking at the dark, finely carved wood, studying the figures of human beings, and heavenly beings, and hellish beings.

To my surprise, James Harker spoke aloud. "Do you know anything about angels, then?"

"Uh, no, sir. I don't really know anything about them."

"They're all called angels, aren't they? But really, there's nine orders of celestial beings, and only the lowest order should properly be called angels."

"I see. What should the highest order be called?"

"Seraphim. The next step above the seraphim is God. So they tell me. They tell me that God's up there."

"I believe that."

"You do? Why? Because your mum and dad told you to?"

"At first, yes. But lately I've been having my own experiences. Weird experiences. Unexplainable. Unless, of course, they come from God."

"Is that right? Well, I have had no such experiences. I

have sat here every day for sixty years and talked to God, but I haven't heard back from him yet."

"What do you talk about?"

"I ask forgiveness for my sins."

I waited a long moment before asking, "For one sin in particular?"

I expected another angry explosion, but he answered calmly. "That is correct. But God has not deigned to reply to my request. Perhaps he's too busy to bother with a janitor."

I walked around the wooden bench and sat next to him. He half turned toward me. It seemed like the right time to get to the point. "Mr. Harker, what do you think happens when you die?"

His blue eyes registered surprise. He answered, "I expect you're dead. And that's that."

"But you're not sure?"

"I'm not sure," he admitted. "Who knows for sure? Look at Hitler. He killed tens of millions of people; destroyed the lives of millions of others. Then he shot himself, and he was dead. But he was no deader than anybody else, was he? They were all *equally* dead. Does that mean he bloody got away with it?"

"No. I don't think so. I think he had to answer the question. And I think the answer, for him, was a damning one."

"What are you on about?"

"The question is *What did you do to help?* And he didn't do anything to help. He had to answer for all he had done to hurt people. If there's a hell, he is in it."

James turned so that he was looking right at me. "Who are you?"

"I am an American boy who, somehow, met your son Jimmy."

"No. You did not."

"Yes, sir, I did."

He hissed, "You're bloody ten years old!"

"I'm thirteen." His eyes bored into mine. "I met him . . . back in time. In 1940. I traveled there."

"You're off your head. Leave me be now."

"I will. I'll leave you in peace. But I have to tell you some things first. Some things from Jimmy."

"Jimmy? What are you talking about? My Jimmy?"

"Yes, sir. Jimmy wants me to tell you—"

"Stop using his name!"

"He wants me to tell you that he's sorry."

"Sorry?" he whispered.

"Yes."

"For what?"

"For going outside that night, that December night, against your orders. For making a bad decision. For ruining his life, and yours."

James seemed to look within himself. Then he concluded, "You're preying on the old. That's it. Because the old want to believe there's something, don't they? Because they're knocking on death's door."

We sat in silence for a few moments. Then I made one last try. "Mr. Harker, put aside everything I've said to this point, and just listen to this. This is why I'm here, to tell you this. Are you listening?"

He slowly turned toward me.

"You think you killed a man. A man named Harold

Canby. An air-raid warden. You think you killed him on the night of twenty-nine December, 1940, the night of a massive German air aid, the night your son died in the surface shelter."

James Harker's eyes opened wider. His lower lip dropped.

I went on, "But you didn't. You knocked Mr. Canby down, and he lay there like he was dead. But he was just pretending. He was hoping you would go away, which you did when the ambulance left. Then he got up. But he never got out of the rubble. A big man came back. He was angry. He accused Mr. Canby of cheating with his wife. Mr. Canby swore he didn't, but the man wouldn't listen. He picked up a block of concrete and smashed it against Mr. Canby's bald head. That knocked him to his knees. Then he smashed him with it again. That broke his skull open."

James shook his head slowly, robotically. He stammered, "No . . . no."

"The big guy threw more bricks on his head and on his body, making it look like he'd been crushed to death in the shelter. Then he took off." I stopped to let my words sink in. "And I think you know who that man was."

"No! It can't be."

I tried to look him in the eye, but he turned away. "A big man," I said. "A footballer. A good fellow most of the time."

James Harker could no longer resist my words. He finally croaked, "Bill Lane."

"That's right. Bill Lane. He got killed himself the next month, in a fire at Potters Fields."

James whispered, "Yes. He did."

259

"He died before he got up the courage to tell you about that night, didn't he? So I'm here to tell you now. You never killed anybody. Mr. Canby's blood is on Bill Lane's hands, not yours. You've been asking God for forgiveness for sixty years for a crime that you did not commit." I leaned forward. "Mr. Harker, there's nothing to forgive."

He looked right at me. All the blood was drained from his face. "Who told you this?"

"I was there. With Jimmy. Your son, Jimmy Harker." His look demanded more. I added, "A skinny boy. Maybe eight years old. Liked the Gunners, and Vera Lynn. Used Brylcreem. Had a dog named Reg that got put down."

James Harker's eyes widened a little more with every fact.

"Jimmy brought me to that spot, on that night, and he made me stay there and watch so that I could tell you here, today."

All anger was gone now from James Harker, and all suspicion. He simply asked, "Why? Why now, after all these years?"

"Because it's your time now, Mr. Harker." I swallowed hard. "So if you are ready to see your son again, I think I can help you do that."

Mr. Harker's eyes came into clear focus as I spoke. He nodded his understanding, and his consent. After a few moments, he stood up and took one last look around at the Quire; then he started out.

I walked with him down the length of the nave. I saw Dad sitting in one of the wooden chairs in the back, near the exit. His eyes had a strange, faraway look, too. Was he praying? He sat up at attention as we approached. I said, "This is it, Dad. We're at a point here. This is why we've come."

James Harker, standing beside me, let his gaze take in the rest of the great cathedral.

Dad struggled to his feet, pushing several of the wooden chairs out of alignment. "What do you need me to do?"

I thought of all the confusion that had filled my life for the past six months. I thought about Nana and her phone calls about a boy named Jimmy. I thought about sleeping in my grandfather's office next to the radio. And I thought about my own long struggle to comprehend this incomprehensible task. Now I was on the brink of doing it. Now my mind was completely clear. I knew what Dad needed to do, and what James Harker needed to do, and what I needed to do.

I was ready.

I was ready to do my bit.

DAY OF RECKONING

I asked Dad, "Will you go back to the Wayfarer and get the box with the radio? Will you bring it to Mr. Harker's flat?"

Dad answered with enthusiasm. "Sure, Martin. I'll do that right away." He led the three of us through the wooden exit doors and into the sunny day outside. Then he took off at a brisk pace, leaving James Harker and me to wend our way slowly through the streets of the ancient city.

James Harker continued to look around, as if taking everything in one last time. I understood then that he truly believed me. When I thought the moment was right, I interrupted him to ask, "Mr. Harker, when did you first know that I was telling the truth?"

He smiled apologetically. Then he winked. "I suspected it, almost from the first. When you said that Arsenal beat Fulham up at White Horse Lane."

"Why then?"

"Don't know. I have been having . . . thoughts lately. Like maybe something was coming, but I didn't know what.

Then you showed up, with your Arsenal Gunners shirt. I said to myself, 'This could be it.' "

"Yeah?"

"That match, that day, was my last happy memory of Jimmy. He liked the Gunners, as you know."

"And you liked the Spurs."

"Aye. Still do." He shook his head sadly. "That day is one that I go back to, over and over, more than any other. We were all laughing. Even the bloody air raid was a laugh that day." He looked sideways at me. "Those are the days you remember, lad. Have yourself as many of them as you can."

As we approached his building, the blue door opened and the landlord emerged, dressed in his gray sweats. He announced, "I'll be round to check the flat tomorrow, Mr. Harker. And every Saturday from now on. I know that you're smoking in there, and I won't have it."

Mr. Harker paid no more attention to him than he had to me back in 1940, when I couldn't be seen or heard. As the landlord walked slowly away, though, he commented, "He's always sniffing round here, like a fat bloodhound."

He stuck his key into the door and turned it. Then he swiveled his head and directed a steely-eyed gaze at me. "You're absolutely certain you saw Bill Lane do that? You swear to God?"

"I swear to God."

We entered the small vestibule and started up the stairs. "I had always suspected that there was something goin' on between Alice Lane and Canby. Them wardens and volunteers and all, they was all having it off. I couldn't say nothing to Bill, though, unless I knew for certain."

"Did Bill still work with you after that day? After December twenty-ninth?"

"No. They gave me three days off then to bury my Jimmy. Three bloody days. When I went back to work, he was gone. Another lad was posted with me. I didn't see Bill at work, and I didn't see him at home. We was on different shifts entirely."

We reached the door to flat number two. Mr. Harker opened it and let me in. "But I heard, through talk, that he was acting . . . reckless-like. The other firefighters didn't want to work with him. He took too many chances. That sort of thing."

"How did he die?"

"Climbing a ladder. So I heard. He put a ladder up against a warehouse wall over in Potters Fields, like you said, and he climbed up. The wall collapsed, and that was the end of Bill." He wandered over to the table and closed the book of Bible stories. "I went to his funeral. So did Alice, of course." He picked up his father's medals and placed them on top of the book. "Bill was a good man, in his own way. He talked a lot, but he'd stand by you when you needed him. I believe, once he had it all sorted out, that he'd have told me what he done."

"I believe that, too."

"He never got the chance to say it, though, did he?"

"No."

James ran his fingers over Jimmy's book. "Our paths never crossed again."

"No."

"Remember that, lad, if you never remember anything else. We all touch each other's lives, for better or worse. So say the things that you have to say to people while you still have the chance."

"Yes, sir."

James busied himself putting some other personal things in order. I drifted over and looked through the bedroom door. The room had the same faded wallpaper as the living area. Inside, to the right, was an iron cot with a brown wool bedspread. Next to that was a night table with an empty glass on it. On the back wall, I could see a collage of photos. I asked, "Do you mind if I look at the photos?"

"Suit yourself, lad."

The collage had yellowed over the years, but it still showed great care in the making. There were smiling faces that I recognized and some that I did not, but I could guess who they were. There was Jimmy with a football; there was a younger James, with a pretty woman who had to be Peg, standing in front of St. Paul's Cathedral; there were older people—probably his and her parents—including a man in uniform wearing three medals; there was even a photo of Bill and Alice Lane in a happier time, posed in front of a hotel door that said SAVOY.

Beneath the wall collage, James had a two-shelf bookcase. It was filled with titles about World Wars I and II. I bent to look at a row of matching red books—all six volumes of Winston S. Churchill's *The Second World War*.

James came in and joined me. He reached into the bookcase and pulled out the second red volume. Then he held it up to show me the title: *Their Finest Hour*. He spoke without rancor. "Churchill wrote his own history books and made himself the hero. FDR wrote his letters and did the same. But they wasn't the heroes. My Peg was a hero, and my Jimmy. Anybody who went out in the cold and wet, and faced death, and got nothin' for it in return, they was the heroes."

James picked up the empty glass and led me out of the bedroom. His back seemed to be straightening, like a great load was lifting. He deposited the glass in the sink; then he pointed to an old wooden table with a pair of mismatched chairs. "Pull them out for you and your dad to sit on. I've got another one over here." He walked over to a corner where a piece of furniture sat covered by a white sheet, like a squatting ghost. He yanked off the sheet and tossed it to the floor, revealing a chair that I knew well—the Queen Anne wing chair.

I pointed at it. "Jimmy sat in that chair, listening to the radio."

James was no longer amazed by my revelations. "That's right. Five-forty-two every night on the BBC. 'London Calling.'"

"You've had it all this time?"

"Mostly. I left it with Alice Lane. But once I got a job and a flat, I had it shipped up here." He sat on it carefully. "Ol' Alice was glad to be rid of it, I expect. She was about to remarry."

"To Sergeant Dennis Hennessey."

"Was that his name? I hope he made more money than Bill, or she'd have made his life a misery."

"She liked her gin and It."

"That she did. I was a very lucky man in that regard. My Peg was a treasure. They don't make many like her." James's voice got very low. "We was just kids ourselves when we had Jimmy. But she made a right good mother. She put Jimmy and me before her own self." A tear rolled down his lined face. "Yeah. I was very lucky there."

A tinny ring sounded from a rusty little box on the kitchen wall. James whispered, "That'll be your dad. Or the bloody landlord." He walked into the kitchen and pressed a button, unlocking the door downstairs.

It was Dad. He carried the box into the flat. He placed it on the small table by the window, carefully sliding the Bible book and the medals to one side.

I said, "I have a piece of furniture to show you, too, Mr. Harker. It'll go well with your chair." I slid the Philco 20 Deluxe up out of the box and into view. James's face broke into a wide smile. "Cor! That's the one, isn't it?"

"This was your radio."

"It's the very one!"

"When did you last see it?"

"I expect it was the night I brought it back to the Embassy." James leaned forward and touched its mahogany knobs.

Dad looked confused. He asked me, "But . . . that's your grandmother's radio, from Brookline, right?"

"Right."

Then he asked James, "So how did you get it?"

"I got it from the Embassy's storeroom. A kind of a lend-lease program."

"Sorry?"

"My mate pinched it from a Yank."

I looked at Dad before asking. "Mr. Harker, was the Yank a skinny young man named Martin Mehan?"

"That was his name, yeah. We took off his nameplate, in case we got caught."

I kept my eyes on Dad. "What do you remember about Martin Mehan?"

James grinned weakly. "All's I recall about him . . . is that he would set up the big shots with girls."

"General Lowery, and people like that?"

"Yeah. Him. Joe Kennedy. All of 'em."

"That's all he would do?"

"I don't know. That's all I ever seen him do. Bill and me called him the ponce."

Dad and I exchanged a puzzled look.

"Do ya not know that word, Jack?"

"No. Never heard it."

James looked back and forth between us. "It's like . . . I don't mean to be indelicate, Martin, but like . . . a purveyor of women."

"A pimp?" I suggested.

James winked at me. "There ya go, lad."

Dad stared back at me until he finally understood. Then he smiled broadly. "I can't believe it. Not the sainted Martin Mehan?"

"I'm afraid so."

He emitted a short, dry laugh. "I heard his shrine was closing anyway."

"That's right. It never should have opened."

Dad shook his head back and forth several times. He touched the war medals lightly. Then he took the book of illustrated Bible stories, opened it, and began reading.

James moved closer to the radio, examining its grillwork. He caressed the curve at the top of it like it was a child's head, and he spoke with great emotion. "Jimmy loved to listen to this. When I'd let him. But I wouldn't always let him."

He paused as tears came to his eyes. "You shouldn't be too hard with little boys. You should treat them as precious, because that's what they are." He picked up the medals. "I always told Jimmy not to be afraid—of the bombs, or the Nazis, or the dark. But he was just a little boy. He should have been afraid of those things."

James looked through the window, into the distance. "I was afraid of those things." He turned and looked at the bedroom. "I'm only afraid of one thing now." He asked me, "Tell me, lad, aren't you afraid of death?"

"No, sir. Not anymore." I dared to add, "You shouldn't be, either."

"No?"

"No."

"And Jimmy . . . he told you to tell me that he was sorry?"

"That's right."

"When I'm the one that needs to be sorry? For all my harsh words? And deeds?"

I couldn't think of an answer to that.

"Just like his mum, he is." James nodded thoughtfully for a long moment. Then he pulled his shoulders back, like a soldier. "So then, lad? What do we do first?"

I pointed at the Philco 20. "First you'll need that."

"What? The radio?"

"Yes."

"What else?"

"That's it. That's how I met Jimmy, every time."

James's face registered surprise, just like Jimmy's face had so often. He put both hands on the radio and tilted it slightly, to see how heavy it was. Then he picked it up, carried it into the bedroom, and set it carefully on the table. I reached into the box, pulled out the adapter, and followed him in. Dad did not move. He continued to read the Bible book like he was transfixed.

James sat on the creaky bed and whispered hoarsely, "Just tell me what to do, exactly, and I'll do it."

I knelt down and plugged the adapter into an outlet behind the table. I told him, "The way it worked for me is, I'd tune to a spot between the stations. I'd lie with my eyes looking at the dial and my ear listening to the static. Then . . . it would happen. I'd be with Jimmy."

James nodded his understanding. "Tune it in for me, will you, then?"

"Yes, sir. All right." I knelt down again and found a place on the dial that emitted a soft stream of static. I heard it crackling in my ear. I felt the warm glow of the orange dial on my face. I stood back up and looked at James, but words failed me beyond "Goodbye, then, Mr. Harker. Goodbye and good luck."

He lay down heavily, on his left side, with his head near the radio. "Thank you, lad."

But I couldn't bring myself to leave. Not yet. I finally stammered, "Please, sir, if you think of it, tell him that . . . Johnny did his bit."

I don't know if James Harker was still listening or not. He faced the orange dial, with his eyes wide open, and waited. I turned away and hurried out.

Dad was still immersed in the Bible book. He looked up at me with awe in his eyes and in his face, like he was in the presence of a higher power.

I felt the same way. I felt that, for the first time in my life, I had done something great.

I walked to the door and waited there until Dad joined me. Then I led him down the stairs and into the street.

About halfway across, I stopped, turned, and looked back at James Harker's windows. Was it happening now? Was Jimmy Harker in there, smiling his crooked smile? Was he chattering on about football, and pop songs, and the war news? Or was he now telling his father what to expect on the other side? Was he telling him about the next phase in the journey of his immortal soul?

Dad pulled me back slowly to the far curb to let a van drive by. That's when I finally allowed myself to look away. I believed that my job was now finished. I believed that the rest was up to God.

But I also believed this: that I, pathetic, basement-dwelling Martin from Princeton Junction, New Jersey, had just served as His messenger.

THE HAUNTED CITY

Dad and I spent the rest of that day together. By silent agreement, we did not mention the events inside James Harker's flat after we left there. Instead, at Dad's suggestion, we studied the history of the medieval city of York. We toured its Viking museum and climbed its Roman ruins. Dad clearly wanted to stay as busy as possible, so we kept up a rapid pace. By six o'clock, the city was dark and we were exhausted.

When I woke up in the morning, though, the bottle of Napoleon brandy, still half full at bedtime, was completely empty. I looked over at Dad's sleeping body and felt a deep, bruising disappointment.

I brushed my teeth, got dressed, and hurried out the hotel door. I ran to James Harker's flat on Stonegate, stood in the street, and stared up at his windows. I could see the back edge of the table and one corner of the Queen Anne wing chair, but that was all. I thought about pushing his buzzer, but I couldn't bring myself to do it. If James Harker answered the door and told me to get my stupid bloody radio out of there, then I would go right back to being crazy. So I took off running again, sprinting all the way to the York Minster.

I had to wait at least fifteen minutes until the door was unlocked. As soon as it was, I squeezed in past a volunteer who said, not too kindly, "Aren't you the eager one today?"

I hurried past the donation desk without paying. I walked to the top of the nave, turned, and saw Sylvia sitting at the desk by the stairs. She greeted me with a smile. "First customer of the day."

I plunked down a one-pound coin. "Yes, ma'am. Can I go up?"

"You can. Helen is already up there."

"All right. Thanks." I threw myself into the 275-step climb with great urgency, taking the steps two at a time, arriving at the top red-faced and gulping for air.

Helen was sitting in the small office. As soon as I caught my breath, I walked up to her, trying to sound as casual as possible. "Good morning."

"Good morning to you. You're up here bright and early."

"Yes, ma'am. Do you know if Mr. Harker is working today?"

"I believe he does work on Saturdays. He prefers to have the weekdays off. I do, too. It helps to get things done."

"Yes, ma'am. It's just that I saw him last night. My dad and I saw him at the pub."

She arched her eyebrows.

"Outside of the pub, really, nearer to the gutter, and he said he was not feeling too well."

"No?"

"Anyway, I'm worried about him. I'm worried that maybe he has overslept?"

"Maybe."

"I wouldn't want him to lose his job."

"No. Certainly not."

"Perhaps you should call him?"

"He doesn't have a phone. He can't abide them."

I persisted. "You said you help him out sometimes, when he doesn't show up for work. How do you do that?"

"I walk over there. It's not far." She looked at her watch.

I prodded her. "Could you walk over there now?"

"Well, yes. I suppose I could do that and get back in thirty minutes. Don't you think?"

"I think so."

"All right, then. That's what I'll do. I'll tell Sylvia on the way out. But if anybody else asks, say I'll be right back."

"Yes, ma'am, I will."

Helen grabbed her purse, walked to the stair entrance, and disappeared.

I waited a moment and then slipped into the office. I checked under the counter and found the pair of binoculars. Then I ran across the roof to my previous spot, the spot where I could see Stonegate and a blue door.

I was watching that door when Helen arrived. I watched her push the buzzer and wait patiently. Then I watched her back out into the street and look up.

I turned when I heard a sound. A group of tourists had joined me on the roof.

I looked back through the binoculars and watched Helen

pull out a cell phone and make a call. A few moments later, she made another one.

Sylvia arrived on the roof and announced, breathlessly, that the tourists were free to go back down. She stayed in the office after that, and I stayed at my spot until another group of tourists arrived.

I looked again through the binoculars, and I saw the lights of a police car parked on Stonegate. The policeman and Helen had been joined by the large gray-and-black figure of the landlord. At that point, I knew what was happening at James Harker's flat, and I began to cry.

Five minutes later, an ambulance pulled up to the blue door. I focused as best I could through my tears as two men carried a stretcher inside. Then I dried my tears on my coat sleeve, turned, and ran back to the office. I spoke loudly to Sylvia. "Here! I borrowed these. Please, I have to go down. Now!"

"Sorry, love. You'll have to wait."

"No! I can't wait. I have to go." I ran to the door and hurtled myself back down the spiraling steps. I made it halfway down before I encountered a clump of tourists. I forced myself past them, and then past a second group, before I arrived at the bottom. There, I slowed from a run to a brisk walk through the nave and out the heavy door.

Once on the street, I sprinted full out all the way to Stonegate. I arrived just as the stretcher bearers were coming back out. I stood and watched as they lifted up James Harker's body and placed him in the ambulance. He looked very calm and collected, like Nana had at her viewing. He looked like he had died at peace.

Helen walked out right after that. Her eyes were red and puffy and filled with tears. She looked at me and shook her head sadly. "Did you hear what happened?"

"No."

"He died in his sleep. Poor man."

"He did look peaceful."

"Yes. They say that's the best way to go. In your sleep."

"Yeah."

"He prayed every day. I'm sure he has gone on to his reward."

"So am I."

"Forgive me, now—" The woman stopped and looked at me. "What is your name?"

"Martin, ma'am. Martin Conway."

"Forgive me, Martin. There's much to be done. I need to speak to a solicitor. And I need to get back to the Minster." Helen hurried off in the direction of the cathedral.

I turned and looked at the blue door. It was ajar. Someone had placed a wooden stick between the door and the doorjamb, propping it open so the police and ambulance guys could get in.

And it was still there.

I checked left and right and then slipped inside. I took the stairs two at a time to James Harker's flat. The door was wide open, and I could hear someone inside, moving.

I stepped quietly into the doorway and looked around. There was the landlord, big and menacing, and still in his black jacket. He was huffing around the flat, checking in drawers, touching things, moving things. But the most troubling sight of all was right in front of me. He had dragged the Queen Anne wing chair to the center of the room. The Philco 20 Deluxe was perched awkwardly on its leather cushion. So were the World War I medals and the six-volume set of *The Second World War.*

I barked at him, "What do you think you're doing?"

The landlord whirled around, startled. His hand shot involuntarily to his heart. Then he growled, "Who the devil are you?"

"I'm a friend of Mr. Harker's."

"Mr. Harker don't live here no more."

"I know that. He just died, about five minutes ago. What are you doing touching his property?"

"I'm collecting money he owes me. Now bugger off."

"Money he owes you? For what?"

The landlord looked me up and down. Then he turned away and muttered, "I caught him smokin' in here. He owes me a cleaning fee for the drapes and the rug. They all stink of smoke, don't they?" He pointed at his pile of loot. "These'll fetch something. To cover my expenses."

"No! You have no right to steal his property!"

"I've heard about enough from you. Back off, my boy, or you'll get hurt."

I wasn't about to back off. "That radio isn't even his, it's mine!"

"Is it, now? It has no identification on it."

I stepped into the flat and walked to the radio. "Yes, it does. It has my identification number right here: 291240." I clutched the sides of the Philco 20 and spun it around. "Look!"

Instead of replying, though, he suddenly reached over

and grabbed the front of my coat, up near my neck. "I don't need to look at nothing. And you're leaving, boy, now!"

He dragged me two steps toward the door before I could dig my heels in and stop. Then I grabbed his thick wrist in both of my hands and twisted it with all my might. That made him let go of my coat, but he managed to grab the back of my neck with his left hand. We lurched around the room together like that, twisting and snarling, until I heard a shout: "Take your hands off of him!"

I looked up and saw Dad standing in the doorway, with a horrified expression on his face. He flushed bright red with anger and tightened both of his fists.

The landlord was so startled by the sound of Dad's voice that he let go of my neck. I changed my stance and gave his wrist one more mighty twist, turning his whole body toward Dad. Dad took one step forward, reared back, and hit him with a right-hand punch, full in the stomach, his hand disappearing momentarily into a roll of flab. The landlord exhaled a short, loud, sickening sound, like he was about to throw up.

I pushed him toward the door as hard as I could. At the same time, Dad grabbed him by the shoulders and pulled. The landlord's doubled-over body pitched out into the hallway and partly down the stairs. He grabbed at the wall with one hand to keep from plummeting the rest of the way. He slid down the wall like a wet slug, all the way down to the doorway and out into the street. Dad yelled after him, "Don't you come back here!"

Dad stared at the door a few moments longer. Then he turned and asked, "Are you all right, Martin?"

278

I rubbed the back of my neck. "Yeah. He was all blubber. A big nothing."

"What on earth happened here?"

"Mr. Harker is dead, Dad."

His face turned pale. "Dead?"

"Dead. The ambulance just took him away."

"My God, Martin." He stared toward the empty bedroom. "Did we . . . did we do this?"

I answered confidently, "Yes. We did. I believe we did this."

Dad leaned heavily against the doorjamb. "God in heaven."

I waited for him to speak again, but he seemed totally lost in thought. After a few minutes, though, he finally looked back at me, and the Queen Anne chair, and the mess in the room. "But why did that man attack you?"

"I caught him stealing Mr. Harker's stuff. He was trying to steal my radio, too."

"And you fought with him?"

"Yes. Or I'd say *we* fought with him."

Dad straightened himself and looked around. "Yeah. Well, we should take that radio with us now. If you want to keep it."

I thought about the harrowing times I had had with Jimmy—the terrors, the night sweats, the petit mal seizure—but I told him, "Yeah. I want to keep it. Definitely." So we packed up the Philco 20 once more. After a last look around, I pulled the door to Mr. Harker's flat closed and we returned to the hotel.

Back in our room at the Wayfarer, Dad set the box with

the radio down very gently. Then he opened the top of my suitcase, rummaged for a few seconds, and pulled out the sheaf of papers. "I hope you don't mind, but I was looking at these papers of yours."

"No. That's okay."

"There's one in particular." He extracted one from the pile. "This. It looks like you started out with some doubts. Right?" Dad showed me the paper. It was my original list, done on the computer the morning after my first time travel to Jimmy Harker's, the one I had edited and re-edited in red ink with *Rights* and *Wrongs* and *Maybes*. He pointed some of those out. Then he said. "In the end, they all became *Rights*, didn't they?"

"Yeah. In the end."

"Even though no one believed that you could possibly be right. Not even me."

I shrugged. "I can't blame people for that. It was pretty crazy."

Dad pressed the paper between his hands. "Martin, can I keep this paper? Or a copy of it, if you don't mind?"

"You can keep the original. I don't mind."

He put it into his own suitcase. "Thank you. Thank you very much."

I waited a moment before adding, "Dad, a higher power was at work here. I think you know that."

He gulped. "Yeah."

"But I thought you knew that last night, too."

"I did."

"Then why did you have to drink?"

"I didn't."

"I saw the bottle."

Dad shook his head. "No. No. I didn't drink that brandy, Martin. I dumped it out."

"What?" I looked at the mantel and the bottle was gone.

"I did. Last night, before I went to sleep. I dumped it down the bathroom sink. The bottle was too big for that little trash can in there, so I tossed it out downstairs."

"Really?"

"Yeah. Really. I've made up my mind, son. I've had my last drink. I don't expect you, or your mother, or anyone else to believe me, but it's true."

I believed him. I believed that he would do exactly what he said. But I also thought it best to keep us very busy after that. So first Dad and I went for a walk to the Internet café. I wrote to Margaret:

> Things have gone very well in York. I got to interview James Harker again, right before he died. He confirmed everything that I learned over the last three months. Thank Mr. Wissler for his letter. Tell him that the raised seal really worked. Tell Mom that I am fine. Tell her that Dad is fine, too. Martin

Our next stop was at an old inn on the river Ouse where we had a late lunch of roast beef and Yorkshire pudding. We talked a lot about James and Jimmy Harker, and fathers and sons in general.

Then we talked about fathers and sons in particular, about him and me.

We took a rambling walk after lunch that led us into different parts of the historic city. However, wherever we were, the skyline was dominated by one sight, the York Minster. Inevitably, we arrived at its door.

Dad and I paid our donation to Sylvia. I apologized for my behavior that morning. She said, "Think nothing of it, love. Helen told me what happened. Of course you were upset about Mr. Harker. We all are."

We joined up with an official tour led by one of the volunteer ladies. We learned all about the cathedral's history, and its carvings, and its stained glass. Dad must have been thinking about the Mehans and the Lowerys when he whispered to me, "Some families are impressed that a guy worked at a desk job for thirty years, or that a rich guy gave some money to a school. But think about this: Nine generations of a family worked their entire lives, gave everything they had, to build this cathedral. *That's* impressive. That's astounding."

After the tour, we sat in the back row of chairs for a long time, taking in the awesome power of the cathedral, until I heard "Hello, Martin" from behind us.

It was Helen.

I stood up. "Hello, ma'am." She looked at Dad, so I added, "This is my father, Jack Conway."

Dad stood, too, and shook her hand. She said, "Helen Mills. Nice to meet you." Then she turned to me. "A sad business about Mr. Harker. Old as he was, it's still a shock. Did you get to complete your interview with him?"

"Oh yes, ma'am. I completed it."

"Good."

Dad asked, "Is there anyone left to make his funeral arrangements?"

"I am Mr. Harker's executor. He had no one else, you know. I'll be arranging for a service here at the Minster, and then a burial."

"When will that be?" Dad asked her.

"I expect on Monday."

Dad looked at me. "We'll stay for that, Martin, if you want."

"Yes. Absolutely."

Helen seemed touched. "That would be lovely, Martin. Now, tell me, are there are any items of Mr. Harker's, historical items, that you'd like for your encyclopedia article?"

I answered immediately. "Yes. There are, ma'am. Unless they belong to you now."

"I suppose they might, technically, but they're not really mine. What would you like?"

I looked at Dad. To my surprise, he spoke up first. "I would like the *Illustrated Bible Stories*. I was looking at it the other day, and I'd like to continue looking at it."

Helen nodded. "All right. I'm sure that would be fine."

Dad added, "And I'd hate to think of that guy stealing Mr. Harker's medals and pawning them, or selling them on eBay."

She looked alarmed. "What guy?"

"The landlord. We caught him in the flat after Mr. Harker died. He was helping himself."

"Oh no! No. I'll put the police on to him straightaway. Mr. Harker had no use for that man, I can tell you." She assured us, "Those medals will find a proper home. Perhaps at the Duke's Museum." She turned to me. "How about you, Martin?"

I told her the truth. "Ma'am, anything I take would not be for the encyclopedia, it would be for me."

"Oh? Well, I think that would be fine, too."

"Then I'd like to take the photo collage. And the Arsenal program. And the 'Very Well Then, Alone!' poster. I have a room at home with bare walls. I can put them up there."

"That would be lovely."

"And I have room for that chair, too."

"A chair?"

"The Queen Anne wing chair."

"That old one? With the sheet over it?"

"Yes, ma'am."

Helen looked troubled. "I don't know how you'd manage a big thing like that, all the way back to America. It would be terribly expensive."

Dad told her, "I'll call my brother Bob. He'll take care of it."

Helen cocked her head momentarily, but then she just said, "Well, then. That's done. I'm glad we've found those items a happy home."

After Helen left us, we sat for a while longer. Then Dad made a curious comment: "Life is complicated."

"What? What do you mean?"

"I was thinking about that radio. And all of its travels."

"Yeah. It's really gotten around."

"And now it's going back to you."

"Right."

Dad stood up, so I followed. "Will you always keep it?"

"Always. Definitely. Always."

He exhaled into the vastness of the cathedral. "That's reassuring to me."

My smile turned into a look of puzzlement. "Why?"

"I might need it." He looked up to the ornate ceiling. "I might need to contact you someday for some help."

I nodded emphatically. "Absolutely. I'll be there. And I'll be totally receptive. I *will* hear you."

"Yes. I believe you will."

We walked together to the back of the nave. As soon as we pushed open the cathedral door, we saw a portentous sight—the man in black with the high black hat. He was collecting coins for the evening ghost tour. Dad made a surprising suggestion. "Martin? What do you say we take this tour again?"

I shrugged and fell in line with him.

Soon we were part of a pack of a dozen tourists, walking briskly through the darkening streets of York. This time around, the mortician's stories fascinated us, and they touched us. There was a story about a lost child boarded up in a basement and left there to die all alone. And there was one about an orphan who was worked to death by a heartless employer because the child was thought to be worthless. There was a story about a drunken, foolish husband who set fire to his own house, killing his wife and children. And one about another drunken husband who stumbled in the snow on a Christmas Eve and drowned in the river Ouse.

At one point Dad turned to me, with tears in his eyes, and said, "Please, Martin. I don't want my life to be a story about a fool. I don't want my life to be just a joke told by a guy in a funny hat."

I replied with all my heart. "It won't be. I know that for sure. It won't be."

"And I don't want my son's life to be some stupid cliché where's he's nothing but the son of a son of an alcoholic."

"It won't be that. I swear. It won't."

"It had better not. Because I'll know about it, and I'll haunt you."

We stayed with the tour until the very end. At that point, the mortician's assistant appeared and offered to take Polaroid photos of people for one pound. Dad and I each ordered one. We waited our turn and then posed on either side of the mortician.

The quality of my photo has faded over the years, but our expressions remain the same. The mortician looks lifeless, and goofy, and so comical an embodiment of death that no one could possibly fear him. Dad and I, however, both look very much alive. We are shining with an inner wisdom, and with hope, and we are filled with an unshakable purpose.

EPILOGUE

Back when I registered at Garden State Middle School, I re-claimed my first name. Only Aunt Elizabeth resisted the change, and only she continues to call me Martin. Margaret, Mom, and Dad respected my wishes; they never called me that again.

After college, I went to work for the United States Foreign Service, doing the same job my grandfather once did, in the same city. I like to think I do it better, though, with more personal integrity, and with a unique sense of history.

Margaret married the IT guy, Steve, and had a son named Stevie. She has since risen to a position right below Mr. Wissler's at the Millennium Encyclopedia.

Mom still manages her money well enough to live a comfortable life. She forgave Dad for all his broken promises. They had a cordial relationship, but they did not get back together.

Dad did stop drinking, and he did turn his life around. He quit the restaurant business and got a job at a Catholic high school in West Orange, New Jersey, where he taught history. He just didn't do it for very long.

His body, burdened by so many years of alcoholism, broke down while I was at the Walsh School. Mom called me on a rainy Sunday night and gave me the sad news. I took the train up from Union Station in Washington. Mom, Margaret, and her family got on at Princeton Junction.

The funeral director showed us one special request in my father's burial plan. He wanted an envelope placed in his suit pocket. The director let me examine the envelope before the viewing. It contained two items: the other photo of Dad and me in York, with the mortician standing between us; and my folded-up computer paper, listing everything I had learned during my time travels with Jimmy Harker. I smiled to see my own teenage handwriting again: *Right, Right, Right.*

After a small, dignified service, we buried my father near a marble wall inscribed with the Twenty-third Psalm: "Yea, though I walk through the valley of the shadow of death . . ." An elderly priest articulated what I already knew—that the temporal body dies, but the spirit lives on.

Nowadays I pass through Newark Airport often, on my way to London, and I always take a side trip to see my father's grave. I talk to him on those visits. But it's funny, I don't talk to him like one adult would to another. I talk to him like he was a lost boy. Which he was. Which I was. Which Jimmy Harker was.

I truly believe my father was at peace with God when he died. I know he had at least one answer to the question

What did you do to help? Because he did help me to do something astounding. However, just in case, I always kneel beside his temporal remains, and I always say a prayer for his everlasting soul.

John Martin Conway
United States Embassy
Grosvenor Square, London
January 2, 2019